ONE SWEET KISS

"We'd better head out," she said, grabbing Jax's hand and tugging him to the door.

She wasn't thinking about the consequences of that.

Not until all the good-byes had been said, and she was standing on the porch, her hand still wrapped around his.

Warm skin to warm skin, and all she could think about was that moment in the car when his hand had been on her knee.

Maybe he was thinking about that, too, because his gaze dropped to her lips, his palm sliding from her hand to her elbow to her waist. It settled there like it belonged. Like *they* belonged, standing on the porch together.

She should have moved away.

Not because it was such a bad thing to be standing there thinking about how it would feel to be in Jax's arms, but because she had an entire life planned out. This wasn't part of it.

He wasn't part of it, but when his lips brushed hers—a featherlight touch that had her leaning into him, her palms resting on his chest—she forgot that.

She forgot everything but Jax. . . .

Books by Shirlee McCoy

The Apple Valley Series
THE HOUSE ON MAIN STREET
THE COTTAGE ON THE CORNER
THE ORCHARD AT THE EDGE OF TOWN

The Home Sweet Home Series
SWEET HAVEN
SWEET SURPRISES
BITTERSWEET

THE MOST WONDERFUL TIME
(with Fern Michaels, Stacy Finz, and Susan Fox)

Published by Kensington Publishing Corporation

Bittersweet

SHIRLEE MCCOY

ZEBRA BOOKS
KENSINGTON PUBLISHING CORP.
http://www.kensingtonbooks.com

ZEBRA BOOKS are published by

Kensington Publishing Corp.
119 West 40th Street
New York, NY 10018

All Kensington titles, imprints, and distributed lines are available at special quantity discounts for bulk purchases for sales promotion, premiums, fund-raising, educational, or institutional use.

Special book excerpts or customized printings can also be created to fit specific needs. For details, write or phone the office of the Kensington Sales Manager: Attn.: Sales Department. Kensington Publishing Corp., 119 West 40th Street, New York, NY 10018. Phone: 1-800-221-2647.

Zebra and the Z logo Reg. U.S. Pat. & TM Off.

First Printing: August 2017
ISBN-13: 978-1-4201-3931-0
ISBN-10: 1-4201-3931-2

eISBN-13: 978-1-4201-3932-7
eISBN-10: 1-4201-3932-0

10 9 8 7 6 5 4 3 2 1

Printed in the United States of America

Chapter One

Willow Lamont woke bathed in sweat and gasping for air. She lay still, listening to the silence of the apartment, inhaling the familiar scent of furniture polish and age. She was back in Benevolence, Washington. The place where the nightmare had begun.

Back and wishing that she wasn't.

Five mornings spent gulping coffee like it was oxygen and she was climbing Mount Everest. Five evenings reading recipe cards and wondering why she couldn't produce a good batch of chocolate to save her life.

Five nights of hell.

And it would all begin again in . . .

She glanced at the bedside clock—four hours.

She shoved the covers aside and climbed out of bed, the wood floor cold beneath her feet. It reminded her of childhood visits with her grandparents and of the way that it had felt to be young and happy and naïve.

She'd grown up fast.

Her father's illness had been the beginning of the

process. His death from brain cancer had been the end of it.

The thing that had happened in between?

That had made her who she was.

She might hate the nightmares and the fear, but she didn't hate what she'd become because of them.

She did hate being sleepless, though. Especially in the darkest part of the morning when the blackness outside the windows seemed to pulse with energy. She snapped the curtain into place, making sure not even a hint of night was visible through the heavy fabric.

"Five days down," she murmured. "Nine to go."

Two weeks. Fourteen days. Three-hundred-thirty-six hours. She'd calculated the time that she'd spend in Benevolence down to the minute. She'd explained it to her grandfather, to her sisters, to her mother. She'd told anyone who happened to be anyone who loved her family that she could only devote two weeks of her time to Chocolate Haven. Sure, it was the family legacy. Sure, she'd been the Lamont sister everyone had thought would eventually take over the store, but she'd grown up and moved away. She had a life and a career that she loved. Neither included chocolate or fudge or the little town she'd grown up in.

Everyone needed to understand that.

Everyone meaning Granddad.

When he'd called to ask for her help, she'd offered to give him money to hire someone to work part-time in the shop until one or both of her sisters returned to work. She'd pointed out that it was a practical solution to the problem. He'd pointed out that the chocolate and fudge recipes were top secret, need-to-know, and only for family. If he wanted some blasted stranger making them, he could afford to hire someone himself. He wanted family.

She was family.

Chocolate Haven was her legacy.

Plus, he missed her.

The last part had gotten to her.

She'd told herself that she was being manipulated. She'd reminded herself that she did not want to end up like her sisters Adeline and Brenna—living in Benevolence, working at the family store, settling into small-town life. She'd gone over all the reasons why she should not let Byron Lamont trick her into returning home.

And then she'd agreed to do it.

"Because you're an idiot," she muttered, walking out of the bedroom and into the hall. She'd left a light on over the stove. Its muted glow cut through the darkness, but even the light couldn't chase away the remnants of the nightmare. Probably because the nightmare had been her reality, and the dream was nothing more than memories of it.

She hurried through the hallway, ignoring the dark corners that the light didn't reach, the open doorway that led into the bathroom.

The living room was small and quaint. Just like the rest of the apartment. It smelled like chocolate and looked like a page out of a 1970s Sears catalog—plaid sofa and easy chair, small television with antenna ears. Just like Chocolate Haven, it never changed. The sofa had been there for as long as Willow could remember. The stove and cabinets and counters in the little galley kitchen were all the same. She could remember spending time there as a kid, eating cookies and drinking hot chocolate and listening to her grandmother talk about how fortunate they all were to have one another.

If she could have, Alice Lamont would have lived forever. Just to make sure that none of her grand-daughters ever forgot what it meant to be family.

But, of course, no one lived forever.

Including Byron.

The patriarch of the Lamont family was getting older, and he was slowing down. Willow had noticed that when she'd come for her sister Brenna's wedding. She hadn't said anything to either of her sisters, but she was certain they'd noticed as well. They hadn't put any pressure on Willow, but they'd hinted that she should spend more time at home. They hadn't seemed to realize that Willow's home wasn't Benevolence, the chocolate shop, the big house on the hill that they'd grown up in. Maybe because, to both of them, home *was* all those things.

Not a surprise when it came to Adeline. She'd always loved Benevolence. Brenna, though . . .

She was an enigma.

One that Willow wasn't going to solve at two in the morning when her stomach hurt and her head was pounding. Migraines sucked, and she'd been fighting one for days.

She stalked into the kitchen, grabbed the old kettle, and turned on the faucet. Her hand shook and water sloshed over the rim, but she managed to get enough water in to make a cup of tea. She'd count that as a victory.

She needed to win at something.

She'd been losing at chocolate making for days.

She scowled, annoyed with herself and with the situation she was in. She could have said no. She *should* have said no.

The phone rang, and she nearly jumped out of her

skin, the kettle clattering onto the stove, more water sloshing through the spout. She grabbed a paper towel with one hand and the phone with the other, the old yellow cord twisting and twirling as she pressed the receiver to her ear.

"Hello?" she barked, her voice too loud.

"I knew you'd be awake," the caller whispered, and for a moment Willow was back in time, another voice whispering in her ear—*Say a word to anyone, and your sisters die.*

Her hand tightened on the cord, her nails digging into her palm. "Who is this?"

"How many people do you know who'd call you at two in the morning?" the caller whispered. This time, Willow recognized the voice, the hint of sarcasm, and the soft coo of a baby in the background.

"Addie? What in God's name are you doing up?" she said, imagining her sister tucked in some corner of the pretty little house she shared with her husband, newborn daughter, and the two teenagers she'd taken in.

"What most mothers of newborn babies do at two in the morning: feeding my daughter. There is no end to her appetite." She didn't sound frustrated by that. She sounded content. "I'm also wishing I had cake. Coconut. With those yummy toasted coconut shavings on top. Just like Grandmom used to make."

"Want me to bake you one?" Willow opened the fridge, eyeing the empty shelves. No eggs. No milk. No butter. She doubted she had flour or sugar in the pantry cupboard, and she knew for sure she didn't have coconut. But if Addie wanted cake, she could run to the next town over, go to the all-night grocery store, and grab the ingredients. It would give her something to do.

"Don't you dare!"

"Why not?"

"First, that would take hours. Second, I'm trying to lose the baby weight. That's not going to happen if I stuff my face every time my daughter eats."

"You don't need to lose weight."

"That's not what Mom says."

"Since when do you care what Mom says?"

"Since winter is over and spring is coming and I can't fit into any of my clothes."

"You gave birth eight weeks ago. You're nursing your daughter, and your boobs are the size of Mack trucks. Of course, you can't fit into your clothes!"

Addie laughed. "I knew you'd cheer me up."

"I didn't realize you needed it."

"Sinclair left on business yesterday morning. The kids have been bickering all day. The baby is colicky, and my boobs are as big as houses, so . . . yeah. I needed it."

"Mack trucks. It would be difficult to walk around with houses attached to your chest," Willow corrected, and Addie laughed again.

"Thanks, Willow."

"For what?"

"Picking up the phone. I shouldn't have called, but you were on my mind. We haven't really talked since you've been back."

True.

They'd both been busy—Addie with her life. Willow with the shop.

"How are things going?" Addie continued, and Willow gave her the pat answer she'd given everyone who'd asked.

"Great!"

"Really?"

"Aside from the fact that Granddad is driving me crazy? Yeah."

"What's he doing? Trying to convince you to move back home?"

"Home is Seattle, and I plan to be back there in nine days."

"You know what I meant," she said easily. "He wants nothing more than to have all of us close."

"Seattle isn't that far away."

"Close. As in—living in town, working in the shop, being near enough that he can stick his nose into all of our lives."

"He already does that."

"You have a good point, but I still think he's going to try to talk you into staying. Brace yourself for it. And, be prepared for . . ."

"What?"

"Nothing."

"Adeline Rose! What should I be prepared for?"

"Him going off on some trip while you're running the shop."

"He wouldn't dare." She hoped not, because she wasn't prepared to run the shop on her own. Not now. Not in a week. Not in a year.

"He went on a fishing trip while Brenna was helping at the shop. Left her alone to figure things out."

"I didn't hear about that."

"You were busy planning your . . ."

"Wedding? You can say it, Addie. It's not a dirty word."

"I didn't want to bring up bad memories."

"Ken is a nice guy. We had a really nice relationship. I don't have any bad memories." She sounded stuck-up and snooty, and that embarrassed her. When had she become *that* person? The one who didn't like any messy emotions or messy conversations, who liked everything neat and tidy and perfect?

"I'm glad," Addie said, and the sincerity in her voice made Willow feel even worse.

"I'm not saying it was a perfect relationship. It's just . . . well, Ken really *is* a nice guy. He made our breakup easy."

"You sound like you're apologizing," Addie said with a quiet laugh. "You don't have to. I had my heart broken once, but Sinclair has more than made up for that. I just want you to be happy, and I was worried that you might feel lonely after living with someone for so many years."

"Is that why you called me at two in the morning?"

"I called you because I've missed you, and I was sitting here nursing Alice, thinking about how we used to sneak into the kitchen together at night when Dad was sick. You'd always make me warm chocolate milk. Remember that?"

"I can make you some now, if you want," she responded.

"I'd rather we have dinner together tonight. I'll cook. You bring dessert."

"I'll cook *and* bring dessert."

"How is that fair?"

"Why does it have to be fair? You have a newborn and your husband is out of town. I'll make lasagna, and I'll be there at seven."

"You're going to make lasagna *and* work at Chocolate Haven all day?"

"I'll manage. If I don't, I'll swing by the diner and

have Laurie Beth plate up some of whatever the special is. Are Chase and Lark going to be home?"

"Lark will be. Chase has a new girlfriend. So, we'll see."

"A girlfriend? Isn't he a little young?" She grabbed a bottle of Tylenol from her purse, popped three in her mouth, and swallowed them with water. She'd taken so much of the stuff the past few days, she was probably going to OD on it. If she didn't die of caffeine poisoning first.

"He turned twenty last week."

"Time flies." She grabbed a tea bag, realized she hadn't turned on the burner, and did that. Her hands weren't shaking anymore and the nightmare and memories were where they should be—far off in the back of her mind. Thank God!

"I know! A couple of years ago, I was living in this house by myself, thinking I was going to become the resident cat lady. I blinked my eyes, and now I'm married and have a baby."

"Are you happy?" Willow asked, because she wanted her to be. She wanted both her sisters to have what she'd never quite been able to find—contentment and peace.

"Very." Addie yawned, and Willow could picture her, red hair sticking up in a hundred different directions, the baby curled up on her chest.

"You're exhausted. You need to finish feeding the baby and go back to sleep."

"You need to go to bed too. The shop opens in a few hours, and Granddad hates to get off his schedule."

"So he's been telling me. I'll see you tonight, Addie."

"See you, then. Love you, sis."

There was a soft click, and the line went dead.

Outside, the wind whistled through the alley and rattled the old shutters, the sounds familiar and oddly comforting. She walked to the living room window and looked out onto Main Street. It hadn't changed. Not a bit. Same streetlights. Same sidewalks. Same businesses. Mr. Murphy still had a bench outside of the five-and-dime. Eunice Simms still had a wreath of flowers hanging from the door of her florist shop.

And Willow? She still had an ache in her heart when she looked at it, a longing for what used to be.

Two blocks down, a car turned onto Main. She watched as it crept toward the shop. Most people in Benevolence were tucked safely into their beds. If they weren't, they sure as heck weren't trolling along Main at the speed of a slow-moving turtle.

She stepped away from the window as the car rolled past, but she kept an eye on it, following the headlights as they slid along the blacktop. She watched as it disappeared around the corner a block up, holding her breath for whatever would happen next.

Of course, nothing did.

Five minutes. Ten. She turned off the burner, poured water over the tea bag, watched as the mug filled with tan liquid. Told herself everything was fine, because this was small-town America, and nothing bad should ever happen here.

It did, though.

Even if her childhood hadn't proven that, her job did. As the King County prosecuting attorney, she'd helped put away hundreds of criminals. She knew that horrible things happened in the nicest places— upscale neighborhoods in the wealthiest areas of

Seattle, rural hamlets at the edge of the county line, anywhere people lived, crime happened. But, Benevolence was about as safe as any place could be.

She grabbed the tea and turned away from the window, because waiting for something to happen in a town like this one was like waiting for Santa in the summer. He could show, but he probably wouldn't.

The exterior stairs rattled, the sound of metal bouncing against brick so unmistakable she set the mug down and turned toward the door. No way on God's green earth was anyone she knew climbing the stairs to the apartment. She pictured the car that had been crawling along the road. God! Had the person seen her light and come back to . . .

What? Rob her?

It's not like anyone in town would think she'd brought a fortune with her from Seattle. She sure as heck wasn't driving a Lamborghini or Corvette. Nope. She'd ridden into town in the minivan she'd purchased the day she'd completed her foster parenting classes. Nothing fancy. Nothing that would give anyone the impression that she was carrying around trunks of riches.

She did have enemies, of course. What prosecuting attorney didn't? But she'd never experienced any overt threats.

The stairs rattled again, and someone knocked on the door. Just a quick, hard rap, but it was enough to prove what she'd already known. She had an unexpected and completely unwanted visitor.

She flicked off the living room light and grabbed the phone. She'd been a victim once. No way in hell did she plan to be one again.

She dialed 911, her finger shaking, her eyes glued to the door.

"Nine-one-one. What's the nature of your emergency?"

"I need the police," she responded as the stairs rattled again. "Someone is . . ." *On my apartment stairs* didn't seem like a good way to get help. "Outside my apartment."

"Is he trying to get in?" the operator asked.

"He knocked." That sounded way less urgent than she wanted it to.

"What's your address?"

She gave it quickly, her eyes glued to the door.

"Hey, that's Chocolate Haven!" the caller exclaimed. "Is this Willow? I heard you were back in town. It's Jason Morgan. We went to high school together."

"Yes, it's Willow." And she might remember a Jason, but she was too busy being scared out of her mind to think about it.

"Man! It's been ages. How are you enjoying being back?"

"I was enjoying it a lot more a few minutes ago."

"I bet, but don't worry, the police are on the way. Can you hear the sirens?"

Not over the frantic pounding of her heart, she couldn't!

"Not yet," she murmured, staring at the door as if doing so could keep an intruder from bursting in.

A weapon! That's what she needed!

She opened the kitchen drawer and took out the sharpest knife she could find.

"You still there, Willow? Don't hang up until the police arrive, okay?"

"Okay." She could finally hear the sirens. She could

see emergency lights, too. "The police are here. Thanks for your help, Jason."

She hung up, dropping the phone into the cradle and running to the door. She almost pulled it open. Almost. Then she remembered that she'd heard someone on the stairs, and that whoever it was could still be out there.

A minute passed, the stairs rattled, feet pounded on metal, and someone rapped on the door.

"Sheriff's department," a man called. "Everything okay in there?"

"Yes." She yanked the door open and looked into a familiar face. Silvery blue eyes, jagged scar, short-cropped blond hair. Jax Gordon. The kid who'd always been the outsider. The teenager who'd kept to himself, done his own thing, made his own way. A rebel in the eyes of the town. She'd always admired him for that. He'd left town after graduation and had returned a few years ago to help care for his uncle. She'd seen him several times during previous visits, but that was the extent of their contact.

And, now he was here, standing on the icy landing, waiting for her to tell him what was going on. Which was great. Except that nothing much had happened. Just someone knocking on the door and leaving.

"I shouldn't have called," she said.

"How about you tell me what happened before we decide that?" he responded, his gaze dropping from her face to the knife she was holding.

"I heard someone on the stairs. Now that you're here, that doesn't seem nearly as threatening as it did when I was in the apartment alone." She tried to smile and failed miserably.

"Threatening or not, someone knocking on your

door at 2 in the morning is unusual. But, maybe not worth digging holes in your palm over." He uncurled her fingers from the knife, took it from her, and turned her palm so she could see the marks her nails had left.

"Right. I guess the knife was a little overboard."

"I didn't say that, Willow," he responded, his calm tone exactly the kind she used when she spoke to crime victims.

"I know. I'm saying it. This was a mistake. An over-reaction. I'm sorry I wasted your time."

"How about you tell me exactly what happened, and let me decide if it's been wasted?" he repeated.

"I saw a car driving very slowly down Main Street. It went around the corner, and a few minutes later, someone knocked on my door." She shrugged, happy that she sounded as calm and reasonable as he did. "That's the entire story. Nothing intriguing about it."

"It was intriguing enough for you to call for help," he pointed out. "Did you see anyone on the stairs?"

"I was too chicken to open the door," she admitted.

He smiled. "In my line of work, we call that smart." A drop of rain splattered on the landing near his feet. Another fell on his cheek, sliding down the curve of the scar before he wiped it away.

"Why don't you come in?" she suggested, stepping aside so he could walk into the apartment.

He stayed where he was, head cocked to the side, his smile fading. "Hear that?" he asked.

As if his question had conjured it, a faint mewling drifted through the darkness.

"What was it?" she whispered.

"Damned if I know," he responded as the thing—

whatever it was—mewled again. "It sounds like a kitten. Wonder if someone dumped it in the alley."

That made all kinds of sense. The car. The stairs. The knock. Someone with a box of kittens to dump but not quite heartless enough to leave it where it wouldn't be found.

She was so relieved, her knees felt weak.

"A kitten," she murmured, leaning past him and staring down into the alley. "I guess I should go find it."

"How about you let me do that?" He reached past her and set the knife on Granddad's recliner. "Stay here. There's no sense in both of us getting wet."

The rain fell in sheets as he moved down the stairs, plastering his blond hair to his head. She could have stayed where she was—warm and dry in the apartment, but the kitten mewled again, the sound shivering along her spine and making the hair on her arms stand up.

It didn't sound all that much like a kitten.

Not now that she was really listening.

She followed Jax down the stairs, her feet slipping on the ice-coated steps as she neared the bottom. She stumbled, probably would have taken a header, but Jax caught her arm, holding her steady while she caught her balance.

"Careful," he said, flicking on a flashlight. He trained it toward the end of the alley and the Dumpster that stood against the wall there. "I think the sound is coming from there."

He strode forward confidently. Not even a hint of hesitation in his steps. No fear. No caution. She'd heard that he'd worked on a drug task force in LA for nearly a decade. She didn't guess there was much that would scare him.

She was scared, though.

She wasn't going to lie.

She hated surprises. The car, the sound on the stairs, the cat's cries, they were all surprises, and her heart was thrumming along at high speed, threatening to jump right out of her chest.

She didn't realize how close she'd gotten to Jax until he stopped and she nearly plowed into his back. She managed to pull up short, her feet slipping a little in the icy slush that was forming. Shoes would have been good, but it was too late for that. They'd reached the Dumpster, and Jax was shining his light inside it.

"Nothing there."

"How about behind it?" she asked, peering into the space between the Dumpster and the wall. Jax's light illuminated an old fruit crate covered with a blanket.

"That's got to be it," he muttered. "Hold this." He handed her the light, his fingers warm against her chilled skin. Then, he was on his stomach, his head and shoulders disappearing behind the Dumpster.

Abandoning an animal might not be number one on the list of cruel things Jax had seen during his years working law enforcement, but it sure as hell was right up there at the top of the stupid list. There was a no-kill shelter just outside of town, and there wasn't a person in Benevolence who didn't know it. Of course, people did stupid things all the time. Even in a town like this one. Usually, though, the stupidity didn't have the potential to hurt anyone or anything.

He snagged the edge of the rain-damp crate and

gave it a quick, hard jerk. It slid across cement, the scratchy sound of it mixing with the kitten's mewling cry.

Only, it didn't sound much like a kitten anymore.

It didn't sound like a cat.

It sounded like . . .

He pulled the blanket off, looked down into the scrunched-up face of a newborn baby. His heart stopped. He was damned well certain of that, and then it started again, pounding frantically as he lifted the baby from the box. No injuries that he could see. Clean footy pajamas. No coat. Cold hands. Cold cheeks.

"Dear God," Willow breathed, kneeling beside him, her hair plastered to her head, her eyes wide. "Who would do such a thing?"

"I don't know." He kept his voice steady, his hands steady, but he was fuming inside, quaking with the kind of rage that came from seeing someone abused or used or . . .

He looked into the baby's pale face.

Abandoned.

He shrugged out of his coat and wrapped the baby in it. A girl maybe, because there was a tiny bow attached the peach fuzz on her head.

Willow touched the baby's cheek, brushing moisture away with the palm of her hand. "She's freezing. We need to get her inside."

"We need to get her medical attention," he responded. He didn't know much about babies, but this one looked smaller than most, her little hands flailing as she cried, her lips an odd purple-blue.

"I'll call for an ambulance," Willow said, and she would have darted away, but he grabbed her wrist. She had tiny bones and a delicate build, but he'd never thought of her as anything but tough. That had been the persona she'd shown to the world when she was a teen, and she still seemed to wear it. Shoulders back, head up, gaze direct. Kind of an I-dare-you-to-mess-with-me stance.

"I'll call. Can you bring the baby up the apartment? I need to take some pictures of the scene and collect evidence."

"Sure." She lifted the baby from his arms, the beam of the flashlight jumping in a dozen different directions. Something fluttered at the very edge of the light, and he bent to retrieve it, frowning as he saw black marker bleeding through soaked paper.

"Do you think that came from the crate?" Willow asked, moving closer, her arm bumping his as she tried to read the blurry words.

"It could have. Go on up to the apartment. I'm going to get the evidence kit. I'll send the ambulance crew up when they arrive."

He knew he sounded dismissive.

He didn't mean to, but he had a job to do, and sometimes in a town like Benevolence, that was more difficult than it had been in Los Angeles. People here meant well. He knew they did. But they tended to want to help. A lot. Sometimes that meant getting in the way, contaminating evidence, offering unsolicited advice.

To her credit, Willow didn't argue. She didn't offer anything but a quick nod and a fast retreat.

And she *did* move fast—her long legs sprinting across the pavement, her bare feet slapping against metal stairs as she took them two at a time.

Seconds later, she was in the apartment and the door was closed. She'd taken the flashlight with her, and the alley was gray-black, rain falling steadily. Late March, and winter still had a tight-fisted grip on eastern Washington. The temperature was hovering just above freezing, and the wind made it feel colder than that. No one in his right mind would leave a baby out on a night like this.

He strode to the cruiser, calling for an ambulance and then for his boss, Kane Rainier. He could see a few lights on in the residential section of town. Probably people woken by his sirens and currently manning their scanners to see what they could find out. Eventually a few of them would make their way to the scene. That was the way things always were in Benevolence. No criminal case was ever private. No crime ever went unnoticed.

He loved it just about as much as he was frustrated by it.

He snagged his evidence kit from the back of the car, pulled out a bag, and put the soaked paper in it. He'd have liked to take a look at it, but it was too wet and too delicate. He'd let it dry a little first.

He snapped a few pictures of the crate and the blanket, crouched to look behind the Dumpster again. Maybe whoever had abandoned the kid thought it would be warmer and safer back there, but it was a piss-poor place to leave a baby. A few hours, and the infant would have succumbed to the cold.

Just the thought sent rage surging through his blood again.

He tamped it down, lifting the crate with gloved hands. There was something wedged into its corner. Looked like a dollar-store doll. Small. Drawn-on face that was about as cute as the back end of one of Ander Smithfield's prize hogs.

"Poor baby," he muttered. "No wonder you were crying."

Butt-ugly doll. Cold. Rain. And parents, or parent, who had their heads up their behinds.

Sirens screamed and lights flashed as Benevolence's finest arrived. Ambulance. Fire truck. Sheriff's car. Everyone rushing in, the EMTs running up the stairs to the apartment. Sheriff Kane Rainier walking toward him.

"What have we got?" he asked, his expression as grim and hard as Jax had ever seen it.

"Abandoned newborn. Found in this crate." He held it up and Kane nodded.

"Looks like something from the farmers' market. Probably had fruit in it at one point. Maybe we can trace a vendor, but I've got a feeling the thing is as old as me. Was there anything else with it?"

"Blanket. Doll. Possible note." He handed over the plastic evidence bag. "Willow Lamont may have seen the vehicle the baby was transported in."

"Did she give you a description?"

"Not yet. We were distracted."

"I bet." Kane eyed the crate, his gaze moving from it to the Dumpster. "Not a very nice place to leave a baby."

"Would any place have been?"

"The police station is a mile away. The fire department is just a little farther. Either would have been a better option. Let's get the vehicle description from Willow. We'll give it to the local media along with a photo of the baby. Someone somewhere knows the mother."

"She could have been passing through," Jax pointed out, but Kane was right. The sooner they got the information out to the public, the sooner they'd start getting leads on the identity of the mother. From there, they could work out who had abandoned the baby and why.

"Could have been, but anyone coming through town has probably been here before." Kane swiped rain from his cheek. "We'll figure it out. Eventually. For now, go ahead and get the vehicle description. We'll work from that."

He strode away, moving toward a small crowd of curious onlookers. Half of them were still wearing pajamas. The other half had managed to dress in street clothes before they came running to the scene.

Jax turned away.

Let Kane deal with the community. He was good at it. Jax? He was good at doing his job. Finding the bad guys. Putting them in prison. Making sure they paid for their crimes.

The rest . . . all the political crap that went with being a deputy in a small town . . . he was still trying to figure out.

Even now. After four years back home, he wasn't sure he'd gotten the hang of it.

He jogged up the metal steps and walked into the apartment.

Willow was sitting in the old recliner, the baby in her arms, wrapped snuggly in a white blanket. His jacket hung over the arm of the chair, the baby's soft curls brushing against it. He could see the little bow dangling from a few strands of downy hair. For some reason, that bothered him. It was as if someone had been trying to say, *I love her. I want her to be okay. I want her to have all the things a little girl should.*

Anyone who'd wanted to say that, wouldn't have been stupid enough to leave the kid out in the elements. That was Jax's opinion, but he couldn't discount the bow or the blanket that had been tossed over the crate. Not much by way of protection, but the gesture itself spoke of concern.

"How's she doing?" he asked, and Willow looked up, her eyes a deep midnight blue in her pale face.

"Still a little purple in the fingers and lips. The paramedic thinks she has a heart condition." She tucked a strand of hair behind her ears. Not strawberry-blonde like her sister Brenna or orange-red like Adeline's, Willow's hair was a deep true red that reminded him of fall leaves and quiet autumn evenings.

"Actually, ma'am," one of the EMTs said, "I said it was a possibility. That doesn't mean she has one." He closed the medical kit. "We'll let the doctors make the diagnosis."

"Of course," Willow murmured, her gaze focused on the baby.

"The ambulance is waiting," the EMT continued. "I'll take her from here."

He moved into her space, leaning down to lift the baby from her arms. Willow flinched back, the reaction so quick and subtle, Jax wouldn't have noticed if he hadn't been watching so intently.

She must have felt his stare. She met his eyes as she handed the baby over, offering a tight smile. "Thanks for coming out so quickly, Jax. Another fifteen minutes in the cold, and who knows what would have happened to her."

No need to thank me for doing my job, he almost said, but Willow was already up and moving away, snagging a purse from a hook near the door and following the EMT outside.

Jax grabbed his coat and followed, shutting the door and making sure it was locked.

There wasn't a lot of crime in Benevolence. It was one of his favorite things about the place. Sometimes, though, a petty thief broke into an empty home and took a few dollars, some jewelry, or a big-screen television. Malcom Finch had managed the last one, carrying the TV out through the front door of his vacationing neighbor's house and weaving down Main Street in a drunken stupor.

Yeah. Petty crime happened in Benevolence. Sometimes worse. And for a woman like Willow—a prosecuting attorney who was known for always winning her cases—caution was an imperative. He had no doubt she'd made enemies. He sure as hell had. Thank God none of them had followed him from Los Angeles.

He walked down the stairs, moving into step beside Willow. She was still wearing pajamas, the cuffs of the pink flannel pants dragging in puddles of melting ice and rain. She had to be cold. Hell! *He* was cold and he was used to the weather. She'd only been back in town for a week, and from what he'd heard, she'd spent most of her time in Chocolate Haven or in the apartment.

The blue-haired ladies at the diner were calling her a hermit. The men who'd had hopes that the oldest Lamont sister was back looking for a guy to hook up with were spending all their spare change at the chocolate shop hoping to catch a glimpse of her and maybe convince her to go for a drink. Everyone in town was whispering that she'd changed. She wasn't the girl who'd left town nearly fifteen years ago. She was different.

Jax didn't see it. But, then, he'd thought she was different before she'd left for college. The happy-go-lucky sixth-grader he'd met when he'd moved to Benevolence to live with his uncle and aunt had become quiet and introspective in the middle of eighth grade. Instead of letting her hair hang loose while she swung from monkey bars and jumped rope, she'd tied it back in a tight bun. She smiled less, laughed less, was silent more.

It was possible everyone else in town had been caught up in the tragedy of her father's illness and had failed to realize just how different Willow had become. Jax had noticed, because he'd noticed everything—the shift of shadows across a window, the haunting cry of a mourning dove, the way that old man Rhodes and Jemma O'Rourke looked at each other when they thought no one could see.

They'd eloped a year after Jax went to college. He was the only one in town who hadn't been surprised. Being hyperalert had it benefits. It also had its detriment. He'd spent the second half of his childhood sleepless, every night filled with a million potential dangers.

When he'd slept, he'd heard the first gunshot and then the second echoing through his dreams. His mother. Then his youngest sister. Killed quickly while he slept in the tent in the backyard—earning a Boy Scout badge on one of the hottest nights of the summer.

The worst night of his life.

He pulled the thought and the memories up short and shoved them all away, tucking them back in the corner of his mind where they had been since he was eleven. Even then, he'd known that if he let them, they could destroy him. One more victim of the drug-thugs who'd murdered his family.

He ducked under yellow crime-scene tape that Kane had strung up across the alley entrance. A few people in the crowd called out questions. He ignored them. Willow had already climbed into the ambulance, and he slid into his squad car.

He'd get her statement at the hospital.

Then he'd go back to his office and file it.

That might just be enough to keep him from hearing the gunshots as he drifted off to sleep.

His mother.

His sisters.

His brother.

And the high-pitched, brokenhearted keening of his father, the horrible sound that had filled his ears as he'd raced into the house.

Jax had almost saved his father.

Almost saved his baby sister, too.

Almost.

He touched the scar that bisected his cheek and then let his hand fall away.

Twenty-two years.

And he still wondered what life would have been like if he'd managed it.

He scowled, shoving the keys into the ignition and following the ambulance out of the parking lot.

Chapter Two

Shoes would have been a good idea.

And, maybe, a coat.

Willow eyed her still-frozen toes, rubbed her chilled arms, and told herself that the hospital wasn't nearly as cold as it felt. Mind over matter. That's what this amounted to. She just needed to imagine that she was somewhere warm and dry and comfortable, and she'd feel better.

The problem was, she wasn't somewhere warm or comfortable.

She was soaking wet and freezing, pacing the empty NICU waiting room. She hated the hospital scent, the ammonia floor cleaner and the lemony furniture polish that thickened the air. She hated the nighttime quiet, the empty corridors, the shadowy doorways. She could swear she heard someone crying. Not a baby. A woman, the soft sound so faint it might have just been her imagination.

But probably not.

This was a hospital.

A place where people came for second chances, for healing, for help, and, sometimes, to die.

As a prosecuting attorney for King County, she'd interviewed many crime victims in hospitals. She should have been used to the tears, the sadness that often seemed to hang in the air. She should have been used to the silence and the hallways and the doorways that opened into darkened rooms.

But there were memories in those things. There were secrets hidden in the dark corners, whispers lingering in the silences.

She shivered, her teeth chattering as she rubbed her arms more vigorously. If she asked, a nurse would probably find her a blanket, but the nurses in the NICU were busy, and asking would require stepping out into the long hallway filled with all those closed doors.

"You're being ridiculous," she muttered, swinging toward the door and screaming as a tall, broad-shouldered man stepped into view.

Jax.

His identity registered before her scream died, and she blushed. She was a grown woman hanging out in a hospital waiting room. She should *not* be screaming because a man appeared in the doorway.

"Holy crap," she said. "You scared me!"

As if it needed explanation. As if the scream hadn't been clue enough that she'd been terrified.

"Sorry." He stepped into the room, his hair dark with melted rain, his cheeks ruddy from the cold. "How's everything going?"

"With the baby? I haven't heard anything since they brought her into the NICU."

"The baby, and you. Are doing okay? You look a

little pale." He was a foot away, his eyes a mix of gray and blue that reminded her of tropical beaches and the honeymoon she and Ken had been planning a lifetime ago.

"I'm a redhead. Pale goes with the territory."

"There's pale and then there's what you are," he responded. "Which is about as white as I've ever seen a living, breathing human being. How about you sit for a few minutes while I go see what I can find out about Baby Doe?"

"I'd rather come with you." She tried to add energy and life to her voice. She failed miserably. She hated that. Hated being vulnerable or needy or scared.

"Suit yourself. I can't promise anything, though. Usually, they only let family into the intensive care, but we might be able to change their minds since she has no family. At least not any family that we can contact." He shrugged out of his coat and draped it across her shoulders, tugging it closed, his knuckles brushing her collarbone and sending heat through her chilled blood. She felt it like she felt the cold floor beneath her feet and the tepid air chugging out of the heating vent.

He must have felt it, too. He'd stilled, his hands falling away, his eyes looking straight into hers. Her pulse jumped, but Jax was just a guy she'd gone to school with, someone who'd known her before and after, but who didn't know her anymore. Whatever she was feeling, it was more to do with fatigue and adrenaline than the man who stood in front of her.

At least, that's what she was going to tell herself.

He finally stepped away, and she could breathe again. Only she'd never realized she wasn't breathing, and she was suddenly dizzy, suddenly desperate to drop into one of the vinyl-covered chairs. Jax was moving away, and she'd said she was going with him, so she followed, moving across the room and out into the hall. Her legs were wobbly, but she didn't fall.

A small victory, but after the last few days of failure after failure in the chocolate shop, she'd take it.

Earlier she'd gotten as far as the double doors that led into the NICU. Now she waited while Jax pushed a button on the wall and the doors swung open.

A nurse sat at a tall counter a few feet away, staring at a computer screen and scribbling something on a notepad. She looked up as they approached.

"I'm sorry," she said before either had a chance to speak. "Unless you're family, visiting hours are over."

"I'm here on official business." Jax flashed his police badge and a smile. The nurse glanced at the badge and took notice of the smile. Of course, she did. Jax had that kind of smile and that kind of looks. The kind that seemed dark and dangerous and a little mysterious. It was the scar. And the eyes. The strong line of his jaw, the sharp edges of his cheekbones. A chick magnet. That's what he'd been called in middle school and high school. He'd been the only freshman invited to senior prom. The way Willow had heard things, he'd been invited by four different girls. He'd turned them all down.

It might or might not have been true.

She'd been preoccupied, struggling with night-mares and fear and anxiety.

A long time ago.

Sometimes she had to remind herself of that.

"Is this regarding Baby Doe?" the nurse finally managed to say. She seemed a lot more eager to help now, her dark eyes alight with interest.

"Yes," Jax responded.

The nurse typed something into the computer, then scanned the screen. "She's currently in radiology having a sonogram of her heart. They should be back up shortly. Or, if you're in a hurry, you could go down and wait. I'm sure one of the doctors will speak with you when they wheel her out."

"I'll do that." Jax smiled again. "Has anyone else asked about the baby?"

"In the fifteen minutes since she arrived? No."

"I'd like you to call me if anyone aside from law enforcement does." He slid a business card from his wallet and handed it to her.

She scowled, apparently no longer enamored with Jax's smile.

"Do you know how busy I am, Officer"—she glanced at the card—"Deputy Gordon? I work twelve-hour shifts with barely enough of a break to pee. I don't have time to call your office every time someone shows up asking about that poor kid."

"Someone left her behind a Dumpster. In the rain. With nothing but a thin blanket to keep her warm. I want to find that person, because there isn't a human being on this planet who deserves to be tossed away like that."

Her face softened, the hard lines of irritation smoothing away.

"I'll call." She tucked the card into her pocket. "You can wait in the NICU lounge or you can head down to radiology. Like I said, they should be finished there soon."

"Thanks," Jax said, cupping Willow's elbow as he turned away. Under normal circumstances, she'd have shrugged from his grasp and forged her own path. She planned to go to radiology, and she was perfectly capable of making it there on her own.

But these weren't normal circumstances.

Everything felt odd and off and strange, and for a moment, she let herself enjoy the contact—his hand on her elbow, his arm brushing her shoulder. He was taller than her by several inches, and she felt protected in a way she never had when she was with Ken.

Ken who'd called her twice since she'd left Seattle, who'd asked how she was doing and made small talk because he'd felt obligated. They'd promised that they'd stay friends after they broke up.

After all, they'd been together for eight years. Nearly a quarter of their lives. There was no need to cut the bond completely. Like Willow had told Addie—Ken was a nice guy. They got along well.

But the calls? They'd felt awkward and forced, the silences in the conversations stretching out a little too long. Ken was dating someone else. He'd met April four months ago, and they were already planning a fall wedding.

Funny how that had happened.

Or not.

Four months of dating, and Ken and April were committed to forever together. Eight years of dating, six years of living together, and Willow hadn't gotten more than a half-hearted "we should get married" from the man.

Not that she'd wanted more.

Obviously.

She'd been the one to break the engagement just a few months shy of their wedding. She'd been the one to pack her bags and leave the house they'd shared for six years.

And she'd been the one to decide that she didn't want another relationship.

So why was she walking through the hospital, with Jax's hand on her elbow? Why was she enjoying it, for God's sake?

"Thanks for your help tonight," she said, easing away.

"Are you going home?" he asked, raising one sandy-brown brow.

"That would be difficult to do, since I don't have my car."

"Have you called your family?"

"Not yet." And she didn't plan to. Adeline and Brenna were both busy with their new families. Grand-dad needed his sleep. And Mom . . .

Yeah. Janelle would be a problem.

"Then would you mind if I get your statement now? That will save you a trip to the station tomorrow. It will also help expedite the release of information to the public."

"How much are you planning to release?"

"Enough to catch people's attention. The make and color of the car, a picture of the baby." He fished a small notepad from his shirt pocket and wrote some-thing on the page. There were faint scars on his knuckles and a longer, deeper one that sliced across his palm and wrapped around the side of his hand.

Defensive wounds. Not something she'd realized when they were kids, but her work had taught her a lot about violence and its aftermath.

"You did see a car, right?" he prodded, and she real-ized that he'd seen the direction of her gaze, that he was trying to draw her attention away from the old scars.

"Yes, but I can't say for sure that the baby was ever in it."

"We'll figure that out. Did you get the make or model? The color? A partial or full plate number?"

"It was an old Plymouth or Chrysler. Long hood and trunk. You know the kind? Maybe nineteen-sixties or seventies. Not sporty or a roadster. Just old. Dark blue or black."

"We've got about a dozen of those in town, and I'm not sure how many are stashed away in barns outside of town. It'll be interesting to see how many calls we get about the vehicle."

"I'm guessing hundreds."

"That'd be a call from just about everyone in Benevolence."

"I know. People like to be part of stories like this."

"It's not a story, Willow." He tucked the notepad away. "It's a life."

She knew that. Just like she knew that people would want to help. People in Benevolence. People in every town nearby. Small towns. Big hearts. Lots of gossip. Someone somewhere knew something.

It was just a matter of time before everyone else did.

They were walking again, his boots tapping against the tile floor, the dark doorways to either side of the hall making Willow's skin crawl. She'd overcome her fear of the dark and of halls and of doorways years ago. She'd gone to therapy. She'd talked it out. She'd done breathing exercises and meditation and all the things she'd been told to do to let go of the trauma.

But trauma never really went away. It just hid in the back of the mind, waiting for an opportunity to show itself. Returning to the Chocolate Haven had been the perfect conduit for that. She'd get over it again. Eventually.

They stepped onto the elevator, and she could see herself in the stainless-steel doors—drowning in his coat, hair tangled around her face, the damp cuffs of her pajama pants dragging on the floor.

She didn't look like Willow Lamont, Prosecuting Attorney.

She looked like a drowned rat.

She scraped her hair back into the ponytail holder it was escaping from and pulled her damp pajama top away from her skin. She felt clammy and cold and tired, but she wasn't leaving the hospital until she knew the baby was going to be okay.

"You look fine," Jax said, and she realized he was watching her, his expression unreadable.

"I'm not worried about how I look."

"You were fixing your hair."

"I don't want to scare the baby," she lied.

He smiled at that, the edges of the scar puckering. "It would take a lot of makeup for someone as gorgeous as you to scare a kid."

If another man had said it, Willow would have thought he was flirting, but Jax had never been flirtatious. Not even in high school when girls were falling all over themselves to get his attention. Maybe the years had changed him. They sure as heck had changed her, but she was looking straight into his eyes and all she could see was the man who'd pulled a tiny baby from behind a Dumpster.

"I am my mother's daughter. I like to be presentable," she admitted. "She'd be appalled if she saw me out in public like this."

"Guess it's good you didn't call her then."

"Janelle means well," she said, jumping to her mother's defense despite the fact that Jax wasn't criticizing her.

"Your mother has a good heart," he agreed. "She's been great to Vera and Jim."

"How are your aunt and uncle?" she asked, anxious to turn the conversation away from her appearance, her family, her life.

"Vera is doing well. Jim is frustrated. He wants to do more than he can. The stroke took a lot out of him." The doors opened, and he took her arm, ushering her out into another long, empty hall. "Fortunately, he has really good friends who've come up with creative ways to get him out of the house. The week before last, your grandfather took him to an antique car show in Spokane. Byron probably told you all about it."

Actually, he hadn't.

She'd been busy trying to clear her desk, clean her house, stop her mail, and do all the other things that needed to be done before leaving home for two weeks. Plus, she hadn't wanted to get into protracted conversations about how long she planned to stay in Benevolence.

Forever was the only thing Byron wanted to hear.

It was the one thing she would never say.

"Did Jim have fun?" she asked rather than explaining how busy she'd been, how unable to listen to Byron's stories.

"He always has fun when he's with your grandfather. Jim says they're planning another day trip while you're in town."

"Really?"

"Byron didn't mention it?"

"No, but we've been busy at the shop." And she'd been distracted. Frantic. Trying so hard to get back into the rhythm of the business that had supposedly been bred into her. She knew how to make chocolate, for God's sake! She'd learned the art before she'd turned ten. Byron always said she'd taken to it like a fish to water, like a bird to the air, like a drunk to cheap whiskey. The last part always annoyed Janelle and made Willow smile.

The fact was, she *had* taken to it. She'd loved working in Chocolate Haven. She'd understood everything there was to know about making delicious fudge.

Once upon a time.

Now though . . .

Now she'd been failing. Over and over and over again.

"I'm sure he'll tell you about it soon."

"It better be really soon. I'm only in town for nine more days." *Not a day or hour or minute longer.*

"The way Byron tells it, you're here for good."

"Who is he saying that to?" They rounded a corner, following signs that pointed the way to radiology.

"Jim and Vera. I'm sure most people are like me and figure he's exaggerating."

"I do have a job, Jax, and a house and a life away from Benevolence."

"There's no need to explain or to justify."

She told herself that all the time, but she always felt the need to do it anyway. She'd been the Lamont sister everyone had expected to take over the shop.

She'd failed their expectations.

She'd failed her grandfather.

Some days she thought she'd failed herself.

They reached the radiology department—a closed door with a sign hung from it. HOSPITAL STAFF ONLY.

"Might as well have a seat," Jax said, motioning to a couple of vinyl chairs shoved up against the wall. "A heart sonogram could take a while."

"The nurse said they'd probably be finished soon."

She dropped down beside him anyway, grabbing a magazine from a scuffed table and thumbing through it. It was that or make small talk, and she'd used up her daily quota of *that* about three hours after she'd arrived in Benevolence.

"You okay?" Jax asked, and she realized the magazine was upside down, and that she was staring at the page like it might contain the secrets to the mysteries of the universe.

"Just wishing I'd seen the driver of the car. Or the license plate number. Or—"

"Wishes are dreams without action," he cut her off.

"What?"

"My mother used to say that. A lifetime ago." He took the magazine, turned it right-side up, and handed it back.

"Your mother must have been very wise," she responded, surprised that he'd brought up his past. She'd heard bits and pieces of his story, but not all of it and not from him. Jax had always been notoriously silent about what had happened to him and to his family.

"She was. At least, all my memories of her make me think she was. It's been a long time. It could be I've made a portrait of a saint out of a picture of a very ordinary woman."

"I'm sorry, Jax."

"Yeah. Me too, but that won't change it. Besides, I've had a pretty good life, a pretty great one, really. Aside from that one major blip, I have nothing to complain about."

He pulled his phone out, and she knew the conversation was over. Maybe he'd said more than he'd wanted

to, or maybe was afraid she'd ask questions that he
didn't want to answer.

Whatever the case, he texted someone and she
went back to staring at the magazine. She had her
phone. She could text Brenna or Adeline. Heck, she
could text her mom. Janelle would be at the hospital
in two shakes of a stick, taking control, making sure
things were done properly.

But she didn't really want any of them there.

She wanted to be quiet for a couple of seconds and
think about what had happened. A baby in a crate
behind a Dumpster, and she was knee-deep in the
drama. That wasn't something she wanted, and it sure
as heck wasn't something she could have anticipated.

"Willow!" a man called, and she looked up, expecting to see Byron or maybe Brenna's husband, River.
She sure wasn't expecting to see Randall Custard, but
there he was in all his overinflated glory. Hair gelled
back from his Botoxed forehead, brows shaped about
as perfectly as anyone's could be. The owner of the
Benevolence Times and a self-proclaimed lady's man, Randall had always been cocky, self-assured, and annoying.

Based on the fact that he was snapping pictures
without her permission, she'd say he hadn't changed
much.

"Randall," she responded, standing up as he approached. "It's been a while."

"Not so long. We saw each other at May's wedding.
Remember?"

"How could I forget? You posted a lovely shot of my
sister in her beautiful bridesmaid dress on the front
page of the paper." It had been a horrible photo—
payback for the fact that Addie had refused Randall's
invitations to dinner.

"Right." Randall had the good grace to blush. "I've

changed a lot since then. I won't post any pictures of you without your permission. Of course, I hope"—he raised the camera and snapped two more shots—"that you'll give it. You too, Gordon." He turned, lifted the camera.

"Don't," Jax said quietly.

Randall lowered the camera. "What?"

"I don't want my picture on the front page of the paper, Randall, so don't bother taking one of me. Did Kane contact you?"

"That's why I'm here. I plan to run the story in the morning paper, but I need the baby's picture and other pertinent info *stat*." He snapped two more pictures of Willow and then aimed at the door. "Is the baby injured? What condition was she in when you found her? Is this an abuse case or just abandonment?" He fired off one question after another, and Jax didn't answer any of them.

Finally, his voice trailed off, and he cleared his throat. "Kane said you planned to fill me in."

"I do."

"Anytime you're ready, Gordon," Randall snapped, obviously irritated, "I'll be happy for you to do it."

"There's not much information." Jax took out his notepad and read the description of the vehicle verbatim.

"Hold on. Hold on," Randall muttered, fishing in his pocket and pulling out a pen. "I need to take notes."

"That's it," Jax said.

"What do you mean?"

"I mean, that's all the information we have."

"You don't think I'm going to believe that, do you? I've been a journalist for over a decade. I know when someone is keeping information from me. I can read a person like an open book. I can see through a lie—"

He was cut off by the radiology department door. It swung open, and a nurse pushed an Isolette out. She stopped short when she saw them, her dark eyes flashing with irritation as she glanced at Willow, then Jax, and finally Randall.

Or maybe his camera.

She pointed to it and frowned. "We're not talking to the press."

"I'm here on official business," Randall intoned, his voice about two octaves deeper than it had been before. The nurse was attractive. Randall was between wives. Obviously, he hoped to impress her.

"The press is always here on official business." She pushed the Isolette past, and Willow caught a glimpse of the baby—fuzzy hair, tiny bluish fingers and toes. "We still don't talk to them."

"What I'm saying," Randall persisted, "is that the police have asked me to get a photo of the kid."

"The *kid* is a newborn baby."

"That's what I meant."

"Might be what you meant, but it wasn't what you said."

"Hun—"

"The name is Honor, and just because I'm telling you, doesn't mean you should use it all of the time. Now, if you folks will excuse me, I have to get Little Miss back up to the NICU." She jabbed at the elevator button, her nails short, her cuticles ragged.

"Honor, I'm Deputy Jax Gordon with the Benevolence Sheriff's Department." Jax followed her onto the elevator and Willow did the same. She was hoping that Randall had realized he wasn't wanted, but he stepped on behind her, crowding into her space and making the breath freeze in her lungs.

She hated being crowded by people.

She especially hated being crowded by men.

She stepped back, bumping into Jax in the process.

"Sorry," she mumbled.

"Relax," he responded, his breath ruffling tendrils of hair that had escaped the ponytail holder again.

She resisted the urge to fix her hair, to step away from Jax, and to cower in the corner of the elevator until the doors opened. She did *not* resist the urge to get a closer look at the baby.

She leaned close to the Isolette, watching the rapid rise and fall of the infant's chest.

"She's still a little blue," she said to no one in particular.

"Are you family?" Honor asked.

"I found her. Well"—she glanced at Jax—"*we* found her."

"The doctor will have to decide what information to release, but she will probably keep you informed since you saved Little Miss's life."

"I'd like to get a photo of the baby," Jax cut in. "We want to release it to the press."

"We'll do that upstairs. This little munchkin needs to eat."

"That would be a great shot!" Randall crowed. "The sweet little baby being fed by the beautiful young nurse."

"Not going to happen. I already told you, the police will take the photo." The doors opened, and Honor marched off, beelining it to the NICU doors. She paused there, jabbing her finger at Jax and then Willow. "You two can come on back. You"—she pointed at Randall—"stay here."

For once, Randall didn't argue or try to get his way.

He handed his camera to Jax. "Better get a good shot. That baby has parents, and those parents have family and friends. I want to run a nice, clear picture in the morning paper to give people a chance to recognize her."

Jax said something, but Willow was already following Honor into the NICU, and his words were lost as the doors swung closed between them.

Jax was tired.

That was the problem.

He'd worked graveyard all week because Aunt Vera had had meetings at church almost every day and she hadn't wanted to leave Uncle Jim alone. Jax didn't mind helping. He didn't mind being tired or working graveyard or having the last call of his night be a complicated one.

But he wasn't a fan of Randall Custard, and he wasn't in the mood to deal with him. The guy was a pompous ass who'd been born into money and had spent the entirety of his life throwing that fact around. He'd been married too many times to count, trading in the woman du jour every couple of years. He ran a tiny little newspaper in a tiny little town and thought he could rival any major newspaper in any major city.

And he annoyed the hell out of Jax on the best of days.

Today wasn't the best, and Randall's rambling explanation of how to get a good photo of the baby was making it worse.

"Tell you what," Jax said, cutting into the monologue, "I'll take a picture on my phone and text it to you."

"You can't do that."

"Sure I can."

"If you want the best quality photo, use this." Randall thrust the camera into Jax's hands. "It cost a fortune. Be careful with it."

"Right," Jax muttered.

"And maybe you could put in a good word with that nurse."

"About you?" Jax managed to keep the irritation out of his voice, but he couldn't hide the surprise. Honor was at least a decade younger than Randall. That wasn't as big of an issue as her intelligence would be. She seemed smart, and smart women usually didn't go for guys like Randall.

"Who else? You're not thinking of making a play for her, are you?" he asked, his voice dripping with suspicion.

"Women aren't a game."

"That's not an answer."

"It's *my* answer. Wait here. I'll bring the camera out once I get the shot." He slapped his palm against the silver push plate that activated the door and hurried into the NICU.

He was anxious to get the photo.

He was more anxious to get away from Randall.

"Are you looking for Baby Doe?" the nurse at the desk asked. She was sitting in the exact same position she'd been in when he'd spoken to her before, ramrod straight in her chair in front of a computer.

"Yes. Her nurse said I could go back to the NICU."

"I guess we're bending the rules tonight." She sighed. "Go on back. Third door to the right. You'll have to wear scrubs. Honor can hook you up."

"Thanks." He walked past the desk and into the silent corridor. Nighttime in the hospital was always lonely, the shuffle of feet and the quiet swish of mops on the floor interspersed with squeaky-wheeled medicine carts being pushed through the empty hallways.

He'd been eleven years old the last time he'd spent the night in a hospital, but he still remembered what it was like to wake to the quiet blip of the machine tracking his pulse. He still remembered the yellowish light that seeped under the door. He remembered exactly how it felt to be alone and to know that no one was coming. His mother had been an only child. His father had a much-older brother named Jim whom Jax had never met.

That was it for family.

Jax had known it, and he'd had no idea that Jim and Vera were on the way—contacted by the LAPD five days into their twenty-fifth anniversary cruise to Europe. They'd been airlifted to the nearest port and were doing everything in their power to get to Jax.

For three days, though, he'd been alone. For three nights, he'd lain in bed trying to understand what it meant to have no one. On the fourth night, Jim and Vera had walked into the room—Jim an older, grayer version of Jax's father.

For one moment, Jax had thought it had all been a nightmare—the gunshots, the screams, the knives, the blood. For one euphoric second, he'd believed that his family had been returned to him. He'd whispered, "Dad." Just that one word, because his cheek had been sliced through, muscles and nerves carefully stitched back together, and he'd been in too much pain to say more.

If he let himself, he could still see the stricken look on Jim's face, the tears sliding down Vera's cheeks. He could still feel the yearning and the despair and the wild relief of knowing that he wasn't alone after all.

The way Jax saw things, everyone should have someone to stand beside him in the darkest hours of the night.

Even tiny babies with bows dangling from their hair. *Especially* tiny babies.

He walked to the door the nurse had indicated, knocking once before he opened it. A large sink stood against one wall, a pile of scrubs and shoe covers sitting on shelves beside it. His coat hung from a hook next to the sink. Willow must have removed it when she put on scrubs. He knew the drill. He'd worked the beat in LA for years, and he'd interviewed more than one mother of a preterm baby. Another door separated him from the babies who were too little or too sick to be in the regular nursery.

He slipped into scrubs, washed his hands, and grabbed a face mask from a box sitting near the door. When he finally entered the nursery, he was surprised by the activity there. Several mothers sat in rocking chairs, watching their babies sleep. Two nurses moved from Isolette to Isolette, checking monitors and vitals. It wasn't noisy or busy, but the feeling of loneliness didn't seem to dwell there the way it had in the hallway.

Willow stood near the back wall, watching as Honor pressed electrodes to the baby's chest. Another woman waited beside them, dark hair scraped back into a bun, a clipboard in hand. The lower half of her face was covered by a surgical mask, her eyes nearly hidden by thick-lensed glasses, but he got a sense of maturity, of energy, and of impatience.

A social worker. That was Jax's guess.

Either from the hospital or the county.

She met his eyes as he approached. "Deputy Gordon? I'm Alison Brenner. Director of Whitman County Child Protective Services."

"Nice to meet you, Ms. Brenner."

"Alison is fine, and the meeting would be nicer if we weren't in these circumstances, right?" She gestured to the baby. "Still, she's one lucky kid that you and Willow found her. A sheriff's deputy and a prosecuting attorney. What are the odds?"

She obviously didn't expect him to answer, because she just kept talking. "The media is going to have a field day with this. You're getting a picture for the press, right?"

"Yes."

"Good. You handle finding the missing parents. My department will be handling the civil aspects of the case."

"Meaning the sheriff's office should keep its mitts off the baby?"

"Something like that." She pulled a card from her pocket and handed it to him. "Of course, I understand that you'll need access to DNA and any medical evidence that's gathered, but we'd prefer that any visitors be vetted through the system. That includes law enforcement officials."

"I'm assuming you'll have a list of approved visitors?"

"I've already made it."

"I'd like to be on it."

"Of course." Alison jotted something on a sheaf of paper clipped to the board. "My office is already getting calls from the media, so I'm going to check in with the nurses and make sure that they're not letting anyone enter the NICU without proper ID. I'll be back in a few. Wait here."

It wasn't a suggestion. It was an order, and Jax wasn't all that keen on obeying. Then again, he wasn't all that keen on getting kicked off the case before he'd even begun investigating. If he went head-to-head with social services, that's probably what would happen. Kane was a laid-back boss. He was a good leader. He also liked to follow the rules, play by the book and make sure that everyone who worked for him did the same. He wouldn't appreciate Jax causing trouble with Whitman County CPS.

Not that Jax planned to cause trouble, but he sure didn't plan to follow every command Alison tossed his way.

"Are you going to follow her?" Willow asked.

"I'm tempted. Just to prove that I can."

She laughed quietly. "I get that. Right before you arrived she told me to wait here while she went to look for you. I had the immediate urge to leave."

"I guess neither of us have changed much since high school. We're both still determined to do things our way."

"That's probably a good thing. If we weren't, we'd both have become what people in town thought we should be." The corners of her eyes crinkled. Even with the surgical mask in place, he knew just how her lips would curve, just exactly how the tiny dimple at the corner of her mouth would look as she grinned.

They'd been classmates all through high school, in silent competition with one another for the role of valedictorian, study partners for SATs prep. They'd even critiqued each other's college entrance essays. Back then, she'd been Willow Lamont—Benevolence's golden child, the Lamont girl most likely to take over the family shop. He'd been the guy who people in town thought was most likely to wind up in jail. They'd been as different as two people could be, but they'd both been absolutely determined to achieve their goals. In that way, they had been exactly alike.

"I sure as hell wouldn't want to be in jail, that's for sure."

"And I wouldn't want to be the proprietress of Chocolate Haven. At least not for longer than a few days." She rubbed her temple, her fingers trembling a little. She had dark circles under her eyes. The kind that didn't happen after just one night of missed sleep.

"Why don't you sit for a few minutes?" he suggested, motioning toward a rocking chair that sat near the baby's Isolette.

"I guess I will." She dropped into the chair, a hint of winter rain and chocolate drifting in the air as she moved. It reminded him of cold nights, warm fires, good company, and it made him long for what he'd sworn he'd never have—a wife, kids, the kind of settled-down life that would break a man's heart if he were to lose it.

"Are you planning on staying for a while?" he asked, and she shook her head.

"I have to open the shop in a couple of hours. I just want to make sure the baby is stable, and then I'll go back to the apartment."

"She's been stable," Honor said as she hooked the electrodes to the monitor.

"Maybe I just hate to think of her being left alone," Willow admitted. "Everyone deserves to have someone beside them."

"I was just thinking that same thing," he said, and her eyes crinkled at the corners again.

"Great minds?"

"Two people who know what it's like to be alone?" he responded. He wasn't sure why. As far as he knew, Willow had never been alone. She'd always had her family standing in her corner, helping her through whatever crisis she was facing.

There was something in her eyes, though. Something that reminded him of the nights he'd spent alone in that hospital room.

Instead of responding, she reached her hand into the porthole in the side of the Isolette, touching one of the baby's fingers. "She's so small."

"Five pounds even," Honor said, jotting something in a chart. "Which is a lot bigger than most of the babies in here."

"My niece was eight pounds when she was born."

"Your niece was healthy, right? This little one has a heart condition. She probably weighed more when she was born and lost weight because she didn't have the strength to eat properly."

"How old do you think she is?" Jax asked. He'd been assuming she'd been born hours ago, but Honor seemed to think otherwise.

"A few days to a week. I'm basing that on the umbilical stump. I've got a feeling her mother had her at home and realized there was something wrong. Maybe she didn't know how to get the medical attention that was needed. Of course, that's my optimistic take on things. Visit with me tomorrow when I finish my fourth twelve-hour shift, and I'll be a lot more pessimistic about things. I need to go check on a couple other babies. You two can wait here or head out. If you go, leave your number at the desk, Willow. I can give you a call once we know what's going on with the baby's heart."

"I will. Thanks."

Honor bustled away, and Willow settled deeper into the rocking chair, the scrubs she wore damp from the wet clothes beneath. Her bare toes peeked out from beneath the pant cuffs, and she'd shoved her sleeves up when she'd reached into the Isolette. There were goose bumps on her forearms.

"Still cold?" he asked.

"Freezing."

"I can grab my coat for you."

"No. I really do have to go back to the apartment. I just feel so bad for her. And, honestly? I feel bad for her mother, too."

"I don't have your kind of sympathy. The mother had a choice. The baby did not."

"Maybe she had a choice." She reached into the Isolette again, touching the baby's downy hair. "Maybe she felt like she didn't. I wonder what she's doing while we're here with her baby."

"If she's got any kind of conscience at all? Crying."

"And worrying. She *has* to be worried. Do you think she stuck around to make sure the baby was found? That maybe she was one of the people watching from the alley entrance?"

It was a good question. One he'd been asking himself.

By the time he'd pulled out of the lot, there'd been a dozen people gathered nearby. He knew Kane had followed protocol and taken the names of everyone there. Tomorrow they'd canvas the neighborhood, interview anyone who might have seen anything. They'd also visit every person who was on Kane's list.

"It's possible."

"If she wasn't there, maybe someone she knows was. I'm hoping that someone will come forward with information that will help you find her."

"Me too." He lifted the camera and took a couple of shots of the baby. She was cute in the same way every other newborn was—scrunched-up face, soft-looking hair, tiny fingers and toes. No birthmarks that he could see. No scars or injuries. Just that hint of blue in her fingers and toes, the hint of purple in her lips. He took a photo of all those things and lowered the camera. "I'll bring this out to Randall, and he can get started on his story."

"I'll come with you." She stood, her movements unconsciously graceful, the long rope of her hair swinging as she moved. He smelled chocolate and rain again, and something darker and more decadent. Something that made him want to touch her silky skin, run his thumb over the pulse point in the hollow of her throat.

Maybe she sensed the sudden charge in the air, the sudden tension in him.

She stepped back, put a couple more inches between them. "Or, I can bring him the camera. That way you can stay with the baby."

"There are three nurses in here," he pointed out. "And I need to talk to Randall. I want to make sure he gets the details right."

"It would be a little difficult for him not to. There aren't all that many."

"You've read the articles he's written for the newspaper, right?"

"Long on opinion, short on fact?"

"Exactly."

"This is different. It's not a hot piece of gossip that he can twist into something more."

"I still want to make sure he gets it right." He touched her shoulder, urging her out of the nursery. They were the only ones in the prep area, and he could feel the silence again, the loneliness.

Yeah. Hospitals weren't his favorite places. The sooner he left this one, the happier he'd be.

He pulled off his face mask and stripped off the scrubs, tossing them into a large laundry hamper and turning to face Willow.

She'd turned her back to him and was tugging the top of the scrubs over her head. The damp fabric pulled her pajamas with it, revealing the smooth, creamy skin of her lower spine, the taut muscles of her back. Flawless. Silky. Beautiful.

She yanked the top down, tossed the scrubs into the hamper, her movements brisk and efficient.

When she turned to face him, his breath caught. Just for a moment. Just for long enough for him to wonder how the hell he'd forgotten the way it felt to look in her eyes.

"What do you want to bet Randall is standing on the other side of that door?" she asked, and the moment was gone.

"The nurse wouldn't let him in. I'd say he's pacing the hall outside the NICU, hoping he gets to run his story before the national news gets wind of what's going on."

"How long do you think that will take?"

"About as long as it takes Kane to issue an APB on the vehicle."

"That should make your job a lot more interesting."

"My job is plenty interesting."

"Really?" She raised a dark red brow. Her lashes were lighter. Gold-red in the fluorescent light. "I heard you were working in LA for nearly ten years."

"That's right." He held the door open as she walked into the hall.

"I'd think that Benevolence would be mind-numbingly boring in comparison."

"That depends on what you find exciting. Me? I've had enough murder, rape, gang violence, and drug crime to last me a lifetime."

"I guess you had your reasons for going back to LA in the first place." Her gaze shifted to his cheek, and he knew she wanted to ask questions. Aside from his uncle and aunt, only one person in town knew most of the story. Sinclair Jefferson wasn't the kind of guy who talked about other people's business. The fact that he was married to Willow's sister didn't play into it. He'd keep Jax's confidence. Just like Jax had always kept his.

"And I guess you had your reasons for going to Seattle instead of taking over the family business," he responded.

"Right," she murmured.

"Are they a secret?" he pressed, because he'd always wondered what had driven her away.

"We all have secrets."

"That wasn't the question."

"No. I guess it wasn't." They passed the nurse's desk, and Willow jabbed the button to open the door.

"Should I take that to mean you don't want to share?"

"Would you?" She walked through the open door

and turned to face him. "I mean, if I flat-out asked you why you went to LA and returned would you tell me?"

"Sure."

"So . . . why did you go to LA? And, why'd you return? From what I've heard you'd made a good name for yourself with the LAPD. You had to be making a good salary. I'm sure your friends were there, your home." She'd turned the conversation neatly away from herself.

Which was fine.

He might not discuss his family, but he didn't mind telling her the truth about why he'd left Benevolence. "I went to LA looking for revenge." He touched the corded edge of the scar.

"Did you find it?"

"I found justice. It's a better thing."

She eyed him silently, the freckles that dotted her cheeks dark against the pallor of her skin. "And, typically doesn't get a person thrown in jail."

"There's that."

She smiled, just a quick curve of her lips and a quicker flash of her dimple. "Do you still want revenge?"

"I want what I have here. Peace." That was the truth. Or as much as he ever shared with anyone. He'd come back to help Jim and Vera, but he'd also come because he'd needed what Benevolence offered. He'd longed for the quiet and the predictability, for the nosey neighbors and the low crime rate.

He thought she might say something, but a woman's voice echoed through the hallway—shrill, loud, frantic. He could hear the voice but not the words.

"Oh. Dear. God," Willow whispered.

"What?"

"That's my mother."

"Are you sure?" he asked.

"Listen," she commanded, pulling him to a dead-stop.

The woman was still talking, her voice drifting from the waiting area. Whoever she was, she was trying to get her point across, the words growing louder and shriller.

"I'm telling you right now, this is not just about the baby. There's something else going on. What if she's hurt? Or worse?" she cried, and this time Jax heard what Willow had—Janelle Lamont's voice.

"See?" Willow hissed. "It's her."

She didn't give him a chance to respond.

Pant cuffs dragging, ponytail swinging, she jogged into the waiting room and disappeared from view.

Chapter Three

Janelle drove her crazy.

That was the truth. Plain and simple.

It wasn't that she was selfish or self-absorbed, mean-spirited or spiteful. She was none of those things. It was simply that she didn't know when to leave well enough alone. She wanted the best for her daughter. Not the best things. The best life, and she'd spent most of their childhood trying to explain how they could each have that.

Childhood?

The lessons had stretched on for longer than that. Teenage years and adulthood, too. Every birthday, Christmas, vacation together, Janelle made her opinions about her daughters' lives known.

Willow loved her. She admired her. She knew that when push came to shove, Janelle always came through for her daughters.

But . . .

Sometimes a little space was a good thing. Sometimes being left alone was easier than being hovered over.

Case in point: the nice dry clothes Willow was

currently wearing. The warm socks. The comfy tennis shoes. The brushed hair. The lip gloss. All of which were wonderful, and all of which Janelle had insisted needed to be donned immediately.

She'd shooed Willow out of the waiting room, followed her to the bathroom, told her to make sure she brushed her hair before she returned. All of it in front of Jax who'd watched with a mixture of amusement and pity.

Unless Willow missed her guess, Janelle was still waiting in the corridor, ready to approve or disapprove of the transformation.

Or, maybe, not.

She hadn't just shown up at the hospital. She'd arrived with Willow's sister Brenna, Brenna's husband, River, and, of course, Granddad.

They were in the waiting area.

Expecting Willow to return.

And she would.

Eventually.

She eyed herself in the bathroom mirror, then splashed warm water on her face, trying to force some color into her cheeks. It didn't help, but at least she no longer looked like death warmed over.

She *did* look like she was going to cry, her eyes red, her cheeks hollow. Being back at Chocolate Haven obviously didn't agree with her. That was no surprise. She'd known that it wouldn't. What she hadn't known was how frequent the nightmares would be, how often she'd wake frantic and sweating.

Nothing a little makeup can't fix.

That was one of Janelle's philosophies of life. Maybe it was true or maybe the makeup just hid what nothing could fix. Either way, a little blush wouldn't hurt.

She reached into the bag Janelle had packed and pulled out a handful of makeup. There was something beneath them, and she lifted it, too.

Shortbread cookies. Zipped into a small plastic snack bag.

Willow's favorite.

Her eyes burned, and she blinked back tears. God! They were cookies for crying out loud! Cookies shouldn't make a person cry. But, she wanted to cry. She wanted to walk out of the bathroom, find some quiet place where no one could find her, and sob.

She dropped the cookies back into the bag, dropped the makeup in with it. She knew what the tears were about. Not the damn cookies. The past. The childhood that had been stolen from her. The secrets she'd held in for so long she could never let them out.

This was why she hated being back. It was also why she'd had to return. She was nearly thirty-two, for God's sake, and it was way past time to face her fears. Her grandfather wasn't getting any younger, and she'd missed out on a lot of time with him because she hadn't wanted to be reminded of something she knew she'd never be able to forget.

And then there was little Alice. Addie's daughter. Her birth had been the catalyst that had set everything else into motion. Willow wanted to be there to watch her niece grow up. She wanted to be the aunt who came through in a pinch, who always had the right thing to say, bought just the right gift. The one who understood when parents didn't. She wanted to be someone her niece knew and loved and respected.

That would be hard to achieve if she only visited once or twice a year.

Yeah. It was time to get over her aversion to Chocolate Haven. It was time to let go of the anger and the fear and the humiliation that gripped her every time she walked into the shop. Not forget. She was never going to do that. Reclaim her space, push him out of it.

Eric had been dead for ten years.

She knew because she'd made sure to know.

She'd read news stories, followed the younger Williams brother's political career, made sure that she knew exactly where the family was. She wouldn't call it stalking. It had been more like an obsession driven by fear and by her need for some sort of closure.

Maybe Eric's death had been that.

He'd been killed in a single-car accident and had left a wife and two young kids behind. It should have been over. Willow should have had the closure she'd wanted.

She had had it.

For a while.

And, then someone had walked into Chocolate Haven and asked for her. He'd given an envelope to Brenna and asked her to pass it along. There'd been a check and a note in it.

Willow hadn't wanted either.

She'd told Brenna to burn them, and she'd told herself she wasn't going to think about what they might mean. She wasn't going to imagine how they might be connected to the past.

But, of course, she'd spent way more time imagining it than not. Eric was dead, but someone in his family must have known what he'd done, because the check? It had been twenty-thousand dollars' worth of pay-off money.

She shivered, her skin clammy with fear and memories.

Someone knocked on the bathroom door. Her mother or Brenna, coming to make sure she was okay.

She shoved her pajamas into the bag, smoothed her hand over her hair, and flung open the door.

Jax stood there, every shade of handsome—gun strapped to his waist, shadowy beard on his chin, jagged scar on his cheek, light blue eyes that seemed filled with secrets and shadows.

He looked good.

Maybe even great, but that wasn't something she should be noticing.

"I thought you were someone else," she murmured.

"I'm not," he responded with a half-smile, his silvery eyes dropping to her feet. "I see you've got shoes. That's a nice addition to the ensemble."

That made her smile, some of her fear seeping away. "I've also got yoga pants and a T-shirt. Mom is good that way."

"I'm sure she's good in a lot of ways." He took the bag from her hand. "Sorry for rushing you, but Alison is looking for you."

"Is the baby okay?"

"As far as I know, she's fine. Alison is a little overwhelmed, though."

"With?"

"Your family. Your grandfather wants answers and your mother wants to start a collection. They're talking at just about the same time."

"And, Brenna and River trying to get one or the other to quiet down?"

"Good guess."

"I know my family well. What kind of collection is Janelle wanting to start?"

"Clothes. Bottles. Baby stuff."

"That sounds like Janelle."

"And you sound tired."

"I passed tired about three days ago," she said.

"Being back home doesn't agree with you?"

"The apartment isn't home."

"Figure of speech."

"Did Alison say why she was looking for me?" she asked, purposely changing the subject.

"They've moved Baby Miracle out of the NICU and into a private room."

"Miracle?"

"That's what they're calling her."

"If they've moved her, she must be doing better."

"They moved her because a private room is easier to secure than an entire wing. Or so Alison says."

"She's calling the shots?"

"She is in her mind. I'm not planning to tell her anything different. The woman terrifies me."

She laughed, and he smiled again.

"There you go, Willow. It's not so hard to relax." His put his hand on her shoulder, steering her down the hall. She could feel the warmth of his palm through her shirt, the heat of it spreading through her still-chilled blood, and she wanted more of him. Or, at least, of *it*. That heat, that comforting feeling of connection, that heady knowledge that she wasn't alone.

She should have moved away.

She *should* have, because she knew what she didn't want. She didn't want the kind of relationship that would pull her back to the small-town life she'd left. She'd watched it happen to Brenna, and she'd wondered how her sister had gone from "I'll never live there again" to "It's the only place I want to be."

She hadn't asked, because Brenna and River were making a good life together. If that life happened to be in Benevolence, who was Willow to judge?

On the other hand, it wasn't something Willow planned to have happen to her. She'd established herself as one of the top prosecuting attorneys in the country. She made better than good money, had a cute little rental in Seattle, had finally been certified as a foster parent for the state. All the goals she'd set for herself, she'd achieved. She was happy and content, and that wasn't going to change because a good-looking guy walked into her life.

She pulled away, pretending to tie a shoelace that was obviously not untied. He noticed. Of course, he did.

And she felt like an idiot, her cheeks heating as she straightened up again.

"I don't bite," he said, and her blush deepened.

"I'll keep that in mind," she responded, walking down the hall as quickly as she could without actually running.

Janelle and Alison were deep in conversation when she entered the waiting room. Brenna, Byron, and River were huddled a few feet away from them, talking quietly. They'd left their beds and their homes to be there for her, and thinking about that made her eyes burn again.

No tears.

Not now, because she wasn't much of a crier, and if

she did let a few tears fall, her family would be worried sick.

"There you are!" Janelle exclaimed. "I was beginning to worry."

"Sorry. I'm running on slow-speed tonight. Thanks for bringing me clothes, Mom." She dropped a kiss on Janelle's cheek. "I really appreciate it."

"It's no problem, honey. I was happy to do it. As soon as you're ready, I'll give you a ride home. You have another busy day ahead of you. I'm sure you'd like to nap before you start it."

"I know you probably do want to get home, Willow," Alison interrupted, "but they've got little Miracle settled in her room. The nurse is planning to feed her in a few minutes. I thought you might like to do it."

"Me?"

"Unless you'd rather not."

"I'd be happy to. Do you mind waiting a little longer, Mom?"

"Of course not. You go ahead. I'm going to grab some coffee."

"Did someone say coffee?" Brenna walked toward them, her long legs covered by a skirt that fell to her ankles, her oversize sweater falling to her hips. She may not have brushed her short hair. It was poking out in a dozen different directions. Somehow she still managed to look slim and stylish and beautiful.

"You want a cup?" Janelle asked. "We can see if the cafeteria is open."

"Whiskey would be better," Byron said, and River laughed. Even Janelle was smiling. They all seemed so in sync, so connected, and Willow suddenly felt like an outsider. The broken cog in a wheel that should be moving beautifully.

She waited until they left and then walked into the hall, Alison beside her, Jax following.

"Now that we're alone," Alison said as they reached the elevator and stepped on, "I have a few things I need to go over."

"Like?"

"Just the rules of the game. So to speak."

"I don't consider this a game, but go ahead."

"Information about Miracle is to be disseminated by my office or the sheriff's office. We're working in conjunction on that." She jabbed the button and the doors slid closed.

"And?" She schooled her voice to keep from sounding impatient. Alison called the shots when it came to the baby. If she wanted access, she'd have to cooperate.

"If you feel like you can't keep information to yourself, it would be best if you remove yourself now."

"I deal with highly incendiary information every day. I think I can manage to keep my mouth shut." She sounded cool and calm. She felt annoyed.

Alison cocked her head to the side, studying her for a moment before speaking. "That wasn't meant to be an insult. It was simply a statement."

"It was warning," she corrected.

"That too. This is going to be a big media story. There is no help for it. There will be fundraisers and GoFundMe accounts. And, of course, more press coverage than any of us probably want."

"From my perspective," Jax said, "press coverage isn't a bad thing."

"It will be when an entire contingent of journalists camp out in your tiny little town hoping for breaking news. I'm sure the Benevolence sheriff's department isn't prepared for that kind of crazy."

Jax's jaw tightened, the edges of his scar going white. He was annoyed, too. Unlike Willow, he didn't seem worried about hiding it. "You'd be surprised at what our office is prepared to handle."

Alison sighed, smoothing her hand over her perfectly styled hair. "I see I've managed to offend both of you without even giving it a good effort. Let me start again. This time by saying, don't be offended by my bluntness. I've been at this job for a long time, and I've learned that there isn't always time to couch things in the nicest terms." The doors opened onto the fourth floor, and they stepped out into the pediatric unit. Miracle's room was in critical care, her door closed, a security guard stationed outside it. He nodded as they approached, asked for IDs, and checked a list.

Alison worked fast and she was thorough.

Willow would give her that.

They all scrubbed down again, following instructions issued by a nurse who sat in a chair beside Miracle's Isolette.

"Masks too," she said. "The baby will be having surgery in the next couple of days."

"They'll be closing a hole in her heart," Alison explained as she put on a face mask and approached the baby. "She looks better, though. Nicer color."

"The oxygen is doing its job. You're the foster?" the nurse asked, lifting Miracle from her bed and handing Willow a tiny bottle.

"I'm—"

"She's certified with the state. We haven't assigned a foster yet."

The nurse didn't seem impressed or put off by the explanation. She adjusted Miracle's heart monitors, checked tubes that were feeding oxygen into her nose, and then nodded toward a chair that stood against the wall. "Have a seat. I'll hand her to you. The lines will reach, no problem, but sometimes they get pulled out if a parent is walking around with the baby."

Willow did as she was told, perching tensely on the edge of the seat, the oversize surgical scrubs bagging around her ankles.

"This is great," Alison said. "Really good. I'm meeting with a couple of my team members. Prepping a statement to the press. You'll be okay here, right?" She was already in the hall as she asked the question, the door closing firmly behind her, the room suddenly quiet except for the soft hiss of oxygen and the quiet beep of the heart monitor.

"All right, looks like you're ready," the nurse said. "She should take an ounce. If you can get her to take more, that will be even better." She handed Willow the baby, checking the electrodes and leads before she left.

And then it was just Jax and Willow and the tiny little life they'd found behind the Dumpster.

Willow settled back against the seat cushions and looked into Miracle's face. The baby's eyes were wide open, and Willow could swear they were looking straight into hers.

"Hungry, beautiful?" she murmured, offering the bottle.

Miracle took it immediately, her eyes drifting closed as she ate. And for the first time since she'd left Seattle, Willow relaxed. Really, truly relaxed. No tension in her muscles. No knot in the pit of her stomach. She was looking into the face of a newly formed life, listening to the soft suckling sound of Miracle eating and the quiet music of the machines. She wasn't thinking about the past. She wasn't worrying about the future. She wasn't doing anything but holding a baby who needed to be held and enjoying an almost stunningly perfect moment.

She touched Miracle's soft cheek, smoothed her brown hair.

"That's probably not a good idea," Jax said, and she looked up, meeting his eyes.

"What?"

"Falling for a kid who isn't yours." The words were harsh, but the tone was gentle. He pulled a chair over, sitting so that they were knee to knee. "It can only break your heart."

"'*The world breaks everyone and afterward many are strong at the broke places,*'" she responded.

"Hemingway. I'd quote the rest of the passage, but it's depressing."

"I guess it is."

"So is loving someone deeply and saying good-bye."

"No," she corrected. "That's just sad. It's also part of life. We all have to say good-bye eventually."

He nodded, but didn't say anything else. Maybe he was letting the silence settle again, the hissing and beeping falling into the backdrop of the peaceful moment.

Whatever the case, she found herself sitting in that silence and, instead of looking down into Miracle's face, looking into his. She was lost there for a moment, studying the edge of the scar that was visible above the mask, the tiny white lines near his hair that must have been other, smaller wounds. He had the longest lashes she'd ever seen on a man, the bluest eyes, and she was looking into them, feeling that same thing she'd felt in the NICU—heat and excitement and interest.

She pulled her gaze away, forced herself to focus on the baby, because she'd made enough mistakes in her life, and she wasn't going to make another one.

Sitting knee to knee with Willow?

It was a mistake.

One that Jax could easily correct. All he had to do was stand up and move away. Of course, he didn't. Uncle Jim had always said he had to learn things the hard way. Maybe it was true. He'd sure as hell taken the long road to learning that revenge was never the answer.

So, yeah, he should stand up and walk to the other side of the room. But he didn't. Willow was falling. Hard. For the tiny little girl she was holding. The one who'd be healed—hopefully—by skilled surgeons and then be placed in a foster home where someone else would grow to love her.

And it was beautiful. The softness in her eyes, the contentment. He couldn't quite make himself move away from that. Or from her.

"Are you sure you know what you're getting yourself into?" he asked, and he wasn't certain if was asking her or himself.

"No, but this is what I got certified to do. Love a child and let her go."

"How many kids have you fostered?"

"None. My certification was issued a couple of weeks ago. I celebrated by buying a minivan."

"I'm not sure if I should congratulate you or tell you I'm sorry."

"Minivans are a lot cooler than they used to be."

Her eyes crinkled, and he knew she was smiling. He also knew that his closeness was making her uncomfortable. She didn't move back, but she'd tensed, all her Zen gone.

The fact that he'd done that to her bothered him.

Willow didn't seem like the kind of person who'd get nervous around others. Her job put her in contact with people from all walks of life. It would be really difficult to be successful at what she did without an ability to connect on a variety of levels.

But she was definitely nervous around him.

He stood, putting a little distance between them.

"Was being a foster parent always part of your plan?" he asked.

"When I was a kid, yes. Then I met Ken, and he really didn't like the idea, so I put it on hold for a while."

"Ken is the ex?"

"Yes. We're still friends." She added the last hurriedly.

"Okay."

"Sorry. I always feel like I have to explain it."

"Your relationship?"

"The fact that we were together for so many years, and now we're not." She shrugged, a silky strand of red hair falling across her shoulder.

"You don't have to explain to me."

But he *was* curious.

He'd heard the rumors. He knew Janelle Lamont had been planning her eldest daughter's wedding. Reception hall. Flowers. Dresses. She'd talked to all her friends about it. Since Aunt Vera was one of her friends, Jax had heard enough of the details to get the gist of things—big, ornate, fancy.

Not going to happen.

"I don't have to explain it to anyone, and yet, I find myself doing it. Over and over again." She sighed. "I guess it comes from having a family that is always asking questions. I'm primed and ready to answer."

"Do you always tell them everything?"

She laughed, the sound rough and a little harsh. "No! But I guess you know how that is."

"My family is pretty small, and Jim and Vera aren't the kind to pry into other people's business. The questions they do ask, I'm usually willing to answer."

"And when you aren't?"

"They let it go. Which is nice, because there are a lot of things I can't share with them. There are other things I won't."

She wanted to ask more questions.

He could see that in her eyes, but the nurse returned, taking the empty bottle and the baby, and handing Jax a note.

"I was asked to give this to you," she said.

"Thanks." He unfolded the piece of paper and scanned it for a signature. There wasn't one, so he read the scrawled handwriting:

Janelle is on a rant about that bastard Custard and his damn camera. He's been taking photos of Brenna, and Janelle is about to lose her everlasting mind. I'm making an executive decision and bringing her home before that happens. Told her that you needed to ask Willow a few questions and would give her a ride when you finished. I've got a couple of nice cigars to thank you.

Byron Lamont.

Had to be.

He was the only person who ever offered Jax cigars.

"Problems?" Willow asked, her gaze on the baby. The nurse was settling her back into the Isolette, and Willow looked like she wanted to lift her right back out.

"Your grandfather suggested that I give you a ride back to town."

"Suggested, huh?"

"He offered me a nice cigar in exchange."

"Wow. He must be really desperate."

"He thinks Janelle is going to do bodily harm to Randall and he wants to separate the two."

"Mom wouldn't hurt a hair on anyone's head, but she's had a bone to pick with Randall since he ran that photo of Addie on the front page. Remember it?"

"It's a little difficult to forget. The dress was really orange."

"And tight."

"And shiny."

She chuckled. "That too."

"She made it work, though. Even in that god-awful picture, she had her head up and a smile on her face." He'd always liked Addie, but when he'd seen her walking down the aisle of Benevolence Baptist Church wearing the shiny orange monstrosity, he'd fallen a little in love with her. In a completely platonic way.

"Yeah. I thought the same. Mom was horrified. Of course. She's still horrified."

"What does Addie think?"

"She swears that dress won her the man of her dreams, so she framed the picture and hung it above the fireplace mantel."

"Sounds like something out of a fairy tale. The shoes or hair or dress wins the man," he said.

"And leads to happily ever after. You forgot that part."

"I remembered." He just hadn't mentioned it because, in his experience, happily ever after almost never happened.

He walked to the Isolette and looked at Miracle—tubes in her nose, electrodes on her chest. She was a prime example of what could happen when happily ever after didn't work out, a sad testimony to the frailty of human relationships. The frailty of humans in general.

He understood that good people made mistakes.

He understood that they often regretted them.

But finding a baby behind a Dumpster? It still pissed him off.

"I'm going to give Kane an update. Text me when you're ready to leave," he said.

She nodded, accepting the business card he handed her without comment.

He walked out of the room, because he had to. He was getting too emotional about something that couldn't be changed.

He could find Miracle's parents. He could help determine what charges would be filed against them—if charges would be filed. But he couldn't turn back the hands of time and make sure they had what they needed to make a better decision.

If he had *that* superpower, he'd have gone back in time years ago. He'd have returned to the summer he'd turned eleven, to that little tent pitched at the corner of the backyard, and he'd have done things differently. Instead of lying on top of his sleeping bag the humid air making his skin sticky, he'd walk in the house before he heard the first gunshot, and he'd whisper a warning in his father's ear:

That friend you like so much? The one you graduated from the police academy with? The one who works on the anti-gang task force with you? He's dirty, and he's going to betray you, because if he doesn't, the gang leader who called a hit on you is going to make him pay. He's going to use the house key you gave him, and he's going to let five thugs into our home, and they're going to carve gang symbols into Mom's chest and into little Liberty's stomach. They're going to shoot Maverick, and poor little Dot and they're going to make you watch before they kill you.

And your friend?

He's just going to stand at the corner of the yard while they do it, because he's in their pocket, and he's afraid for his own wife and his own kids.

Jax scowled. Yeah. If he could go back, that's what he'd do. But he couldn't. Things had played out the way they had, and there'd been nothing he could to do change it.

He couldn't change things for Miracle, either. The beginning of her story had already been written.

What he *could* do was make damn certain the next chapter of it was better.

Chapter Four

Willow stayed with the baby for an hour. She'd probably have stayed longer if Alison hadn't returned and not so subtly suggested that she go home.

"The baby needs quiet to heal," she'd said. "Go home and go on with your day. I'll call you if anything changes."

So, of course, Willow had walked out of the room, texted Jax, and waited for him to return. It had taken seconds, and she'd thought he must have been somewhere close by, just waiting to be summoned.

She didn't ask, and he didn't explain.

They'd walked to his car in silence, and he'd held the door as she'd climbed in. Icy rain had turned to fat snowflakes, and they drifted from the pitch-black sky as he pulled out of the hospital parking lot.

It was a forty-minute drive back to the apartment.

Ten minutes into it, and neither of them had spoken. She should have been fine with that. She wasn't the kind of person who felt the need to fill silences. For some reason, though, she wanted to do it now. She pressed her lips together. If Jax wanted to talk, he'd be doing it.

He wasn't. Obviously, he had his reasons. Probably ones that had something to do with how abruptly he'd walked out of Miracle's room.

She was tempted to ask him.

Tempted, but she wasn't going to do it, because they didn't need to be friends to make sure Miracle was taken care of. She didn't need to know what was bothering him to accept the ride home. In a few days, she'd be back in Seattle, back at her job, living her life as if she hadn't just faced her biggest fears and darkest memories. She'd be free—finally. That was her only objective. Finding someone she clicked with, someone who seemed to have as much baggage and darkness as she did, that wasn't part of the plan.

She stared straight ahead, watching snowflakes swirl in the headlights. It was kind of sickening, really, the way they danced and twirled, turning around and around in endless waves of grayish white. Or maybe it was just her migraine that was making her think that. It was back with a vengeance, sending throbbing pain through her left eye, pulsing in time with the swish and whoosh of the windshield wipers. She closed her eyes, pressing her fingers to her temple.

"Are you okay?" Jax asked, finally breaking the silence.

"Dandy," she moaned.

The car swerved and rolled to a stop. For a moment there was nothing but silence again, and then leather creaked and a warm, dry hand pressed against her forehead.

"I'm fine," she muttered, brushing his hand away.

It felt too nice against her skin, and she was too aware of that and of him.

"You look a little green around the gills."

"Just what every woman who has ever lived wants to hear," she ground out, and he chuckled.

"Sorry. That didn't come out right." His knuckles slid down her cheek, his fingers coming to rest on the pulse point in her neck. "Your pulse is fast."

Of course it was. It hiked up a couple of notches every time he touched her. Weird, because it had never been that way with Ken. What they'd shared had been nice and easy. Unchallenging and pleasant. It hadn't been breath-stealing, heart-pounding, pulse-racing. She hadn't wanted it that way.

"I have a migraine." She let that be her explanation because she sure as hell wasn't going to admit that her pulse was racing because of him.

"Anything I can do to help?"

"I'll be fine." She didn't open her eyes. The radio played some soft country ballad and the darkness felt as peaceful as it ever had. There was no need to look at the swirling snow or the gray-black night or Jax.

He shifted in his seat, leather creaking again as he tucked his coat around her shoulders. It was warm from his body, as comfortable as it had been in the hospital, but her mind was busy putting things together where they didn't belong. She was alone with a man she didn't know all that well, his coat a heavy weight on her arms and chest. And suddenly she could smell stale nicotine and alcohol and BO.

She took a deep breath, inhaling the scent of Jax's coat, the subtler scent of leather from his gun belt, fighting to get her thoughts back under control.

"It's okay," Jax said, his hand settling on her knee, his voice chasing away the memories.

He pulled back onto the highway, the car picking up speed as they headed back to Benevolence. Back to the shop. Back to all the things she'd spent years hiding from.

By the time Jax exited the freeway, Willow was asleep, her head resting against the window, his coat tucked up around her chin. He could hear her soft breathing, steady and even. It hadn't been like that thirty minutes ago. It had been shallow and quick, her skin so pale he'd thought she might pass out.

She'd said it was a migraine, and maybe it was. But there'd been something else there, something that had filled the car with panicked energy. For a split second, he'd thought she might open the car door and run. Thank God she hadn't! He'd have had to follow, and that would have made a bad situation worse.

He turned onto the country road that led into town, passing a few farms and a couple of old trailers. Main Street was a left turn off the road, a few blocks of almost nothing and then the little town with its touristy shops and pristine sidewalks. The first time he'd seen it, he'd been in too much pain to laugh, but he'd wanted to. After nearly three months in the hospital fighting infections, he'd been desperate to go home. Of course, home had been his parents, his siblings, the little house on the outskirts of LA. It was the balmy air, the traffic, his buddies knocking on the door and asking him to bike to the 7-Eleven. He'd talked about that incessantly during his recovery, and

Jim and Vera had let him. It had only been during the last two weeks of his hospital stay that they'd begun talking about *their* home—about the house and the yard and the school with new friends for Jax to make.

He hadn't wanted new friends, a new house, and a big yard. But Jim and Vera had been all he had, and he'd been afraid to tell them that. As soon as he was released from the hospital, they'd left LA. He hadn't had a chance to say good-bye to anyone or anything. Now Jax could understand why. He'd been the only survivor of a brutal attack that had left five people dead. His testimony would eventually put his father's police buddy in prison for life. Jim and Vera had wanted to keep him alive, so they'd kept him out of the media and the limelight. They'd taken him away from the danger. They'd given him what they could, and it had been plenty, but that first day? Compared to the suburbs of LA, Benevolence had looked like a movie set. Prissy and fake and a little too cute for an eleven-year-old kid to appreciate.

Now it looked like home.

Fluffy flakes of snow coated the grass and sidewalks and drifted lazily through the air. A few lights were on, but most people were still tucked into bed, sleeping soundly. The weather seemed to have sent the gawkers away. The area in front of Chocolate Haven was empty, the people who'd gathered there dispersed. Yellow crime-scene tape stretched across the entry to the alley, but there were no cars parked at the curb.

He pulled around to the back lot. It was empty. Just like he'd hoped, the lights in the upstairs apartment were off. Jax parked near the shop's back door and touched Willow's arm.

"Hey," he said, "we're here."

She didn't respond, and he gave her shoulder a gentle shake. "Willow?"

She was up like a shot, screaming and swinging, her fist coming within an inch of his chin, her terror pulsing through the car. Her eyes were wide open and empty, her hair flying from its ponytail holder as she scrambled away from him. Still shrieking. Still fighting.

God!

He wanted to grab her shoulders, tell her it was okay, but she was scrabbling at the door, trying to escape. One scream after another tearing from her throat.

"It's okay," he said, not touching her. Not trying to stop her. "You're okay."

She didn't hear, probably couldn't hear. She was yanking at the door handle, and he was afraid she'd rip the nails from her fingers. He popped the lock, and she stumbled out. He was out, too, rounding the side of the car, worried that she'd dart into the road, run screaming down Main Street. She didn't need that. Didn't need the gossip that would come from it.

"Willow," he tried again, stepping in front of her, blocking her path.

"Willow," he repeated, keeping his voice calm, and moving in closer. "Wherever you are, it's time to come back."

He wasn't sure if it was his voice or the cold that did it, but he watched her return—her arms dropping to her sides, her eyes focusing. She brushed her hair from her face, her hands shaking, and when she met his eyes, he saw humiliation and frustration and the last remnant of fear.

"God," she said. "Twice in one night."

She turned away, stumbling toward the edge of the

lot, retching before she even reached it. She dropped
to her knees, vomiting into snow-coated grass.

He cupped her shoulders, feeling the narrow width
of her back, her scapula jutting from her too-thin
frame. Feeling her muscles tremble in the aftermath
of whatever terror she'd been in.

And he knew.

God! He knew, and he wished he didn't, because it
changed everything about the way he saw her and
nothing about what he could do to help.

She swiped her mouth with her sleeve, but didn't
make any move to rise. Just knelt where she was, snow
slowly coating her hair and her back.

"Who was it?" he asked, because whoever the hell
had hurt her had better be in jail. If he wasn't, Jax
would be happy to put him there.

She ignored him, finally getting to her feet and
trudging back to his car. Her purse was there, and she
grabbed it, digging keys out and heading to the alley
and the stairs that led to the apartment.

He knew she didn't want him to follow.

He didn't give a damn.

She tripped on the first step, nearly falling to her
knees. He caught her arm, keeping his grip light
enough not to spook her but firm enough to keep her
from going down.

"Slow down, Willow. The metal is icy."

"It's not the metal. It's this damn migraine." She
touched her left temple, her voice breaking.

"Is that the game we're playing?" he asked. "We
pretend I didn't just see what I saw?"

"You saw it. I lived it. My head is about to explode,
and I'm not discussing anything else," she growled,
moving up the stairs more slowly. She couldn't get
the key into the lock, and he took it from her hand,

pushed the door open for her, and waited while she stepped inside.

"Where's your medication?" he asked, walking into the apartment behind her. He tossed the keys back in her purse, waiting for her to reply. Her skin was leached of color, her lips nearly white. She had the hollow, glassy-eyed look of someone who'd been through hell and barely survived it, and he wondered if she was actually capable of giving him a response.

"Willow?" he said more gently. "The medicine?"

"In the kitchen. I'll grab some in a minute. First, I need to get ready for work."

"You don't really think Byron's going to let you work when you look like hell, do you?" he asked, frustrated because she was tying his hands and there wasn't a thing he could do about it.

"I'm working. Whether Byron likes it or not," she muttered, and he wasn't sure if she was talking to herself or to him. "That's why I'm here."

"You're here to help Byron. What kind of help will you be in this condition?" He strode to the kitchen, yanking open cupboards one by one until he found a bottle of Tylenol and prescription medicine that he thought might be for migraines.

Willow didn't try to stop him. She just stood in the center of the living room, her hair scraggly around her pale face, her hands fisted at her sides.

"Is this the right stuff?" he asked, holding up the bottle.

"Yes, but—"

"Juice?" He opened the fridge. It was nearly empty. Just a half-full quart of creamer and a half dozen eggs. No wonder she was skinny. "I guess we're going with water."

"Jax." She finally moved, stepping through the

living room and into the galley-style kitchen. "I don't need you to do this for me. I can handle it."

"Sure you can, but you don't have to." He tapped a pill into his palm and handed her that and a glass of water.

She swallowed the pill and thrust the glass back into his hand. "*Now,* I need to get ready for work. You can stay or go. Whichever you want to do."

She sounded weary. Not a word he'd usually use, but it fit, because her tone was more than tired or exhausted or any of the things that came from working too much or getting too little sleep. It was tinged with a hint of sadness and despair, and if he'd had the right, he'd have pulled her into his arms and told her it was going to be okay.

She walked down the hall, and he let her go, waiting to hear the bedroom door close. It didn't, and he waited another couple of minutes, pacing the small living room. The knife he'd taken from Willow still sat on the arm of the chair. He carried it into the kitchen, found a spot for it, and wandered back out of the room. Still not a sound from down the hall.

To hell with waiting, he was going to find out what was going on.

He found Willow's bedroom easily—it was the one with the light on and a human-shaped lump lying in the center of the bed. The floor creaked as he stepped over the threshold, the old building groaning in protest.

"Go away," Willow mumbled, a pillow pressed over her face, her body only half covered by a blanket.

"Okay," he replied, flicking off the light and approaching the bed. There was another blanket at the end of it, and he pulled it over her.

"I mean it, Jax." She removed the pillow, the light from the hallway illuminating her face. "I am trying to get myself together, and I need to be alone to do it."

"I get that," he said.

"I doubt it."

"Do you?" He touched the edge of his scar, and her gaze followed the movement, her eyes nearly black in the dim light.

"Okay," she muttered, pulling the pillow back into place. "I take that back. You do. Which means that you should be willing to let me do what I need to do."

"I'm willing. If you let me do what I need to."

"What's that?"

"Call Byron. You're in no shape to work this morning."

"Like hell I'm not." She moved the pillow again, this time just enough to peek out with one eye. "And if you tell him differently, I'm going to be royally pissed."

"I'll bring you a crown later today."

"Look," she said, and shoved the blankets aside and sat. "Granddad needs my help opening the shop. He's counting on me to be there, and if you call and tell him I'm not coming, he'll drive over in that rattrap car of his, get into an accident because of the icy roads, and that will be on your head and mine. Is that what you want?"

"I want you to rest," he said. "I won't call Byron if you agree to do that."

"That's blackmail!"

"And?"

"It's against the law."

"Only if you can prove it happened." He grabbed her alarm clock and headed back across the room.

"Hey! Where are you taking that?"

"Into the living room."

"You don't seem to understand. I can't leave my grandfather hanging. He's not a young man. He doesn't have the energy he used to have. He'll show up at the shop, expecting all the prep work to be done, and it won't be. That's going to cause him a lot of stress that he doesn't need." She stood, her face so pale he was surprised she didn't fall back down again.

"My shift ended an hour ago. I'll stick around and prep what I can. Then help Byron with the rest when he shows up," he offered, surprising himself almost as much as he'd probably surprised Willow.

"You're kidding, right?"

"Byron has been a good friend to my uncle. I can sacrifice a few hours of sleep to help him." It was a sound reason, a good one, but he wasn't sure it was the *real* reason. Willow's screams were still echoing in his ears, the image of her fighting her demons etched into his brain. He knew how that felt, and he knew how difficult it was to pull everything back together once it had come apart. She needed time, and he happened to be able to give it.

Maybe there was something else.

Something about the way it felt when he touched her hand and looked into her eyes—as if they hadn't spent the last two decades as close to being strangers as two people who knew each other could be.

Maybe, but he wasn't going to explore that. He wasn't going to pursue it. He sure as hell wasn't going to let it influence the decisions he made.

"Jax, Chocolate Haven is a chocolate shop," she said, enunciating the last two words.

"And?"

"There's a heck of a lot of work that needs to be done before the doors open."

"I'm assuming there's a list somewhere."

"On the whiteboard in the kitchen, but there's no way you can do what's on it."

"Why not?"

"Have you ever made chocolate?"

"No, but there's no time like the present to learn." He closed the door, because that was as much of an argument as he could give, and it wasn't a good one.

She didn't open the door or call out for him to return. Hopefully, she was doing what he'd asked her to.

And hopefully, he wouldn't destroy Chocolate Haven while he was trying to help. The truth was, he didn't have much in the way of kitchen skills. Vera had tried to teach him, but he hadn't been interested in learning. As a kid, he'd been focused on one thing and he'd pursued it with dogged determination. As an adult, he hadn't had the time or the patience to learn how to cook elaborate meals. He could grill a burger and scramble an egg. He had a couple of pasta recipes that weren't all that difficult. In a pinch, he could probably roast a chicken. But chocolate making was an art, and he was pretty damn sure he didn't have the talent for it. He'd give it a try, though, because he'd said he would.

He snagged the keys from Willow's purse, made sure the alarm clock was off, and set it on the coffee table. His muscles were tense, his cheek throbbing, the nerves that had been severed all those years ago misfiring. Even after all this time, there was pain. Physical and mental.

Damn! It had been a long night.

He walked outside, breathing in lungsful of cold air, clearing his mind of all the baggage that he'd spent years unloading. He knew what it was like to suffer. It made him good at what he did. It gave him compassion and empathy.

But making chocolate for Willow?

That went above and beyond the call of duty.

Sure, his shift had ended an hour ago.

Sure, he was wide awake and in need of something to keep him occupied, but chocolate? That should be last on his list of things he could do, because Willow could become a problem if he let her. She could take up a little too much space in his head and that could lead to things that he didn't want.

Or shouldn't want.

His cell phone rang, and he answered, glad for the distraction. "Hello?"

"Jax? You delivered my granddaughter to the shop?" Byron Lamont whispered as if he were a Mafia godfather asking about an illegal distribution of funds.

"To the apartment. Is everything okay?"

"Why wouldn't it be?"

"You're whispering."

"I'm at Janelle's place. I don't want her to know I'm planning to leave. She might feel the need to come with me."

"The roads are messy. You might be better off staying there until the sun comes up."

"You think I'm too old to drive?"

"I didn't say that."

"You may as well have. I've been driving on slick roads for longer than you've been alive. Besides, it's a mile to the shop, and I don't want Willow to do all the prep on her own. She's had a long night."

Probably longer than Byron knew, but Jax wasn't going to tell him that. "She's not feeling well. I offered to help out."

"At Chocolate Haven?"

"I'm afraid so."

Byron laughed. "No need to be glum, kid. We'll manage just fine together. You have a key?"

"Yes."

"You go on in, then. Take a look at the whiteboard. That'll give you some idea of what needs to be done. Do what you can. I shouldn't be long."

He disconnected, and Jax walked down the stairs and into the alley. Snow swirled on the cold pavement, collecting near the edges of the building and the Dumpster. If they hadn't found Miracle, she wouldn't have survived the weather. He was very aware of that, and very aware of his obligation to find the person who'd left her there to die.

Or to be found.

Either way, it was a criminal act. He stepped around the corner of the building, walking to the back door of the shop. There were only three keys on Willow's key chain. He'd used one for her door. That left two other options. He tried one that looked old and scuffed. The door swung open easily, the heady scent of chocolate, vanilla, and sugar drifting out.

He flicked on the light, letting the door close behind him. The whiteboard was hanging on the wall near the sink, a list of ingredients on one half of it, a list of candies on the other. Bonbons were first. Milk chocolate. Peanut butter. Raspberry. Three dozen each.

He searched the shelves and the pantry, gathering all the ingredients listed on the board, then walked into Byron's office. It was small. Just a closet-sized room with a few shelves, a desk, a file cabinet, and a computer. He eyed the shelves, realized they were lined with recipe books. One might contain a bonbon recipe.

Not that he anticipated that helping any more than a manual on landing a plane would have helped him touch-down a 747 on a landing strip. He wasn't a quitter, though. Byron hadn't appeared. Bonbons needed to be made. Jax was there. So were the cookbooks.

He pulled one off the shelf, flipping through to a page-marked recipe. Chocolate Truffles. Not what he wanted, but he figured the bonbons were in there somewhere. He thumbed through the rest of the book, found a recipe for chocolate bark that he thought he might need. Pulled down a second book, and was thumbing through it when he heard the back door opening.

"You in here, Jax?" Byron called.

"In the office."

"You're not trying to find my top-secret fudge recipe, are you?" Byron appeared in the doorway, his salt-and-pepper hair brushed back from his forehead, his glasses speckled with melted snow.

"What else would I be doing? Once I find it, I'm planning to hold it for ransom. Payment to get it back will be a lifetime supply of the stuff," Jax deadpanned, and Byron laughed.

"Good for you! Would have been here a couple of minutes sooner, but Janelle was on the phone with Kane. She wants Randall Custard arrested."

"For what?"

"He was in the bushes outside the house, snapping photos."

"I should be surprised, but I'm not."

"Me neither. He's harmless enough, though. Looks like you have things under control. I'll go up and check on Willow, and then I'll show you a few tricks of the chocolate trade."

"It might be better if you let her rest," he suggested, and Byron frowned.

"Why?"

"She looked like hell. Near as I could tell, she felt like hell. If she knows you're here, she'll feel like she needs to come down."

"You're right about that. Girl is too stubborn for her own good sometimes. You think she needs to go to the hospital?"

"She said it was a migraine."

"Migraine, huh? She used to get them when she was a teen. Didn't realize she still had them. Poor kid. I guess we can make do until Chase comes later this morning."

"We? I'm here to help prep. Not to help run the shop."

"Son, do you know how hard it is to get around once you bust a femur?" Byron patted his left leg. It might or might not have been the one he'd broken over a year ago.

Jax didn't think it was.

As a matter of fact, he was almost certain it wasn't.

Far be it from him to point that out. "I'd imagine pretty hard."

"You'd imagine right. Thing hurts like a bugger all day every day. It's all I can do to keep moving."

It hadn't seemed to be hurting all that much the

previous Sunday when Jax had seen Byron riding a bike through the park, Laurie Beth from the diner riding along beside him.

He decided not to point that out, either.

"You could try a wheelchair," he suggested instead, and Byron scowled. Just like Jax had known he would.

"Like hell I could. You going to stick around or not?"

"I am."

"Good. Put this on, scrub your hands, and let's get to work." Byron pulled an apron off a hook near the back door and handed it to him. "We'll need about five pounds of milk chocolate to start. White sugar. Corn syrup. Vanilla. Grab that big mixing bowl from the shelf."

He issued orders like a drill sergeant, and damn if Jax wasn't compelled to follow them.

Maybe because he liked Byron.

Maybe because he wanted to help Willow.

Maybe just because he was there, and the place smelled like chocolate, and he was a little more curious than he should be about what it was like to work in the most iconic shop in Benevolence.

Whatever the case, he tied the apron over his holster, washed his hands in the sink, grabbed the bowl, and got to work.

Chapter Five

Willow woke to the sound of voices. Male. Female. More than one of each. They sounded close. Maybe outside the window. Which would be possible, except that she was on the second floor of the building.

Wasn't she?

She opened her eyes, wondering if she was back in Seattle and if the last twenty-four hours had all been a dream. The work in Chocolate Haven, the crazy night and the newborn baby. Jax. Seeing her at her worst. Helping her up the stairs. It was all there, the memories fuzzy from the effects of the medicine she'd taken.

How many hours ago?

She looked for the alarm clock, remembered that Jax had taken it. Looked for her cell phone, but it was in her purse. She had no idea where that had gone. Bright sunlight filtered in through the shades, illuminating the old rocking chair, the pale yellow walls, the 1960s prints framed and displayed on either side of the door.

She was most definitely in the apartment in Benevolence, and she was most definitely hearing voices.

She got to her feet, waiting a few seconds to see if pain would jolt through her head again. The headache was there, but less incessant. She could function. She could think. Hopefully, she could make chocolate.

She shuffled to the window that looked onto Main Street. There were cars, news vans, and people everywhere. The national news must have picked up the story about the baby. It was going to be a busy day, and Byron was on his own in a shop that was probably overflowing with people.

She grabbed the first thing she saw in the closet—a soft gray sweater dress that was perfect for a cold day but maybe not so perfect for working in a kitchen. She didn't have time to look for something else. She took a quick shower, pulled her hair into a tight bun, and yanked the dress over still-damp skin.

No makeup.

No lip gloss.

She couldn't find her keys, but Granddad was already in the shop, so she didn't waste time with an all-out search. She was hours behind her schedule and hours behind her grandfather's, but she still felt sluggish, her body moving in what felt like slow motion as she stepped outside.

Cold air stung her cheeks and seeped through the knit fabric of the dress, but it did nothing to wake her up. She needed coffee. Stat!

"Ms. Lamont?" someone called.

She glanced toward the end of the alley that opened onto Main. A group of people had gathered there, pressing close to crime-scene tape that had been strung between buildings.

"Willow Lamont, right?" the person continued. "You found the baby?"

She wasn't sure who was asking, and she really didn't care. In her line of work, dealing with the press was a necessity, but in Benevolence, she wasn't a high-profile prosecutor. She was a chocolatier.

Or, at least, a chocolate maker.

If what she'd been producing the past few days could be called chocolate.

She frowned, hurrying down the stairs and into the alley, ignoring the flashing camera and the shouted questions. Everyone wanted the inside scoop, the newsworthy information that could rocket their ratings into the stratosphere.

They weren't getting it from her.

She hadn't spoken to Kane, and she didn't know what information he'd released to the press and what he wanted to keep a lid on. Until she found out, she was keeping quiet.

She hurried past the Dumpster and into the back lot. It was empty, the sheriff's car blocking the entrance. Kane stood near it, talking on his phone. He waved but didn't seem in a hurry to chat. She'd have to check in with him later. She had a few questions to ask about the investigation. Right now, though, Byron needed her.

She shoved open the shop door, the scent of chocolate filling her nose and clogging her throat. She nearly gagged, the migraine pulsing to life again, the memories scrambling to come out of hiding.

Keep calm.

Keep focused.

Don't think about it.

She'd made it through nearly a week by doing that. She'd make it through another day. Eventually it had to get easier.

She hoped.

The front of the house was full. She could hear the crowd of people, the excited chatter and soft clank of the old-fashioned cash register. She pulled an apron from a hook near the door and tried not to look at the hallway. Even when the shop was filled with people, even when the lights were on and people she loved were nearby, that opening, that little passageway between the front of the shop and the back seemed like the portal to hell.

She frowned, putting on the apron and going to the whiteboard list. Every item had been crossed off. Byron must have been working fast.

There were a few dishes in the sink, and she went there instead of the front of the house. She needed a minute to get herself together, to gather up all the stores that had carried her through the years. Once she did that, she could walk through the hall. She could pretend this was any other place, and she was just a regular person doing regular things. Not a victim fighting to hold herself together.

She heard footsteps as she scrubbed a pot, but she didn't turn around. She was afraid Byron would see the fear and the sickness in her face. She was afraid he'd ask questions that no one had thought to ask when she was thirteen. She'd kept her silence then, and it had only grown deeper and harder to break since. At this point, she couldn't see any reason to talk about what had happened. It would only hurt her family to know what she'd gone through. And that was the last thing she'd ever want to do.

"It sounds like things are crazy out there, Grand-dad," she called in the fakest, most cheerful voice she could manage. "I'll be out in a minute."

"Take your time. Byron has things under control," Jax responded, his voice so surprising, she spun around, spraying water and suds across the kitchen and him.

"God! I'm so sorry," she murmured, grabbing a hand towel and wiping a few sudsy splotches from his cheek.

"I'm already covered with chocolate. I don't think we need to worry about a little soap and water." He took the cloth from her hand and set it on the counter.

"Covered? I don't see a speck on you."

"That's because this is my third apron. I spilled an entire pot of chocolate on the first one. The second met a similar fate."

"Death by chocolate?"

"Death by exploding mixer." He pointed to the mixer that sat on the marble-topped island. There was a bowl under the blades and bits of chocolate and cream splattered on every nearby surface.

"Flourless torte?" she guessed, and he nodded, his beautiful blue eyes looking straight into hers.

"Byron said I win the prize for most ingredients wasted in a single day. Brenna will be happy to know that she's currently in second place for the award."

"Byron may be underestimating my sister's failure. From what Brenna has told me, she wasted hundreds of dollars' worth of stuff."

"*I* may be verging on thousands. Mine is a very special talent," he said, placing his hands on her shoulders and spinning her around.

"What—?"

"You didn't tie your apron." He tugged the strings tight, his fingers gliding along her waist as he straightened the sash. "An untied apron is a safety hazard."

"Words of wisdom from Byron?"

"Rule number fifteen of the company guide. I have a booklet to prove it." He turned her back around, and they were facing each other again, her eyes chest-height with him. She had to look up to see his face, and when she did, her heart skipped a beat.

God! He was handsome. He could have been a model for the cover of one of the romance novels Brenna liked to read.

But he wasn't.

He was Jax Gordon, a guy she'd known for two decades, but who she didn't really know at all. Because the Jax she remembered? He never would have been content to live in a place like Benevolence. All he'd ever talked about was getting back to LA.

"You seem awfully cheerful for someone who's spent the morning being attacked by chocolate," she said, and he smiled.

"There are perks to the job."

"Free chocolate?"

"Laurie Beth brought breakfast. She said it was going to be a long day, and Byron needed sustenance. Since she brought enough for ten people, I got my share of biscuits and gravy. There's more left, if you want to eat before you start."

She shuddered, just the thought of food making her stomach churn. "I'll pass. But thanks. What's left on the inventory for today?"

"We've made everything."

"Really?"

"Is it that surprising? Byron could run this store with his eyes closed and both hands tied behind his back."

"Both hands? That might be tough."

"After watching him work this morning, I'd say it's

entirely possible." He reached past her, grabbing the dish she'd left in the drainer and drying it with a dishrag.

She'd been wrong about the chocolate. There were tiny flecks of it in his hair and a few more on the side of his neck.

She reached out without thinking, rubbing at one of the spots, and feeling something she hadn't expected, something she didn't want. Her fingers wanted to linger. Her body wanted to sway close, and if he hadn't grabbed her hand, she might have done both.

"That's probably not a good idea, Willow," he said quietly, and she thought she heard something in the words, a warning about just how far things could go between them and just how quickly.

"Sorry. I just . . . You have chocolate on your neck."

"I may be terrible at making the stuff, but I'm pretty damn good at cleaning up messes. I'll take care of it later."

"How much longer are you planning to stay?" she asked, turning away to wash another dish, because she didn't want to look into his eyes or his face. She didn't want to feel that thing that seemed to be there every time she did.

Temptation was a good word for it.

Longing.

She could probably think of dozens more, but she had work to do, and she had a life to return to, and Jax wasn't part of either of those things.

"Now that you're here? Not long. Byron needed me to restock product. Once I do that, I'll go."

"Jax!" Byron called, as if mentioning his name had drawn his attention. "You having trouble finding the bonbons? I can get them if you want to work the register."

"I've got them," Jax responded, opening the cooler and pulling out a tray of glossy chocolates.

"Want me to bring them to the front of the house?" she offered, and he nodded, handing her the tray.

"Thanks. I'm sure Byron will be happy to have more proficient help." He smiled, but there was an edge to his voice, a hint of tension that hadn't been there before.

"No problem. I really appreciate everything you've done the past few hours." She smiled, too.

Or, she tried to.

It was difficult with the hallway just in front of her and an entire day of chocolate-making failures looming. Her life in Seattle wasn't perfect, but it was predictable, high-stress but routine. When she was there, she felt confident and capable.

Here, she felt like a colossal failure.

"Like I said, Byron has been really good to my uncle. I don't forget that kind of thing. Tell him I appreciate the chocolate lessons," Jax said as he opened the back door. "I'll give you a call later, let you know what I find out about the baby."

He stepped outside, and cold wind swept in. She wanted it to chase away the cobwebs, clear the air of all the old stuff that seemed to make the sweet smell of chocolate rancid. Of course, it didn't, and she was left holding the tray of bonbons, watching as the door swung closed.

"Jax!" Byron called again, a hint of impatience in his voice. He had high standards. Just like Willow's father had. He liked things done a certain way and at a certain time. Willow was the same. Peas in a pod is what her grandmother Alice had called the three of them. Until Willow's father had died and everything had changed.

She took a deep breath and marched through the hallway, the tray of bonbons in her hands. She wasn't a kid anymore, and all the hurt that had been done to her, all the ugliness that had happened, was in the past.

The past could haunt a person, if she let it.

It could make someone who loved small towns and chocolate shops and the family business despise all of those things.

It couldn't steal a person's future, though. It couldn't take away joy or triumph. It couldn't prevent someone from finding love and contentment and purpose. Of all the things Willow believed, that was the truth she held on to most tightly. She was going to face her demons. She was going to defeat them, but first, she had to bring the damn chocolates to her grandfather.

Jax took a quick nap, ate a late lunch with Vera and Jim, and did a little work on the old house he'd been restoring since he'd moved back. *His* old house. He'd purchased the huge Victorian for a song. Not because he planned to fill it with family, but because it was within walking distance of his uncle and aunt's house. Another year or two of being abandoned, and the place would have been condemned. It was no longer in danger of that, but there was still plenty of work to do.

He liked working. It kept his mind occupied.

He didn't like meetings. And yet, he'd just spent two hours of his day in one Kane had scheduled because Benevolence had gone crazy. Traffic jams.

A fistfight over parking near Chocolate Haven. Three reports of Peeping Toms.

Benevolence was a small enough town to not need a large police department. Right now, that was proving to be an issue. There were news reporters everywhere, talking to locals, staking out the area outside the Lamonts' shop, and trying desperately to get the big scoop, the breaking news that was going to make their station the one to watch.

Jax didn't know what they thought the big scoop would be. Maybe an interview with Willow or him. Maybe a photo of the baby—one that was different from what had been issued to the media. Maybe the name of the person who'd abandoned her. It didn't matter, and he didn't really care. Let them look for the story. Just as long as they didn't destroy the town while they were at it.

The way the day was going, destruction was a distinct possibility, and Kane had asked all his deputies to patrol the streets. It meant overtime and extra pay, and no one had complained. Whether or not the small-town sheriff's department was prepared for the influx of people remained to be seen.

Jax grabbed his coat from the back of his office chair, surprised by the hint of chocolate that clung to it. He hadn't been a quick study at the chocolate-making thing, but he'd given it a good effort. He'd had the chocolate-splattered clothes to prove it.

He hadn't realized he'd splattered his coat, too.

Or, maybe, the scent of chocolate had just permeated the fabric.

Not a bad smell, but it reminded him of Willow, and that reminded him of the way she'd looked when she'd woken from her nightmare, screaming and fighting, empty-eyed and hollow.

He'd seen that look hundreds of times before. On the faces of people who'd been victimized, abused, hurt, and abandoned. He'd seen it on women and children and men. Old, young, and everything in between.

Hell! If he looked back at photos taken the first few years after his family was murdered, he'd see it on his own face!

He'd never expected to see it in Benevolence, and he sure as heck hadn't expected to see it on a Lamont's face.

Willow was an adult, and she knew how to deal with her own crap. It wasn't his right to barge into her life and try to fix things. He wasn't even sure anything needed to be fixed. He just knew what he'd seen, and what he couldn't unsee.

"Knock-knock," a woman said, and Sunday Bradshaw stepped into the office. Petite, with pretty green eyes and soft brown hair, she'd been head of the cheerleading squad in high school and had married Matthias Bradshaw a day after graduation. Everyone in town had assumed the high school sweethearts had wed because Sunday was pregnant, but she'd never had a baby. Ever. Currently, the couple had six children through adoption and ran a profitable organic farm ten miles outside the town limits.

"What's up?" Jax said, looking past her to see if any of her kids were hanging out in the hall. Usually, she had at least one clinging to the hem of her cotton skirt. Today, she was alone. "Hopefully not problems with the press camping out on your property. I thought they'd stay close to town."

"It's nothing like that. It isn't even really a problem." She shifted, smoothing a hand down her loose-fitting shirt and not meeting his eyes.

"Is there something wrong with one of the kids?" If he remembered correctly, the oldest Bradshaw kid was ten. Probably not quite at the age of rebellion, but he'd seen younger kids get into trouble with the law. "Do you need me to talk to one of them? Maybe instill a little fear of God or the law?"

"No," she laughed. "They're all doing great. I just . . . have a few things I wanted to donate to the baby you found."

"Things?"

"Clothes. Nearly brand-new. When we got Moisey, she was tiny. Six months old and barely in newborn clothes. We fattened her up pretty quickly, so most of the stuff is in great shape. A few things were never worn. I'd thought . . ." Her voice trailed off, and she smiled brightly. "Well, whatever I thought, I've got a box of things we're not going to be using. I thought it would be nice for that poor baby to have some of them. I'd deliver them to the hospital myself, but I heard on the news that they don't want any visitors. Someone somewhere in town is collecting stuff, but I'll be darned if I can figure out who it is. Every time I try to make a phone call, one of the kids starts screaming in my ear. I figured you might have heard something. Since you found the baby."

"Janelle Lamont might be in charge of that, but I'll be heading to the hospital at some point. I'd be happy to deliver the clothes for you."

"It won't be any trouble?"

"None."

"Then I'll get them for you. They're in my van."

"I can grab them. I'm on my way out, anyway."

"You're heading to the hospital?"

"Not yet. Kane asked me to work an extra shift."

"I'm not surprised. Matt drove through town this morning. He said it was a madhouse. People everywhere. Reporters. News vans."

"That's an apt description. Is Matt on the road today?"

"He's out on delivery. We have a few clients in Seattle, and he's bringing them some really nice relishes and fruit compote from our greenhouse crop."

"You sell the stuff at stores?"

"It's not *stuff*," she corrected, grinning to take any sting out of the words. "It's high-quality organic product that restaurants are willing to pay big bucks for. We make it all in small batches and with only our own ingredients. This time of year, business is limited by the size of our greenhouses. During the summer and the fall, he drives out to Seattle every week."

"I hadn't realized that."

"Most people don't. Matt is a private person." She glanced at her watch. "And, *I'm* running late. Clementine is going to kill me."

"Clementine?"

"Warren. She rents my parents' rancher. Sometimes she watches the kids."

"The rancher is on the farm, right?" he asked, trying to map it in his head.

"Yes. She and Sim rent the house, and we let them have an acre of land to plant."

"How long have they been there?"

"Nine months."

"They have kids?" he asked, surprised that he hadn't realized they were there.

"No. Just another couple living with them. Elias

and Phoebe are younger, but seem to work hard. They certainly always pay the rent on time."

"They come to town much?" If so, he'd never noticed them.

"Please! As if I have time to notice what other people are doing!" She laughed as she walked outside. "The only one of the group that I've spent any time at all with is Clementine, and that's only because she offered to help with the kids in exchange for an extra half-acre garden plot. She's smart and quick. She mentioned a master's in education, but never said where she got it."

"She an older lady?"

"Young. Probably late twenties. Why?" she asked as she crossed the parking lot, heading toward the old red passenger van she and Matt transported their crew in.

"Just curious. There aren't many new people in town that I haven't met or don't know."

"We're not really in town. Remember?"

"Not too far from the town limits, so we'll include you in the next census."

She grinned. "I'll make sure to tell Matt just how lucky we are."

"Or, you two could move your crew into Matt's house. That place needs a little love." The Bradshaws' house was two blocks off Main Street, the huge old place nearly hidden by overgrown bushes and tangled weeds. Matt and his brothers had been raised there, and they'd left there. One by one until the only person remaining had been Matt's father—a mean miser of a man who'd died a decade ago.

"Matt and I have discussed it. The house is big enough, and it would be nice for the kids to be closer

to their school buddies, but the farm just seems . . .
right. Besides, Matt isn't the sole owner. His brothers
are on the title. We'd have to get all of them to agree,
and we'd probably have to buy them out. That would
cost—"

"There's no need to explain, Sunday. You and Matt
can make whatever decision you want, and you don't
have to answer to anyone but God and yourselves
for it."

"Matt always says that, but I know people in town
are wondering when we're going to clean that property up, and I feel bad that we haven't. I drove by
there a few days ago, and it's becoming an eyesore."
She opened the back of the van and reached for a
cardboard box filled with pink and yellow and white
clothes. "Matt said he and his brothers might clean it
up and rent it out sometime this year. If they manage
to do that, the place will look more like the rest of
the town."

"How does the rest of the town look?" he asked,
taking the box from her hands.

"Perfect. Pristine. Impossibly quaint and charm-
ing. The town voted the fifteenth most wonderful
place to live three years running. But you know all
that, so why ask?" She sighed, the watery sunlight
highlighting a few strands of silver in her dark hair.
They'd graduated two years apart, and Jax knew she
was in her late twenties. She looked older. Or maybe
she just looked tired. She had no fine lines near her
eyes, no commas bracketing her mouth. Her skin
still looked smooth, her cheeks tinged with pink.
Somehow, though, she'd aged.

"You sound like you don't think your family be-
longs here."

"My family is . . . wild. That's on the good days. Other days, it's nuts. Don't get me wrong. I love my kids. I love farm life. I love what Matt and I created, but I don't think the town is ready for the likes of us. Now, I really do have to get back. I'll see you around, Jax!" She hopped into the van and drove away, a cloud of black exhaust following her.

He waited until she was out of sight, then put the box in his cruiser and headed back inside.

He had a lot of questions. Not about the Bradshaw brothers' property. He couldn't care less about the old house. Sure, the yard was a mess, but the Bradshaws had hired a company to paint the exterior of the house three years ago. They kept the place winterized, the windows and doors boarded up to keep vandals out, and had replaced the roof recently. It wasn't like the property was a health or safety hazard. They owned it free and clear, paid the taxes on it every year. They were welcome to do what they wanted with it.

What he was wondering about was Clementine and her group. They'd been at Matt and Sunday's farm for months, but he'd never seen them around town. He doubted anyone else had. He'd have heard people talking. There was *always* talk when newcomers showed up.

He hadn't heard a word.

That was strange, and it made him think the four people who lived on the farm were purposely staying hidden.

Which made him wonder why.

He didn't have much to go on, but he typed Clementine's first and last name into the system. She had a clean record. No criminal history. Not even a parking ticket.

That meant just about nothing, but it didn't give him any reason to go for a visit.

Not that he needed a reason.

He'd just drive on by there while he was on shift, introduce himself, make certain that Sunday's renters weren't growing more than fruits and vegetables in their garden.

Marijuana was his first thought, but Sunday hadn't seemed suspicious. She was a savvy lady. Smart. Quick. Driven.

She also had a boatload of young kids.

She could have missed the clues.

Or maybe her renters were just as innocent as she thought, and maybe Jax had spent too much time working in LA. His cell phone rang, and he glanced at the number and frowned. Chocolate Haven. He'd called the shop a couple of times in recent months, but they'd never called him.

"Hello?" he answered.

"Jax?!" Byron Lamont nearly shouted. "I've got a problem, and I need you to solve it."

"Is it an emergency?"

"You're damn right it is! I caught Randall Custard trying to pilfer the family fudge recipe."

"Why would he do that?"

"How the hell would I know? He probably wants to sell it to the highest bidder."

"You know he's got more money than Midas, right?" Randall was a lot of things. Desperate for money wasn't one of them.

"Maybe he needs more. Or maybe he just wants to plaster it all over the front page of the *Benevolence Times*, so he can ruin my family. Thank God I had it locked up when he broke in."

"He broke in?"

"Walked right in the back door of the shop and straight into my office!"

"Was the door locked?"

"Why would it be locked in the middle of the day?"

"What you're saying is that he *didn't* break in. He just walked in without permission."

"Are you coming or not? I've got him locked in the office. Guy is hee-hawing louder than Clinton Myer's prize mule. If you don't get here soon, I may have to stuff his mouth with a few dozen chocolates just to keep him quiet." Byron disconnected without so much as a good-bye.

"Great," Jax muttered.

"I guess you heard from Randall?" Kane said, stepping into the office. "I just got off the phone with him. He didn't waste any time putting in an extra call for help."

"Actually, that was Byron. He wants me to come free Randall from his office. He's threatening to stuff chocolates into the guy's mouth if he doesn't shut up. Not sure if we'd classify that as a felony or misdemeanor."

"I'd call it a public service, but that wouldn't be the right thing for the sheriff to say." Kane glanced at his watch. "I'd take care of the problem myself, but I got a call from the hospital. The baby isn't doing well."

Jax's heart dropped at the news. "How bad is she?"

"They may do surgery tonight or tomorrow morning. I've got a meeting with CPS and the hospital security team. Once the press gets word of this—and they will—they'll be heading in that direction. You want to deal with Randall and Byron for me?"

"No problem."

"Thanks. The good news? With the press rushing to the hospital, our evening just got a lot quieter. Take care of things at Chocolate Haven, and then punch out. You've worked too many graveyard shifts lately, and I want you to have a night off."

"You know that's not necessary."

"I know you'd work twenty-four-seven if I let you. I'm not letting you. Call me if there are any problems."

"I will," Jax responded, stepping out into the hall and heading toward the exit. The sooner he took care of things at Chocolate Haven, the better. Kane wasn't the only one who wanted to be at the hospital. Jax wanted to be there too. He still thought there was a good chance Miracle's mother would show up. But that wasn't his only reason. The baby needed someone there for her. Someone who wasn't being paid to change her, hold her, feed her.

Not that the nurses and doctors weren't exceptional, not that Alison and her team didn't want the best for Miracle, but he wanted to be that person who didn't need to be paid to show up. Like Jim. Like Vera. The steady presence who stuck it out. No matter how tough things got. With Miracle that would only be necessary until a family was found for her, but he was willing to stand in the gap until then.

He wasn't going to get emotionally invested.

He was simply going to show up, because when he'd lifted Miracle from the fruit crate, he'd been reminded of his life before—mother, father, brother, sisters. All of them living a normal, simple, happy life.

Until they hadn't been.

Some nights, he still dreamed about those times.

Some days, he thought he might like to try to have all the things that he'd lost that day. Then he'd remember how it had felt to lift his dying little sister from her crib and try to breathe life back into her.

God!

Not a good memory, but it was there. Always. Just like the sunrise and sunset, the blue sky and distant mountains, the cold winter and brutally hot summer.

Yeah. He knew it as well as any of those things. Probably better. But he couldn't dwell in it, because that was a surefire way to ruin the life that had been gifted back to him.

He walked outside, letting the crisp, cold air fill his lungs and chase away the blood-tinged memories.

No emotional attachment, but Miracle needed someone, and he might as well be that person. For now.

He climbed into his cruiser, pulling out of the parking lot and making the quick drive to Chocolate Haven. The press had mostly cleared out, all but a few stragglers headed for the children's hospital in Spokane and the next addition to their Miracle Baby story.

He parked on the street a block down and walked around to the back of the shop. He didn't want to call attention to his visit. He doubted Randall and Byron would keep quiet about their altercation, but it was their story to tell. He preferred to deal with trouble quietly and with as little drama as possible.

He knocked on the back door, then opened it.

Chocolate.

Vanilla.

Berries.

Something dark and rich and earthy.

The scents that filled the shop were as alluring as

the woman who stood at the counter, red hair pulled into a neat bun, bright yellow apron tied loose around her waist, soft knit dress hugging slender curves that made his blood heat and his mind go blank.

Willow turned as he'd walked in, and he could see specks of chocolate on the apron, a smudge of what looked like cherry on her cheek, and a weariness in her eyes and on her face that cooled his blood and cleared his head.

"I heard there was some trouble with Randall," he said.

"Trouble? World War Three almost broke out."

"That bad, huh?"

"Slight exaggeration." Her lips curved into what should have been a smile. "No bombs. No guns. No threats of bodily harm. Just puffed-up chests and idle lawsuit threats."

"Did Randall clear out?"

"He and Granddad are in the office. Working out their differences."

"Did you lock them in there?"

She laughed. "Tempting as it was, no. I just threatened to head back to Seattle if Granddad didn't start acting reasonably."

"And that convinced *Randall* to have a deep and meaningful conversation about their conflict."

"I told him that he'd be banned from the store if he didn't work things out with my grandfather."

"He's a big chocolate fan?"

"His new girlfriend will be."

"He has one?"

"Not yet, but he will eventually. When he does, she'll want Lamont fudge.. They always do." She turned back to whatever she'd been doing when he'd walked in. Cleaning a mess, it looked like. Bits of chocolate splattered across the marble work surface and a slick of something dark and oily. No pans in the sink, though. No pots piled up to the rafters. Unlike when her sisters had helped with the shop, Willow seemed capable of keeping things neat and orderly.

She also seemed capable of keeping secrets, because the thing he'd seen in her face earlier? It was still there. Not as stark or as vivid, but he could read it clearly, and—God help him—he wanted to know what had put it there.

"Willow—"

"That you, Jax?!" Byron called, interrupting whatever he might have asked. Good. Great. Because Jax shouldn't be asking questions. He shouldn't be getting involved.

Yet, somehow, he was nudging Willow out of the way, taking the rag from her hand, swiping at the oily brown mess.

"Jax!" Byron called again, this time walking into the kitchen, Randall a few steps behind him. Both were red in the face, breathing hard, and ready for a fight.

Or for work.

Jax had spent a hell of a lot of time doing physically demanding chores when he was a kid. He'd had a chip on his shoulder and a need for revenge that could have turned him away from the law and toward something uglier.

Jim's solution?

Work, work, and more work.

What had been beneficial for an angry kid should be beneficial for two pissed-off men.

Jax grabbed an apron from a hook and tossed it at Randall.

"What's this?" he asked as he caught it, his too-smooth brow furrowed in surprise.

"You trespassed."

"So?"

"This is your community service. You can work here for the next couple of hours while Willow goes to Spokane."

"Since when am I going to Spokane?" she asked, but Jax was too busy fielding protests from Randall and Byron to answer.

Chapter Six

Willow had seen a lot in her life, but she'd never seen anything like this—Randall Custard wearing a frilly white apron, listening intently while Granddad explained the fine art of tempering chocolate. All their anger was gone. All their animosity had disappeared.

From feud to friendship in one-minute flat.

Jax needed to write a book. He'd sell a million copies.

"You're smiling," he murmured, and she met his eyes, saw that he was watching her as intently as she'd been watching Granddad and Randall.

"It's good to see them getting along for a change."

"We're not getting along," Granddad corrected. "We're working."

Randall nodded, but he was measuring scoops of chocolate pieces into a double boiler with a fierce intensity that didn't seem to leave room for words.

"That's the way, son," Granddad said, and the words were an echo of the ones Willow had heard over and over again when she was young.

That's the way, son, as Willow's father created another perfect bonbon, cut another gorgeous pan of fudge, rolled another delicate rose.

She blinked, surprised by the memory. A lot of things had been coming back to her since she'd returned. Some of them good. Some of them not.

She glanced at the hallway, the shivery fear of it still lodged in her stomach.

"You okay?" Jax asked, and Granddad glanced her way.

"*Are* you, doll?"

"I'm fine. Just trying to decide what to make next." She'd been planning on mixing another batch of fudge. The three she'd made earlier had been . . . mediocre. She supposed, in another shop in another town, they would have been good enough to sell.

In this shop, in this town?

No way.

Not ever.

She'd tossed all three batches into the Dumpster. Thank God Granddad had been busy in the front of the house. He wasn't any the wiser.

Sadly, she wasn't either.

She had no idea what she was doing wrong. The smooth, creamy, decadent fudge she'd perfected when she was twelve was now lumpy, dull, lifeless crap.

"Make?" Granddad raised a thick gray brow. "You're not making anything. You're going to Spokane."

Right.

Spokane.

To see the baby.

She couldn't think of any other reason Jax would want to take her there. The only problem was that she didn't plan to go. Not yet, and sure as hell not with him. The man made her insides melt and her thoughts fly away, but that wasn't the reason she wouldn't go with him.

She wouldn't go because he'd seen too much.

He'd heard her scream.

He'd held her shoulders while she'd puked.

He'd looked into her face, and he'd known. She wasn't sure how. She didn't know how much, but she knew that he'd seen the truth. She was a victim. There was no doubt about that, but she didn't want the world to know it.

She didn't want Jax to know it.

Call her a coward, because she was one, but the last thing she was going to do was spend more time alone with a man who seemed to see her deepest, darkest secrets.

"We've been swamped all day, Granddad," she began, knowing that Jax wasn't going to believe a word of it. God willing, Granddad would, and he'd jump onboard her plan. "We've got a ton of product to make. That's going to take hours."

"You think the young man and I can't handle it?" Byron jabbed his finger toward Randall, obviously not understanding his part in the conversation. All he'd had to do was agree. Would that have been so difficult?

"He has no experience."

"He's a natural."

"I am?" Randall beamed, and Willow wondered if she was hallucinating, because Randall looked . . . happy.

"Damn straight you are," Byron announced. "You go check on that baby, Willow."

"I'm here to help you. Not leave halfway through the day to go on a jaunt to—"

"Visit a baby who's going to have surgery tonight," Jax interrupted.

"Tonight? When did they decide that?" She pulled out her cell phone, realized she had three calls from the hospital.

"I don't know. They let Kane know. He told me. Someone else must have told the press. They've all cleared out."

"I noticed how quiet it had gotten out there," Willow said, pulling off her apron and tossing it into the laundry bag near the back door. This changed everything, of course. No way was she *not* going to the hospital.

"Hold on a second!" Randall nearly shouted. "I'm not staying here while I get scooped by out-of-towners!"

"Yeah. You go run to the hospital like all those other idiots," Byron said. "Crowd around outside and wait to get whatever little tidbit of information the hospital decides to give. Or you could stay here and wait for Kane to give you a call with the real information."

"You think he'd do that?" Randall asked, looking hopefully at Jax.

"You're local. If there's a scoop to be given, you're the one he'll want to give it to."

It may or may not have been the truth, but Randall seemed satisfied with the answer. "Fine. I'll stick around Chocolate Haven for a while. Maybe the mother will come in for a piece of fudge."

"Anything is possible," Jax agreed, his palm pressing against Willow's lower spine as he urged her toward the back door. He wanted to go to the hospital with her.

She'd rather go alone. She wasn't afraid to have the conversation, but Byron was watching her, a look of concern on his face. Randall was watching—vulture-like and looking for a story—and she found herself moving. Walking to the back door, grabbing her purse from a hook where she'd hung it, stepping outside, moving across the empty parking area.

"Relax," Jax murmured. "I'm not taking you to jail."

"I know," she said.

"Then, why do you look like I am?"

"Just thinking I should drive myself to the hospital. I wouldn't want to pull you away from work."

"You're not." He opened the cruiser door, and she found herself sliding in. Just like that. Not even a word of protest.

She met his eyes, because . . .

He was there, and she was there, and that quick jump of her pulse? The unexpected catching of her breath? That feeling that she'd been here before—looking straight into his eyes—and that she could be here again a million times and it wouldn't be enough? They were like everything she'd ever wanted with Ken.

She finally looked away, making a big deal out of finding her seat belt and snapping it into place.

He must have gotten the hint.

He closed the door and rounded the car, climbing in without another word.

So, of course, she felt the need to talk.

She stared at her cell phone instead. She'd been too busy to check it earlier in the day. Now she could see that she had four text messages from her family, the calls from the hospital, and a voice mail from a number she didn't recognize.

A reporter, maybe?

She'd check later. When she wasn't sitting in Jax's patrol car.

"I have to drive back to the station and punch out. We can take my SUV from there," Jax said as he pulled onto Main Street.

"It might be easier if we just go in separate cars." She should have said that *before* she'd gotten in his car.

"Easier for who?" he asked.

"I just mean that if we go in separate vehicles, neither of us will have to worry about someone else's timeline. We can arrive when we want and leave when we want."

"I'm not worried. Are you?"

"Well, no, but I still think—"

"That we should do the practical thing and share the ride?"

"Practical is overrated."

"So is fear, but you seem to have a lot of it."

"Why do you say that?" she asked as he parked in a lot behind the sheriff's department.

"Am I wrong?"

"Does it matter?"

He turned off the ignition and turned to face her. She wasn't sure what he seeing, had no idea what he was thinking, but finally he shrugged.

"I guess that's up to you, Willow."

"Then, no. It doesn't matter. Even if it did, it wouldn't be up for discussion."

"No problem. I can think of plenty of other things to talk about." He got out of the cruiser.

"My SUV is there." He pointed to a blue Ford Explorer and then handed her a set of keys. "Go ahead and start it. I'll be out in a minute."

This, of course, would have been the perfect opportunity to tell him to forget it. It would have been the perfect time to explain to him that she wasn't afraid of him or of anything else.

Except the past. And dark hallways. Empty doorways.

It *would* have been the perfect opportunity, but he was already walking inside the building, and she was still sitting in his cruiser, the keys in her hand, the chilly March air seeping through her sweater dress.

A jacket would have been a good idea.

Staying in Seattle would have been a better one.

All this crap about facing her fears? She should have made damn sure she was ready to do it before she'd come.

"You *are* ready," she muttered, climbing out of the cruiser and shutting the door. She thought about taking the keys into the station and handing them back to Jax, but that would have required a conversation she didn't feel like having. One that involved listing all the reasons why spending time alone with him wasn't a good idea.

She unlocked the SUV, pushing the remote start as she got into the passenger seat. The vehicle smelled like leather and sunshine and Jax. For some reason, she found that comforting and nice. Like sitting on a porch during a rain shower, listening to water dripping from the eaves and splashing onto grass and pavement. Like waking to the smell of coffee or doughnuts or both. Like all the small uncomplicated moments in life that seemed absolutely divine.

The door opened, and Jax got in, his hair ruffled, his chin scruffy from a days' beard growth.

He met her eyes and smiled, and her heart skipped about a dozen beats.

"Ready?" he asked, and she nodded, because her throat felt tight with emotions she shouldn't be feeling.

He pulled out onto Main Street, driving through town at a leisurely pace, merging onto the interstate and heading toward Spokane. Unlike the previous night, he wasn't quiet. Neither was she. The conversation flowed the way conversations should. No awkward silences, no uncomfortable questions.

By the time they reached the city limits, Willow felt more relaxed than she had in days.

"You're an easy conversationalist, Jax," she said as he exited the interstate and headed into the city.

"Are you surprised?"

"You were quiet when we were kids."

"So were you. I guess we've both grown up and come out of our shells."

Jax pulled into the hospital parking lot, gestured to a news van that was parked near the front entrance. "Looks like the media is already here. How about we go around back and avoid the chaos? We can probably take the back stairs and avoid the press altogether."

"Sounds like a plan," she responded, and he smiled.

"That's about as lackluster a response as I've ever gotten."

"I could say it again with more enthusiasm, if you'd like."

He laughed. A nice laugh. A big one. No quiet chuckle like Ken's, half covered by a hand or interrupted by a cleared throat or a cough. Nope. Jax went all out, the sound warm and full.

So, of course, she smiled.

She was still smiling as she got out of the SUV and followed him into the hospital.

* * *

Making it to Miracle's room without running into the press? Easy.

Watching the baby being wheeled away for surgery? *Not* easy.

The kid looked tiny lying in the Isolette, her downy curls matted down, her body shrouded by blankets. There were tubes and IVs and people everywhere.

Jax had no idea if the baby was old enough to be scared.

He sure as hell was.

"She's going to be fine," Willow said, and he wasn't sure if she was trying to reassure him or herself.

"Of course, she is," Alison said cheerfully.

She'd been in the room when they'd arrived, sitting in a rocking chair near the baby. Based on her wrinkled clothes, smudged eye makeup, and pale skin, he didn't think she'd left the hospital since Miracle had been admitted.

Miracle Doe.

It was stenciled in black on a little card attached to the Isolette. He could see it as he followed the team of specialists to double doors that led into the surgical wing.

"This is as far as you can go," one of the nurses said. "There's a waiting area just around the corner. I'd be happy to show you where it is."

"We'll find it. Coffee first, though, I think," Alison answered. "How about you two? Up for a cup? We can head down to the cafeteria."

"I'd rather wait here," Willow responded, her gaze tracking the team that was disappearing through the doorway.

"Honey," the nurse said with a sigh. "The surgery is going to be a few hours, and standing outside these doors isn't going to imbue the doctors with magical abilities that will get it done faster."

Willow's lips quirked in a smile that didn't quite reach her eyes. "In other words, you want me gone?"

"Not gone in the most permanent sense of the word." The nurse grinned. "Just not standing right here for so long you fall over. It's happened, and trust me, the end results weren't pretty. Banged-up face, busted tooth."

"Coffee sounds better," Alison cut in. "You have my cell phone number, right?"

"Yes," the nurse replied. "We'll call when she's out of surgery. If things take longer than expected, we'll give you an update. Now, I've got to go."

She hurried away, the doors swinging shut behind her.

For a moment, they were all standing silently, looking at that damn door as if it was going to open and a healthy newborn was going to suddenly appear.

Finally Jax got himself moving.

He stepped away from the door, his hand settling on Willow's shoulder as he urged her to do the same. He meant for his palm to rest on the back of her jacket. But she hadn't worn a jacket. There was nothing between his hand and her skin except a layer of soft knit fabric.

Very soft, and he imagined her skin would be even softer.

He imagined it would feel damn good to let his hand slide along that silky flesh.

He also imagined that he should walk away, put a few hundred steps between himself and Willow, because she was the kind of woman he'd spent a lifetime avoiding. The kind he'd want to build dreams with, the kind he'd want to give the world to, because he'd think she deserved it.

"What do you two think of my coffee idea?" Alison asked, bouncing along beside them, her words an anchor to the real world. The one where Jax avoided relationships that would drag him in deeper than he wanted to go.

He let his hand slip away, his gaze skimming Willow's face as he pushed the elevator button.

Her cheeks were pink, her gaze fastened on Alison as if her life depended on maintaining eye contact with the woman.

"Coffee would be good," she said, nearly running into the elevator as the doors opened.

"And maybe food?" he suggested, because he doubted she'd eaten anything at Chocolate Haven. Except maybe chocolate. He could smell that, the scent filling the elevator as they rode to the main floor. He thought it might be his imagination, but Alison inhaled, her eyes closing.

"Oh. My. Gosh. Someone has chocolate!" she cried.

"I think, maybe, I'm wearing it," Willow replied, brushing her hand down the front of her dress as if she thought she might be covered with the stuff.

He didn't see a speck of chocolate on her.

What he saw was the way her dress hugged her slim curves, the way her legs seemed to go on forever. The way her cheeks went pink again when she noticed he was watching her.

"Too bad. I love chocolate," Alison said. "Maybe I'll come visit that chocolate shop of yours."

"It's my grandfather's shop," Willow responded, her voice husky. She was staring straight into his eyes, and Jax couldn't make himself look away.

He didn't *want* to look away.

He wanted to keep staring into her face. He wanted to trace the angle of her jaw, count the freckles on her cheeks. He wanted to tuck that one loose strand of hair behind her ear and kiss the hollow at the base of her throat.

Her pulse jumped. He could see it thrumming wildly beneath her ivory skin, and if Alison hadn't been standing a foot away, he'd have given in to temptation and pressed his lips to the spot, tasted the sweetness of her skin.

"Oh. I know it is. I've done my research," Alison said as the elevator doors slid open. She bustled out, completely oblivious to the zing of electricity in the air.

"What research?" Jax asked, because Willow didn't. She was too busy striding toward the cafeteria, her low-heeled boots tapping on the tile floor, her muscles taut with whatever she was feeling.

"On potential candidates."

"Candidates?"

"Do you know how many applications for foster and adoption we've received since Miracle's story broke?" she asked.

"A lot," Willow offered, tossing the words over her shoulder.

"Hundreds. By the end of the week, we'll probably have thousands. It's a daunting job weeding through all the information. It's always this way with newborns and babies. Even toddlers. It's the older kids who get the short end of the stick. We're lucky if we get a half dozen applicants for them. It's a shame. There are so many great kids who just need a chance." She shook her head. "But that's neither here nor there. We're dealing with a newborn. A very *new* newborn. Everyone and his brother wants to be her parent."

"She has parents. Somewhere," Jax said, not sure where they were headed with the conversation.

"Parents who may or may not be found. Parents who may or may not be fit to raise her. She needs a home now. Not tomorrow or the next day. The best thing my office can offer is someone who will love her as if she were her own, but who will be willing to give her up when the time comes. Someone who is trained, who has a good heart, who has a good support system. Someone like Willow."

"What?!" Willow spun around. "You're kidding, right?"

"I'm not kidding. You're licensed and approved by the state. You live in the town where Miracle was found. If she's got family around and they're located, that will make visitation easier."

"I don't live in Benevolence," Willow pointed out, and Alison shrugged.

"You're there now, and we want to keep the baby in-county. Your apartment is large enough for you and a child."

"It's not my apartment."

"But you're living there. I could stop by in the next day or two and write up an addendum to your home study that reflects your change in address."

"But it's not a permanent change." Willow sounded confused and, unless Jax missed his guess, intrigued.

"Willow—" He tried to butt in, but Alison was on a roll.

"This isn't a permanent placement. It's an emergency foster. A month or two tops. That *is* what you're licensed to provide."

"I'd only planned to be in Benevolence for a couple of weeks."

"Would you be willing to change your plans for Miracle's sake? Maybe take a little more vacation time? Live here on the weekend and take the commuter flight in and out of Seattle once you go back to work? We're not talking permanently. This will be for a month or two tops."

"All those things are possible, but for the next ten days, I'm working at the shop. I don't have a daycare provider," she said, the fact that she hadn't answered the question giving Jax all the information he needed.

She was going to agree unless there was some compelling reason not to, and that might be a mistake. Or it might not. It wasn't his decision to make, and he sure as hell wasn't going to try to talk her out of it.

On the other hand, if she stuck around town for a month or two, there'd be a lot more opportunities for him to see her, a lot more opportunities for him to overstep boundaries that he'd set into place years ago. A lot more opportunity for heartbreak.

"You have a full-time job in Seattle"—Alison was on a roll and pushing her advantage—"and you still did foster parent training. Obviously, you've thought through your options."

"Of course, I have. They include daycare providers that I trust and a flexible work schedule. I have plenty of personal leave saved. That's when I'm in Seattle. Here, things are different. I can't make chocolate in the apartment, and my daycare provider isn't going to relocate to accommodate me."

"When I spoke with your mother earlier, she said that she'd be happy to offer childcare. She's already gone to have fingerprinting done. Once we get her background check complete, we may be able to get special approval for her to help out. For now, she said that one of your sisters could help at the shop when you can't be there."

"When did you speak to my mother?"

"This morning. Nine-ish maybe. She'd stopped by with some clothes for Miracle and asked if she could take a peek at the little baby that you'd saved."

"I didn't save her."

"Her words. Not mine. Besides, if your mother wants to call you a hero, who am I to argue? Anyway, she caught me at a good time. I'd just had a nice big breakfast. Omelet. Toast." Alison patted her stomach. "Otherwise, I might have told the nurse to turn her away. I get grumpy when I haven't eaten."

"Good to know," Jax muttered.

"I like to warn people." She barely spared him a look. Her gaze was on Willow. She had an agenda, and she didn't seem like she was going to be swayed from it. "Long story short, Willow. Your mother saw Miracle, and we had a nice little chat about what a good foster mother you would be and about how your family would rally around you while Miracle waited for her new beginning."

"New beginning?" Willow frowned.

"She needs a fresh start. You're a good way for her to transition into it. What do you say? Will you consider it?"

"When would you need my decision?"

"Now would be great, but if you need more time, tomorrow will be okay."

"You don't seem to understand. I'm not ready to

take in a baby. I've got no crib. No clothes. No diapers. No formula. I have no idea what kind of medical needs Miracle will have."

"A nurse will come twice a day for the first couple of weeks to help out."

"But that still leaves everything else," Willow pointed out.

"And by the time she's released from the hospital, I'm sure you'll have all of it," she said as if that was the last hurdle, as if the deal was done, an agreement reached.

Willow didn't argue.

She didn't throw up another roadblock, she didn't point out flaws in the plan. No doubt about it. She was going to foster Miracle. She was going to mother her.

She was going to fall in love.

She was going to get her heart broken.

And Jax? He was going to be right there beside her, because what else could he do? Sure as hell not sit around twiddling his thumbs, pretending that he hadn't been part of finding Miracle and that he wasn't just as responsible for helping her get her new beginning.

He could feel the responsibility of it tightening like a noose around his neck, pulling him into a position he'd never wanted to be in.

One where he cared too much, loved too deeply.

"Willow," he began, because he thought maybe he could explain things a little more clearly. Let her know in a little more detail just how tough it was going to be to say good-bye. Not talk her out of it, but sure as hell not help her talk herself into it.

"I know what you're going to say, Jax. I shouldn't do it."

"I was going to say that you need to take your time thinking it through."

"I agree, but we don't have time, do we?"

We?

He doubted she'd realized the wording, and he didn't point it out.

"I'm going to text my mother." She pulled out her cell phone. "She's great at organizing things. We can have the nursery painted and ready by Sunday."

"Wonderful! I'll stop by after church and get the amended home study started. That gives you a full forty-eight hours to prepare!" Alison beamed, grabbing Willow's arm and dragging her toward the cafeteria door. "Now that that's settled, let's go get coffee and pie to celebrate."

Neither woman seemed to realize Jax wasn't following.

He wasn't.

No. He was standing in the middle of the hospital corridor, wondering how in the hell his life had gone from quiet to chaos in just a few short hours.

He was also wondering how he was going to explain things to Kane. One day of overzealous news coverage was about all the town could take. Now it looked like that might stretch on for weeks or months.

They'd have to work extra shifts, assign someone the task of contacting the media and issuing statements. They'd have to protect Miracle's privacy, protect Willow's, and keep the town safe and comfortable for its citizens. They'd have to do it on a shoestring budget with a very small team, all while searching for the person who'd abandoned Miracle.

Not impossible, but it was going to take a lot of planning and coordinating. The way he saw it, there was no time like the present to begin.

He dragged out his phone, punched in Kane's number, and waited impatiently while it rang.

Chapter Seven

Things had gone to hell in a handbasket.

At least, that's what Granddad kept saying.

Over and over and over again.

As matter of fact, he'd said it so many times, Willow thought she'd lose her mind if she heard it just once more.

She didn't have the heart to tell him that.

He meant well.

He really did.

It was just that the apartment wasn't big, and the room they were preparing for Miracle was small, and the two of them had spent way too many minutes trying to assemble the easy-to-assemble crib that she'd purchased last night.

"Easy-to-assemble" must be code for never-going-to-happen.

Except it had to happen, because Alison was coming for a home visit in exactly fifteen hours.

After church on Sunday. Noonish.

God! What had she been thinking when she'd agreed to foster Miracle?

She hadn't been thinking.

She'd been feeling all those ooey-gooey emotions that Adeline claimed to have experienced the moment she'd laid eyes on little Alice.

Only Miracle wasn't Willow's baby, and the ooey-gooey feelings were best left out of the equation. She was doing this because . . .

Well, because she'd been asked, and because she'd spent months taking classes to prepare to do just exactly what Alison had asked her to do.

Plus, she couldn't forget the way Miracle had looked when Jax had lifted her from the box—tiny and frail.

She hadn't looked any better after surgery.

Willow frowned, grabbing a screwdriver and trying to tighten the screw that was supposed to hold the crib together.

No luck. She touched the crib, and it wobbled like a drunken sailor on a storm-tossed ship.

"You know what the problem is, doll?" Granddad asked, holding the instruction sheet at arm's-length and squinting as he tried to read it.

"You forgot your reading glasses?"

"Nah. I can see just fine. The problem is, too many cooks."

"Granddad, it's nearly eleven o'clock at night. I've been up since five. I'm too tired to decipher one of your riddles."

"What riddle? I'm stating it plain as can be. Too many cooks spoil the broth and too many hands ruin the crib."

"You're saying that we've got one person too many working on this job?" she asked, hoping that was what he meant, because once he left, she'd close the nursery door and forget the mess until morning.

God help her if she couldn't figure it out then, because poor Granddad sure didn't seem to be able to lend a hand.

"That's exactly what I'm saying."

"You're right. Why don't you—"

"I'm glad you agree. I've been thinking about those bonbons you made the other day. The ones with the rum-soaked cherries inside?"

"What about them?" It had been the one recipe she'd had fantastic success at. The *only* recipe.

"I sure could use a couple. This is hard work, putting baby beds together. A guy like me? I need my sustenance."

"I'll make some more tomorrow. You go home, and when you—"

"Go home? Now, who said anything about *me* leaving?"

"You said there was one too many cooks."

"Right. Only the one too many is you. I love you dearly, Willow, but you're not quick at bed-building."

Neither was he, but she loved him too much to point it out.

"Maybe not, but I can't let you put this together while I—"

"Go make me a couple of those bonbons? Of course you can, because if I have to get the snack myself, my hip just might give out on me. You know I've been up and down the stairs six times the past few days, right?"

"I thought you were recovered enough to do that."

"That's what the doctor says. The leg?" He patted his right thigh. "It's not convinced. The hip? It likes to try to trip me up. If I fall again . . . well, I might not recover this time."

"Uhmmm-hmmm," she said, and he scowled.

"Now, what in the hell is that supposed to mean?"

"Just that I don't think that hip is going make you fall, and if you did fall, you're too stubborn to do anything but get back up and go right back into the kitchen."

"After I finished putting this damn thing together," he added, and she smiled.

"Granddad, really, you don't have to do this for me."

And she'd really rather he not, because going down into the kitchen and making chocolate at this time of night was absolutely out of the question.

The shop at night? Alone?

It wasn't going to happen.

"I'm not doing it for you. I'm doing it for the baby."

"You don't have to do it for her, either. She's not being discharged until Friday. And that's only if she continues to improve."

"And that caseworker lady is coming tomorrow. What if she doesn't approve the apartment? What if she puts her hand on the crib and it falls into dozens of pieces?"

"Then I guess it just wasn't meant to be."

"Bull crap. This is meant to be. I feel it. Right here." He tapped his chest. "Now, you go make me some chocolates, and I'll put this thing together. If we're both quick, I can be home by midnight."

He took the screwdriver from her hand, nudged her into the hall.

"I could make you grilled cheese instead," she offered. "You love grilled cheese." She didn't have the ingredients on hand to do it, but a drive to the grocery store wasn't out of the question. Not like going down to the shop was.

"I had grilled cheese for dinner."

"When'd you eat dinner?" Chocolate Haven had been busy for hours on end. One customer after another after another. Most of them wanted chocolate and the story about Miracle being found behind the Dumpster.

Most had offered to pay for the story when they paid for the chocolate.

Willow had declined politely so many times, she'd decided to post a sign on the front of the register—NO INTERVIEWS. After they'd closed down the shop, they'd headed to Spokane to see Miracle. Then, of course, they'd come here to put the easy-to-assemble crib together. There'd been no stop for dinner, and no mention of eating.

Apparently, because Granddad had been fed.

"A friend brought it for me." His cheeks were pink. A blush?

Was her grandfather actually blushing?

"A female friend?" she asked, wondering if that friend was Laurie Beth from the diner. Both her sisters had mentioned that she and Byron had a thing going on.

What kind of thing, neither was willing to say.

They sure as heck hadn't used the word *dating*.

She'd have remembered that.

"What's it matter?" he replied. "I had dinner. I want chocolate, and if you don't feel like making it, you can just grab me a couple of whatever we have left from today."

"There's not much. We sold out of almost everything."

"Second day in a row," he said, a hint of pride in his voice. He loved the shop almost as much as he loved his family, and seeing it doing well always made him happy. "Now, how about we implement my plan?

Because you look tired, and I'm feeling it. I want to get this crib built, so we can both catch some sleep!" He closed the door with a quiet snap, turned the old-fashioned skeleton key in the lock.

She could stand in the hall for the next twenty minutes, or she could go make him the bonbons.

She sighed, grabbing her coat from the closet and shoving her arms into the sleeves. She'd been cold for days, the chilly air seeping into her bones and settling there.

Hopefully, the baby would be warm enough in the apartment. Willow had had the radiator serviced to make sure that it was running properly. She'd also paid to have the living room fireplace inspected.

It had checked out, so she'd purchased wood and stacked it in the box beside the fireplace. She had a lighter high on the mantel, kindling in another box. A throw folded over the rocking chair Brenna had brought from the house she and her husband were restoring.

There were diapers in the cute changing table Janelle had purchased. Ointment, clothes, wipes, bottles. All those things had been provided by the community, brought in by the boxload until Willow had finally said *enough*.

Miracle wouldn't be there forever.

Just a couple of months. Maybe a lot less than that.

Jax had called that morning. He'd said they had a few leads that they were following up on. God willing, they'd locate Miracle's parents.

Until then, Willow was a temporary solution to the problem.

Temporary.

She kept reminding people of that.

Her sisters. Her mother. Her old high school friends.
Reporters who stopped in for the story. Church
ladies. Deacons. Shop owners from nearby towns who
wanted to be part of the excitement. She told every
single one of them that Miracle wasn't staying for
long, because she needed them all to remember it.

Eventually Alison would find a more permanent
placement. Then Miracle would move on to some
other town and some other family.

That was the truth, and Willow had spent just as
much time reminding herself of it as she had everyone else.

Because, honestly, Jax had been right.

If she wasn't careful, she'd get her heart broken.

She stepped out onto the landing, inhaling cold,
crisp air and the familiar scent of home—pine needles,
snow, and wood-burning fires.

Home?

Funny that she should think of it that way after all
the years away. She'd settled into Seattle life and into
its weather, and she'd never really thought about what
she was missing—the dry, clean air, the clear sky, the
beauty of nights like this one—stars speckling the
black sky, the moon hanging low on the horizon.

God! It was all so stunning!

How could she have not remembered that?

She stood where she was for just a minute, letting
the night settle quietly around her. She went quiet,
too, her heartbeat slowing, her breathing evening out.

There was nothing to fear in the shop.

Nothing that could hurt her, anyway.

She *could* make a few bonbons. Maybe more than
a few. They'd nearly doubled their sales the last few
days, and there was no sign of that letting up.

Prep work began at five, but if she got a head start on it, maybe she could sleep until . . .

Church.

Tomorrow was Sunday, the shop was closed, any bonbons she made could be shared with friends rather than bought in the store. There was no need to make a huge batch. Just a few for Granddad, a few for friends.

None for her.

She was getting sick of the smell of chocolate, the taste of it, the feel of it on her hands.

Who was she kidding? She'd been sick of it before she'd even arrived.

Granddad sensed it. Or, more likely, he'd guessed based on her abysmal track record with the family fudge. She was batting zero, and the mess from her attempts wasn't pretty. At last count, she'd wasted a few hundred dollars' worth of fine chocolate and heavy cream. The Dumpster was becoming a grave-yard for chocolate crap, and she was becoming the head undertaker.

After her last failure, she'd turned to the Bitter Cherry Bonbon recipe. Her grandmother had taught her how to make it when she was eight, and she'd wondered if she'd lost the touch for that as thoroughly as she'd lost her fudge-making abilities.

She'd been shocked and pleased when she'd produced beautiful glossy confections.

Granddad had been pleased too.

Maybe there's hope after all, his overzealous appreciation seemed to say.

"Not hardly," she muttered, finally taking the first step downstairs. The alley was dark, the exterior light turned off to discourage curiosity-seekers. The caution tape had been pulled down that morning, and there was nothing left to tell the story of Miracle. No box. No snow patted down by a dozen feet. The alley had gone back to what it had always been—a passageway between Main Street and the back lot.

Bitter wind swept through it, scattering bits of debris laid bare by the day's bright sunshine and dry weather. The snow had melted, and the air held just a hint of balmy spring—cut grass, blooming fields, life springing up from the thawing ground. She hadn't planned to be there to see it happen, but now that she'd agreed to foster Miracle, anything was possible. Spring. The beginning of summer.

She wanted to be angry about it. She wanted to regret it. She wanted to feel like she'd left her home, and she was desperate to return to it. After all, she loved her job and her little rental house. She had a good life, good neighbors, good friends.

She didn't have family, though.

Not in Seattle.

She didn't have sisters who stopped by to help shape chocolate hearts or plop pretty little robin's egg–colored white chocolates into tiny coconut baskets. She didn't have a mother setting flowers on her dinette table, cleaning her kitchen when she didn't have time, sticking her nose into every plan she made.

It should have annoyed Willow.

She'd lived independent of her mother's micromanagement for years, and she'd forgotten how insidious it could be.

Somehow, though, she'd found herself more patient with it than she'd expected. She'd found herself looking at her mother's face and seeing a softness that hadn't been there when she was a kid. Or maybe it had been, and she'd just been too caught up in her own drama to notice.

She'd reached the back door of the shop, and she unlocked it, all her good feelings slipping away. This was the part that she didn't like. It was the one thing that she dreaded every moment of every day.

Walking into the empty shop.

Flicking on the lights.

Expecting him to be there, waiting in the shadows of the hallway, telling her that they hadn't finished for the day.

Every night, she dreamed about it.

Every. Damn. Night.

God! Would she ever put it behind her?

Irritated, she grabbed ingredients from the pantry, slammed them on the counter, went to work as if everything in her life depended on making the most perfect bonbons in the whole damn world.

A long day had turned into a long night.

Jax had spent most of it over at the Bradshaws' place, talking to Sunday and Matt's renters. Nice kids. All three of them. There were supposed to be four. One was working in Spokane. At least, that's what her housemates and husband said. She was the one Jax most wanted to see.

Three trips to the farm. Three people who were consistently there. One who was not.

That made him suspicious, so he'd stuck around, asking questions about the organic business the group was trying to start. Something to do with natural fibers and eco-friendly clothing.

He turned off the highway, following the country

road that led into town. He wanted home almost as much as he wanted a juicy hamburger or an oversized milkshake.

When had he eaten last?

Noon, maybe? When he'd stopped in to check on Vera and Jim and been handed a slice of homemade bread covered in Vera's famous grape jelly.

His stomach growled at the memory, and he was half-near tempted to drive over to the house, slip in through the back door, and cut himself another slice.

Jim slept restlessly, though, and he didn't want to wake him.

No. He'd go home and rummage through cupboards that he knew were bare. He hadn't had time to run to the store.

Who was he kidding?

He never had time for that.

He microwaved canned soup or popped bread in the toaster. He might have made an egg last week, but his kitchen usually stayed spotless, the fridge boasting a couple of bottles of water and whatever food items Vera handed him on his way out her door.

He turned onto Main Street, eyeing the dark façades of the shops there. Everything closed down by nine in the winter. In another month or two a few places would stay open later—the custard shop, the five-and-dime, the diner.

He passed one after another, heading deeper into town and closer to his street. Closer to Chocolate Haven, too. It was up ahead, lights glowing from the shop window.

He didn't mean to stop.

He meant to drive by, turn onto his street, continue

along the windy road until he reached the oversize Victorian.

Big enough for a family, Vera said almost every other day.

He never bothered to correct her.

Why break her heart by saying he'd never have one?

He pulled around to the back of the store, saw movement in the shop window. Willow? Probably.

And he should probably not get out of the car and knock on the door, because it was late, he was tired, and he'd told himself a thousand times that he was going to keep things professional between them.

No more looking into her eyes.

No more wondering about her secrets.

No more of anything that could get him into trouble.

But he was there. The light was on, and he had a piss-poor track record for taking his own advice.

He climbed out of the car, knocked on the door.

It swung open, and she was there. Hair pulled back in a tight braid, body encased in another one of those soft knit dresses. Apron hanging loose around her neck, the strings batting her thighs as she stepped back and let him in.

"I saw your lights," he said, turning her around so he could tie the strings, his fingers skimming over fabric warm from her skin. Heat shot through him, and he stepped back, because if he didn't, he'd do something stupid. Like cup her face in his hands, tell her that he'd spent the better part of two days thinking of all the reasons why he needed to keep his distance, and then remembering all the reasons why he didn't want to.

"I saw your car. Otherwise, I wouldn't have opened

the door. Most people don't stop for chocolate this time of night." She smiled, a quick turn of lips that only barely lightened her somber expression.

"You okay?" he asked, because he could see that she wasn't. Her freckles were dark against pale skin, her eyes were deeply shadowed. Her hand shook as she ran a hand over her braid, smoothing it down over her shoulder. He wanted to capture her hand, hold it steady, tell her everything was fine.

But, of course, that would be as stupid as stopping for a visit at eleven o'clock at night.

"Just making some Bitter Cherry Bonbons for Grand-dad. He's upstairs putting together a crib."

"Your inner lawyer is coming out," he commented, walking to the counter and lifting a bowl of dark chocolate bits. "You want this melted and tempered?"

"I was just getting ready to do it."

"See what I mean?"

"About?"

"Your inner lawyer. I ask a question. You sidestep it."

She'd already set the double boiler on the counter, and he poured the chocolate in, grabbing a wooden spoon from one of the drawers. This was the one thing he'd actually learned to do when he'd worked with Byron. Tempering chocolate—candy making 101.

"Is that what I'm doing?" she said, and then laughed. "I guess you're right. It's a bad habit."

"So, should I ask again?"

"If I'm okay? You can see I am." She gestured toward the ingredients on the counter. "Just busy."

"I hear the shop has been busting at the seams the past few days."

"You hear right. We haven't had a break. Both my sisters stopped by to help. Chase skipped a day of school. Granddad nearly took his head off for that one. I don't think he'll repeat the mistake."

"He might not think it was a mistake. He loves your family."

"He *is* our family. We don't separate based on last name," she responded, popping the lid on what looked like a jelly jar filled with candied cherries.

"Bitter cherries?" he asked as she set several on a baking sheet lined with wax paper.

"Rum-soaked. Very sweet with just a hint of naughty. Try one." She held it out, and he took it from her fingers, popped it into his mouth, felt a quick burst of warmth on his tongue, before he tasted the bitter-sweetness of the cherry.

"God!" he said. "Who invented that?"

"I don't know, but my grandmother created this recipe. Layers and layers of chocolate over bitter cherries. That's what she told me when she taught me how to make it. Of course, I was only eight, so she didn't let me taste the final product. We use candied cherries and dark chocolate for the ones we sell in the store. These are special. They're my grandfather's favorite, and Grandma Alice only made them once a month. She'd keep a few for Granddad and sell the rest to her best customers." She washed her hands, opened another jar, set more cherries on the pan.

"So," he said, the taste of cherry and rum still on his tongue, the scent of chocolate in his nose, the feel of that damn soft dress lingering on his fingers. "You're saying we're going to pour chocolate over the top of those?"

"*Layers* of chocolate. We pour. Wait. Pour more. It takes a while. Which is why Granddad sent me down here to do it. He wanted to get rid of me." She leaned across him, grabbing a bottle of vanilla from the counter, her arm brushing against his abdomen, her cheeks going bright red.

"Sorry about that," she murmured, moving back into her space.

Too bad.

He was enjoying her being in his.

He scowled, stirring the chocolate with so much force a couple of pieces jumped from the pot and bounced across the floor.

"Don't stir it, Jax," she said, pouring the vanilla into a bowl with what looked like milk or cream. "Just let it melt."

"Right. Why did Byron want to get rid of you?" he asked, nabbing another one of the cherries, his stomach rumbling with happiness as he chewed it.

"The easy-to-assemble crib isn't all that easy to assemble."

"Maybe, because it's late, and you're both tired?" he suggested, and she shrugged.

"Probably, but try telling Granddad that. He's caught in a battle that he's determined to win, and I was just cluttering up the battlefield." She opened the fridge, pulled out a carton of eggs and a container of heavy cream.

"Eggs in the chocolates?" he asked as she cracked a few into a bowl.

"Eggs in your stomach," she responded. "You look hungry."

"And you look like you don't need to be making me eggs."

"You're tempering chocolate for my recipe. We'll call it even." She beat in cream, added a dash of salt and pepper, poured it all into a buttered pan.

She was quick.

She was efficient.

She was beautiful.

And he couldn't quite stop noticing that.

She finished the eggs, held out a plate and fork.

"You have to eat in the front of the house. We don't want to break any health codes."

"Is this your way of getting rid of me?" he asked.

"If I'd wanted to do that, I'd have never opened the door," she responded, giving him a gentle shove toward the hallway. "Go. I have to pour the chocolate before it cools."

He went, because it seemed a safer bet than standing in the kitchen, the taste of bittersweet cherries on his tongue, the warmth of Willow's back still on his fingers.

Yeah.

Safer.

Maybe not as fun.

He sat at one of the small wicker tables near the storefront window. Someone had set up a display there—a little white baby carriage filled with flowers. Next to it sat a silver display stand that had been covered with all kinds of chocolates earlier in the day.

A shadow moved in front of the glass, and he tensed, all the old habits from his time working in LA jumping into place, his hand sliding to his gun belt. His body up and moving toward the light switch before he realized who was outside the window.

Not some criminal hoping for a clear shot at a cop.

It was Byron. Tall, a little stooped, his face pressed close to the glass.

He spotted Jax, winked, waved, and walked away.

"Interesting," Jax said.

"Talking to yourself?" Willow stepped into the service area, a small plate in her hand, two glossy chocolates bouncing around on it. Not because she was walking. Because she was shaking.

He grabbed the plate, led her to the seat he'd just abandoned.

"Sit," he said.

"So I can stand back up and go in the kitchen? I've got another layer of chocolate to put on the bonbons, but I wanted you to have some dessert." She pulled away, flicked her braid over her shoulder, acted like she wasn't shaking from head to toe.

Maybe she thought he hadn't noticed.

Or hoped it.

And maybe she thought he was too polite to mention it if he did.

She was wrong.

On both counts.

He snagged the back of her apron, stopping her before she could walk away. "What's going on, Willow?"

"I was just asking myself the same thing." She didn't turn around, just stood with her back to him, that red braid settled right in the middle of her narrow shoulders. "I mean, one day I've got a great job in Seattle, a cool rental house that I love, a life that is predictable and easy and nice. The next . . ."

"What?"

"The next, I'm making eggs and chocolates for a guy I should be avoiding, working in a shop I hate, caring for a baby who's going to tie me to a town that I really need to escape."

"You could go back to Seattle," he suggested, not

touching on any of the particulars, because what could he say?

That he should be avoiding her, too?

That he wanted to know why she hated the shop that she'd grown up in?

That the baby was only tying her to the town because she was allowing it?

"I guess I could." She finally turned. "But that would mean leaving things unfinished."

"Someone else can finish the chocolates, foster Miracle, help your granddad."

"And make you eggs?" she asked, a hint of a smile on her lips.

"I know how to make my own eggs, Willow. I also know how to fight the monsters that come out in the darkest hours of the night." The words slipped out, completely unintended, because he'd made it very clear to himself that her problems weren't his, that her crap was hers to deal with.

She didn't need a hero, and he didn't want to be one.

So, they were on the same page, working the same angles, just running into each other and connecting, because it was a small town and there weren't a hell of a lot of ways to avoid each other.

Except for, maybe, driving past the shop instead of stopping in when the lights were on.

"There's no such thing as monsters," she said, but they both knew it was a lie.

"Who was he?" he asked, because—*damn it!*—he wanted to know.

"I don't know what you're talking about." She strode to the threshold of the hall, came to a dead stop there, her hands fisted as if the thing she feared the most was just in front of her.

"You know exactly what I'm talking about. Pretending otherwise is as useless as keeping your silence has been."

"You know the thing about silence, Jax?" She spun around, and he could see the tears in her eyes, the stark whiteness of her face and her lips. "It gets bigger and uglier and harder to break. Eventually, it's its own kind of monster. Eat the damn chocolates, okay? I've got work to do."

She ran through the hall, and he could hear pots banging, water running, boots clicking on the tile floor.

He knew what he should do—leave.

Now. Before things got complicated.

Hell! Things already *were* complicated.

He glanced at the chocolates, lifted one from the plate, Willow's words still hanging in the air.

Eat the damn chocolates.

He popped it in his mouth, let it explode in fiery bits of rum-soaked cherry and sweet creamy chocolate.

Yeah. He knew what he *should* do.

He also knew what he was going to do.

He grabbed the last bonbon and headed back into the kitchen.

Chapter Eight

God! She hated crying.

Hated it, but the damn tears just didn't want to stop. They slipped down her cheeks, dripped onto the marble slab she was cleaning, splashed onto the floor when she leaned over to grab a piece of chocolate that had escaped the pot.

She didn't want to be in the kitchen, surrounded by all the familiar and homey things, because it reminded her of what she could have had. Probably even should have had. The business, the chocolates, the pretty little vintage jars filled with high-quality ingredients. A family tradition that she could have passed down to her daughters and sons.

Only, of course, she wasn't going to have either of those.

Footsteps sounded on the hallway floor, and she knew Jax was returning. She swiped at her cheeks, washed her hands, made a big show of pouring another coating of chocolate over the bonbons.

He didn't say a word. Just went to the sink and washed the double boiler, set it back in the cupboard, put away the bottle of vanilla and an unopened jar of cherries.

When he finished, he grabbed boxes from the neat little stacks that lined the shelves. Pretty ones with muted pink roses on an ivory background.

"Those are for special occasions," she said, her voice raspy from the tears. "Weddings. Showers. Birthday deliveries."

"Good to know," he responded, carefully placing five bonbons in a box.

"Jax, really! The boxes are—"

"Almost as lovely as you." He handed her the box, filled four more flowered ones and a plain white one, and set them in a large cloth bag. When he finished, he wiped down the counter, swept the floor, cleaned up like he'd been doing it his entire life.

And Willow?

She just leaned against the counter, holding the box, and thinking that she should get herself together and help.

"Done," he finally said, grabbing the chocolates and taking her hand. "Let's get out of here."

"And go where?"

"Does it matter?"

"It should."

"You're sidestepping questions again," he responded. "So, I'll try again. Does it matter where we go?"

"I have to bring the chocolates up to Byron and see if—"

"He's already gone. I saw him leave before you brought me the Bittersweet Cherries."

"Bitter Cherry Bonbons. That's what my grandmother called them."

"Right. She should have called them Damn Addictive.

I planned to give you one of the two, and ate it on my way down the hall."

The comment surprised a laugh out of her. "Grandma Alice would probably appreciate the name change. She had a good sense of humor and a bit of rebellious heart."

"She was a great lady."

"You remember her?"

"How could I forget? She was one of Vera's best friends. They used to make Christmas cookies together every year, and Alice always snuck me a couple when my aunt wasn't looking." He strode across the parking lot, opened the passenger door of his police cruiser, helped her in, and then handed her the bag of chocolates.

When he closed the door, she finally realized what she was doing: heading off God-knew-where with a man who was as dangerous to her heart as Lamont Family Fudge was to other people's waistlines.

He slid in behind the wheel, closing the door and sealing them both in the dark vehicle. She expected him to start the engine, drive out of the parking lot and take her . . .

Where?

Does it matter?

That's what he'd asked, and of course, she hadn't really answered. She'd become an expert at side-stepping questions. He was right about that.

"So," he said casually, but there was nothing casual about the way he turned to face her. Nothing casual about the look on his face or the intensity in his eyes. "What's the verdict?"

"About?"

"Our destination. Does it matter or not?"

"Of course it matters." She smoothed her hand over the top of the flowery box and forced herself to relax. This was not a big deal. This was Jax, taking her somewhere with a few pounds of bonbons. "Neither of us has a lot of time to waste, so if we're just going on a midnight ride—"

"Then we'll both be the better for it." He started the engine and pulled around the side of the building. "But I do have a plan. Aunt Vera has always said that the best way to stop feeling sorry for ourselves is to start feeling sorry for someone else."

"Who's feeling sorry for herself?" she asked, and he grinned.

"Is that a rhetorical question, Willow? Because I'm pretty sure I wasn't the one sniffling over the chocolate pots."

"I was sniffling over the marble. I'd never cry over the chocolate pots," she responded, and was rewarded with a quiet chuckle.

"I'd ask you what you were crying about, but I figure you'll share if you want to."

She *didn't* want to, but she felt the strange urge to talk anyway, to tell him things that she hadn't told anyone else. Not about Eric. Not about her nightmares. Just about how much she wanted to love the shop again, to be there and feel like it was home.

"I was just thinking," she said, clearing her throat because the tears were back, and there was no way she was going to let them drip onto the pretty flowered boxes, "that I used to love Chocolate Haven, and I wish I still could."

"You do love Chocolate Haven. You just don't love what happened there."

She went cold at his words, shocked by the accuracy of what could only be a guess.

He was watching her, waiting for her response.

For the first time in a long time, she didn't know what to say.

She could have told him the truth. She could have let him see a part of herself that no one else ever had, but her lips were sealed tight by the silence that had become just what she'd said—its own kind of monster.

"I *have* massacred a few dozen batches of fudge there the past few days," she finally said. "Chocolate making is a messy business."

He didn't smile.

He didn't even blink, just kept watching her as if he could see everything—the dark shop, the black hallway. Eric, his eyes gleaming as she walked toward him.

She shivered and looked away, her heart galloping frantically, her hands clammy, her breathing uneven.

He noticed.

Of course he did.

His hand settled on her knee. The hem of her dress had ridden up her thighs, and there was nothing between his palm and her skin but a thin layer of silky fabric.

Suddenly, every memory of Eric was gone.

It was just Jax in her head. Just his hand on her leg. Just his eyes staring into hers.

"It's okay," he said, and then his hand slid away, and he started the car and they were driving down Main Street, turning onto a side street that led to the west edge of town.

She knew the area. Granddad's new house was just a few blocks away, the cute little cottage sitting on a pristine lot that had once been overgrown with brambles and weeds. She could see it up ahead, every window glowing with light.

"Do you have that plain box of chocolates? The one without the flowers?" Jax asked as he turned into the long driveway. Byron's car was parked near the house, its hood gleaming in the moonlight.

"Yes, but Granddad is probably asleep. He's not as young as he used to be, and it's pretty late."

"All the lights are on," he pointed out.

"Maybe he forgot to turn them off?"

"That doesn't sound Byron-like," Jax responded.

He was right. It didn't.

Which made her wonder if something had happened after Granddad returned home.

"I hope he's okay." She opened the door, and he grabbed her hand, holding her still when she would have hopped out and run to the door.

"If you start banging on his door, he won't be. You'll scare the crap out of him."

"I'm not going to bang. I'm going to knock. Quietly," she responded, the warmth of his hand seeping into her palm and up her arm and into the cold, hard place that had lived in her heart for so long, she barely even knew it was there.

His fingers tightened a fraction, and then he released her, opening his door and climbing out.

She didn't wait for him to come around the car. She jumped out and jogged toward the porch stairs, letting the cold air bathe her face and clear her head.

"Running away from something?" Jax asked, catching up in a few long strides.

"Of course not," she lied, her hands tightening on the chocolate box. If she wasn't careful, she'd smash it and send Bitter Cherry Bonbons rolling across the ground.

"Right," he responded, knocking lightly on the door.

"What's that supposed to mean?"

"Just that you've been running for years. Maybe it's time to stop."

Another totally accurate guess, and she probably would have said something about it, but the door swung open.

"Hi, Granddad," Willow began, and then realized that Byron wasn't standing in the doorway. Someone else was.

A woman.

A very familiar one. Pretty face with just a few wrinkles near the eyes and mouth. Soft brown hair that had a few strands of gray in it. Dark brown eyes that were wide with shock.

Laurie Beth Winslow. Former waitress at the diner. Current owner of the place. She'd been a fixture in town for as long as Willow could remember, but she was a newcomer by most people's standards. There were plenty of stories about her. Most of them revolving around a long-ago husband who may or may not have beat the heck out of her and left her for dead.

"Willow! What are you doing here?!" she cried, and then must have realized how she sounded, because she pulled Willow into a hug, kissed her cheek. "It's so good to see you! I've been to the shop a few times recently, but you're always in the back working, and I never get a chance to say hello."

"Then I guess it's a good thing we ran into each other tonight," she said, offering a smile that she hoped would make Laurie relax.

Was she surprised to find a woman at Byron's house this late at night? Sure, but if her grandfather was ready to pursue a relationship with someone, who was she to stand in the way?

Besides, she'd always liked Laurie.

She was hardworking, smart, and funny.

Since Alice's death, Byron had spent his time working in the shop, running the business, hanging with his guy friends, hunting and fishing and watching football.

Maybe he wanted a little more femininity in his life.

Maybe he was lonely.

Maybe he needed companionship and affection and someone to talk to when no one else was around.

"Is that Steve and Janet?" Byron called from the back of the house. "If it is, send them home. I'm not done making the sandwiches."

"It's Willow," Laurie responded.

"Willow? What's she doing here?"

"You could come out here and ask me," Willow called.

"Give me three shakes of a carved stick. I'm up to my elbows in chicken salad."

"You're making chicken salad?"

"He's putting it on bread," Laurie said. "I made it."

"I added celery."

"You added *more* celery. To my already perfect dish. And you did it just to annoy me," Laurie corrected.

Byron chuckled. "True. Almost done. I'll be right out. Don't let my girl escape before I get there."

"I won't," she said, then she leaned in close to Willow's ear. "He's going to try to convince you to stay for a game of canasta. Take my advice. Say 'no.' He's super competitive. Sometimes, it's not pretty."

"Then why do you play?"

"For the snacks," she said with a laugh. "Your grandfather always provides chocolate. Lots of it."

"You talking about me again?" Granddad stepped into the room, a tray of sandwiches in hand. He'd changed out of the dark slacks and button-up shirt he always wore to work. Now he was wearing jeans and a blue sweater that matched his eyes.

He looked handsome and happy.

He also looked curious, his gaze skimming over Willow and settling on Jax.

"Seems we keep running into each other, Jax," he said. "Is Randall complaining about me again?"

"I haven't heard a word from him since you two made chocolates together."

"Made a mess is more like it, but he's an okay-enough guy. Now"—he speared Willow with a hard look—"back to my question. Are you two ladies talking about me?"

"Only good things, Granddad."

"How could there be anything else?" Laurie added.

"That's what I like," Granddad said, grinning. "Two women who understand my finer qualities. You two are sticking around, right?" he asked. "For canasta. Steve and Janet are okay opponents, but I'm ready to up the challenge."

"Actually, I just stopped by to drop off your Bitter Cherry Bonbons." Willow held out the box, and Byron took it.

"Thanks, doll. I've been craving these damn things since you made the first batch."

"I know. You asked me to make them, remember? And then you cut out on me before they were finished."

"I didn't cut out on you. I left. After I finished putting together the crib."

"You could have come in and said good-bye."

"I didn't want to interrupt."

"Interrupt what?"

His gaze cut to Jax, lingering there for a moment before it returned to Willow. "Whatever was going on in the shop while I was putting together the crib," he finally said.

She could have told him that nothing had been going on, but she wasn't sure if that was true.

She'd made the man eggs, for God's sake!

She'd given him bonbons.

She'd cried because . . .

Because he'd made her think about what life could have been like if she'd been brave enough to stick around.

"Speaking of interrupting," she murmured, anxious to change the subject. "If you'd come into the shop and said good-bye, I could have given these to you there, and I wouldn't have ended up interrupting *your* evening."

"I am always willing to be interrupted for Bitter Cherry Bonbons. And for you," he added with a wink.

"What are Bitter Cherry Bonbons?" Laurie asked. "And are you planning to share?"

"With you? Yes. But Steve and Janet aren't getting a bite. These things are special. They're one of Alice's recipes. Hadn't had them since she passed, and I'd forgotten just how good they are."

"If they're special, you keep them for yourself,"

Laurie said gently. "I can visit the shop and get my chocolate fix anytime."

"The bonbons are special, but so are you." Byron touched Laurie's shoulder, and Willow suddenly felt like a voyeur, watching a private show that she hadn't been invited to.

"We'd better head out," she said, grabbing Jax's hand and tugging him to the door.

She wasn't thinking about the consequences of that.

Not until all the good-byes had been said, and she was standing on the porch, her hand still wrapped around his.

Warm skin to warm skin, and all she could think about was that moment in the car when his hand had been on her knee.

Maybe he was thinking about that, too, because his gaze dropped to her lips, his palm sliding from her hand to her elbow to her waist. It settled there like it belonged. Like *they* belonged, standing on the porch together, the moon dipping below distant mountains, the cold night air wrapping them in its frigid embrace.

She should have moved away.

Not because it was such a bad thing to be standing there thinking about how it would feel to be in Jax's arms, but because she had an entire life planned out. This wasn't part of it.

He wasn't part of it, but when his lips brushed hers— a featherlight touch that had her leaning into him, her palms resting on his chest—she forgot that.

She forgot everything but Jax.

The warmth of his hands.

The intoxicating taste of rum-soaked cherries on his lips.

Chocolate and heat and him, until the porch light went on, and Byron knocked on the window, and she was free of whatever spell Jax had woven.

She backed away. Just enough to look in his eyes.

"What the heck was that about?" she asked.

It was a good question.

Jax didn't have a good answer.

He'd done exactly what he shouldn't have—kissed her.

If Byron hadn't been standing with his face pressed against the window, Jax would have probably kissed her again. As it was, he couldn't quite make himself step away. He still had one hand on her waist, the other on her nape, his lips so close to hers, all he'd have to do was—

"Hey!" Byron rapped on the glass again. "If you're sticking around, come in here and play cards. Otherwise, it's time for both of you to go home. *To your own places.*"

"Shit," Jax muttered.

Not because of Byron.

Not because of the kiss.

Because he wanted another kiss and another.

He wanted long days and longer nights, and a dozen things that he shouldn't even be thinking about.

"I wouldn't say that exactly," Willow responded, her hands on his shoulders, her cheeks flushed.

"What would you say, then?"

"Wow?" she responded.

He laughed.

Which worried him almost as much as the way he

felt when he looked into her eyes—like he'd found something he hadn't even known he was searching for, something he suddenly realized he needed almost as much as he needed to breathe.

He let his hands drop away and stepped back.

"*Wow* is one word for it," he said.

"I take it you have another one?"

"Besides *mistake*? No."

"Mistake, huh? I'm glad we're in agreement on that." She walked down the porch stairs, yanked open the car door, and climbed in.

He figured she'd slam it closed.

He wouldn't have blamed her if she had.

Kissing someone and saying it was a mistake was about as okay as wearing a Speedo to church. Sure, a person could do it, but it was going to leave a lasting impression. And probably not a good one.

Willow didn't slam the door.

She closed it gently and sat stiff as a board as he climbed into the driver's seat and shoved the key into the ignition.

"That was one of the stupider things I've said recently," he admitted as he backed out of the driveway. "I'm sorry."

"A person should never apologize for speaking the truth," she responded. "It *was* a mistake. One we shouldn't repeat."

"Then why are you pissed?"

"I'm not."

"Angry, then."

"I'm not that, either," she responded.

"Unhappy? Irritated? Annoyed?"

"Don't try to make me laugh, Jax. It's not going to

help." But she was smiling, her body relaxing against the seat. "You didn't answer my question."

"I will once I figure it out."

"What's that supposed to mean?"

"That I don't know what the kiss was about."

But he did. It was about finding the right person at the wrong time, and knowing damn well there was nothing he could do about it. A sweet kiss in the moonlight didn't change any of the reasons why he'd decided to stay single. It couldn't change the past, and he sure as hell wasn't going to let it change the future.

"We're heading back to the shop," Willow pointed out as they turned onto Main Street.

"Yeah. We are."

"I still have five boxes of chocolates in this bag." She lifted it from the floor, set it on her lap with a quiet *thump*. She was annoyed, and he couldn't blame her. He'd dragged her out on a mission that was supposed to get her mind off her troubles. Now he was bringing her back. Mission incomplete, chocolates still in the bag, the taste of that kiss still on their lips.

On *his* lips, anyway.

Rum-soaked cherry and chocolate and Willow.

God! He wanted more of it. More of *her*.

"It's late," he said.

"It was late before we left. The only thing that's different now is that you kissed me and you regret it."

"Who said anything about regret?"

"You did."

"I never said I regretted it." He pulled up in front of Chocolate Haven and parked the car, ready to walk her to her door, say good night, move on.

That was the right thing to do.

The safe thing, the thing that would ensure that

the past wouldn't be repeated in the future. No deep abiding love, no wife, no kids, no home.

No risk.

"You're splitting hairs," she replied, reaching for the door handle, ready to go along with his plan.

All he had to do was let her leave.

Of course, he didn't.

His fingers hooked around her wrist, gentle and light because she had her own nightmares and her own demons.

"Not splitting hairs, Willow," he said. "The kiss was a mistake, but I sure as hell don't regret it. I'd make the same mistake again if I gave myself half a chance, but then what? Another mistake and another, until our lives are intertwined and we can't imagine a day without each other in it?"

"I . . . you really don't have to explain," she said.

"I know, but I guess I will anyway." He could feel her pulse thrumming beneath warm skin, and he ran his thumb over the spot, watching as her pupils dilated.

She wanted him the way he wanted her.

And there was no doubt about where that would lead. The path was clear as a neon sign and just begging them both to walk it. Too bad he could only see the beginning and not the end, because he was tempted to damn well step right on the road that led to her.

"You know what I see when I look at you, Willow?" he said. "I see pretty little houses and white picket fences and cute little kids chasing after kittens and puppies. I see Valentine's Days filled with flowers and chocolates and kisses stolen while bunches of kids giggle nearby. I see what my parents had, and that scares the crap out of me. Because what they had? It killed my mother. It killed my siblings, and once my father finished watching them die, it killed him."

"I'd say I'm sorry, but I don't think that's what you want to hear," she said quietly.

"You're right." He'd heard the useless platitude a million times. People meant well, but words didn't change the past, they didn't pour blood back into broken bodies, breathe life back into the dead.

"What *do* you want to hear? That I agree? That any woman who falls for you will be risking her life and her future?"

"I just want you to know the truth."

"What truth? That love isn't worth the risk? There are plenty of people who disagree."

"Don't romanticize it, Willow," he responded.

"I couldn't be a prosecuting attorney and romanticize anything that had to do with hate or murder or innocent people being hurt." She traced the scar he'd gotten trying to do what his beaten-bloody, tied-up father couldn't—protect his family. "But we can't live in our fear, right? We can't give up dreams because we're afraid."

"Are you trying to convince me of that? Or yourself?"

"Maybe both," she said with a shaky laugh. "It's a lesson I've been learning for a long time."

"How long?" he asked, and she stilled.

She was going to sidestep the question or give a nonanswer or tell him to mind his own business.

That's what he thought.

It's what he was prepared for.

He wasn't prepared for the truth, but that's what

she gave him, the words rushing out in hard quick beats that slammed right into his heart.

"I was thirteen. It happened in the hallway of the shop. My father was dying of cancer, and my family was falling apart, and my grandfather hired someone to help out. I still can't walk from the back of the shop to the front without catching a whiff of his damn cologne."

"Willow—"

"I don't talk about it." She cut him off. "Ever. But I do understand the way the past can hold us captive if we let it." Her voice broke, and he reached for her, but she was opening the door, scrambling out into the darkness.

"You were right, Jax," she said, her voice husky with unshed tears. "It's late, and we both have busy days ahead of us. Don't follow me up, okay? I have a lot of work to do."

She closed the door as gently as she had before.

He waited until she reached the corner of the building, and then he got out of the car, walked into the alley behind her.

When she reached the apartment stairs, she stopped.

"You weren't supposed to follow me," she said, and he knew she was crying, knew that if he moved closer, he could take her in his arms and press her face to his chest, let her tears soak his shirt.

She didn't want that, though, and he shouldn't want it, so he kept his distance, standing exactly where he was, moonlight filtering through the space between the buildings, painting gold highlights in her dark red braid.

"I'm just making sure you get inside safely," he said.

"This is Benevolence," she responded. "Nothing bad ever happens here."

"Except when it does?"

"Except when it does," she agreed, heading up the stairs, her footsteps echoing loudly in the silence.

He waited until she was inside. Waited until the door closed. Waited until he saw a light go on in the apartment, and then he went back to his car, and headed for the station.

Because, he had as good a memory as anyone.

And he damn well knew exactly who'd worked in the shop when Willow's father was sick.

Eric Williams.

The former mayor's oldest son.

Five years ahead of Jax in school. Which would have made him five years older than Willow. Eighteen to her thirteen.

He'd have been a full-grown man when he'd attacked Willow. Or pretty close to it.

Tall.

Muscular.

Tough.

He'd have easily overpowered a little girl who'd just started to bud into womanhood.

"Bastard," he muttered, his rage as useless as an umbrella during a hurricane.

Yeah. Forget enraged.

Forget pissed.

They never accomplished anything.

He was going to find the guy, and he was going to have a little talk with him. The last he'd heard, the Williams family had settled somewhere in Virginia. More than likely, Eric had grown up, gotten a job, become what his father had always seemed to expect him to be—rich and successful and popular.

More than likely, he'd also become more of what he'd been when he'd attacked Willow in her family's chocolate shop. Guys who attacked thirteen-year-old girls didn't usually stop until they were caught. They didn't just move on and become stellar citizens. They found ways to keep victimizing people, and they didn't stop until someone made them.

If it hadn't already happened to Eric, it would.

Jax was going to make certain of it.

Chapter Nine

It was only six a.m. Monday, and Willow wanted to quit Chocolate Haven forever.

Or at least for a few hours.

Unfortunately, Byron had made sure she couldn't. He'd left town.

Just for the day, he'd said. *I'll be back by Tuesday opening time.*

"Lies," she grumbled, stirring a pot of melted chocolate and heavy cream. She needed it to boil. Now. Not fifteen minutes from now. Or twenty. Or thirty like the last batch.

She eyed the trash can and the pile of disgusting fudge that was in it.

How had it come to this?

She *knew* how to do this. Or at least she had. She'd done it dozens of times when she was a kid. Now? She couldn't make smooth, beautiful Lamont fudge if the stuff jumped out of the cupboard and plopped itself in the pan.

She grabbed the candy thermometer and attached it to the side of the pan. Byron never used one. He didn't need one. He knew exactly when the mixture was ready. He knew exactly how it should look when it coated the wooden spoon, exactly how much of it should cling to the sides of the pot.

He knew it all, but he was on his way to Seattle. For doughnuts!

Benevolence Baptist senior bus trip.

She'd heard the announcement while she was sitting in church yesterday. Squeezed between Janelle and Adeline, Brenna and River and their crew sitting behind them, she'd heard all about the trip to Seattle, the overnight stay in the gorgeous hotel, the visit to some famous doughnut place. Sightseeing and dinner, and fun.

Yep. She'd sat there and listened, and she'd thanked God that Byron wasn't going, because there was no way she was ready to run the shop on her own.

Only, Byron *was* going.

He'd just conveniently forgotten to tell her until last night. When he'd finally mentioned it, he'd assured her that he'd be back Tuesday morning, but she'd very clearly heard the trip coordinator say that they'd be spending all day Tuesday seeing the sights. The bus would be returning home at seven p.m.

Byron was going on the trip.

He was going to be on the bus.

Therefore, he was *not* going to be back Tuesday morning.

Simple logic.

"And big fat lies," she muttered.

Not that there was anyone around to hear.

She was by herself, the hall right behind her. She'd turned on every light in the place, and that narrow alcove still seemed dark.

I can still smell his damn cologne.

Had she really told Jax that?

Of course she had.

Because of the kiss and the way it had made her feel—as if every possibility was still open to her, as if the life she'd wanted when she was a young kid could still be hers.

She stirred the thick, goopy chocolate mess, eyeing the clumps of unmelted chocolate floating in their bath of cream. Obviously, she *couldn't* have those old dreams. She couldn't even make the Lamont fudge.

She had to try, though, because the shop was opening in a few hours, and she needed twenty pounds of it.

A car drove into the back lot, its headlights splashing across the window.

Hopefully, it was Brenna or Addie coming to the rescue.

She'd texted them both immediately after Byron had broken the news about his Seattle road trip. She hadn't heard from either of them. She'd imagined them both curled up beside their husbands, sleeping the sleep of the innocent while her frantic cry for help went unnoticed. She'd thought about calling their home numbers, but she hadn't wanted to wake them. They deserved their rest. They'd done their time helping with the shop.

Now it was Willow's turn.

Too bad she was failing miserably.

A key scraped in the back door lock, and the door opened, cold air sweeping in. Brenna swept in with it, her dark jeans clinging to long, slim legs, her lilac turtleneck comfortable and soft, her hair speckled with snowflakes.

She looked classy and comfortable and stunning.

"You're here!" Willow hugged her. Hard. Because they'd spent too many years apart, and it was good—*really* good—to be back in the same town, seeing each other anytime they wanted. "I was worried you wouldn't get my text."

"I just got it. I was so tired last night, I went to bed early. Fortunately for you, Ajax woke up screaming—"

"Angel's baby?" The young mother lived with Brenna and her husband. She wasn't the only one. River's aunt had taken in a handful of young people who'd all desperately needed a place to stay. Now they'd become a family of sorts, working on the old house that used to be a home for troubled kids, tilling the fields and building what would one day be a working farm.

"Yes. He's got colic or some da . . . rn thing." She grabbed an apron, pulled a net over her hair. Somehow even *that* looked good on her.

"Are you and River babysitting him?"

"Are you kidding? Angel barely lets anyone get within two feet of the kid. She leaves him with the sitter while she works, and the rest of the time, he's tied to her hip. I heard him crying and woke up. Then I couldn't get back to sleep."

"Too much on your mind?"

"Yeah. River has great plans for Freedom Ranch, but the restaurant addition is a huge project. I'm worried it won't be finished by the time we open for business in the fall."

"Of course it will be. You and River are a great team. You've put together a doable plan. You'll get it done."

"I hope so. River's aunt isn't getting any younger. We'd both like her to see the plans come to fruition."

"Is her health deteriorating?" Belinda had suffered a stroke two years ago, but she seemed to have mostly recovered from it. Willow had spoken to her at church, and the older woman had been cheerful and happy.

"No. Nothing like that. Time just flies, you know? One minute you're seventeen and the world is at your feet, and the next you're nearly thirty, married and caring for a houseful of people who don't have anyone else to love them."

"You sound tired, Bren. Is everything okay?"

"No," she said, and then she burst into tears.

Tears!

Brenna never cried!

"Hun! What's wrong?"

"Nothing," Brenna wailed.

But of course something *was* wrong.

How could it not be when she was sobbing like her best friend had died?

"Is it River? Did something happen between you?"

"Yes! And I don't know what I'm going to do!"

"You're going to tell me what's going on, and we're going to figure it out. *That's* what you're going to do." She pulled her into a hug and wished it had magical properties. The kind that could heal hurts and mend hearts.

But of course, it didn't, and all she could do was stand there and listen while Brenna cried.

God! She wished she were better at this.

She wished she'd spent the past decade learning her sister's heart the way she'd learned criminal law.

The back door flew open, and Addie stepped into the shop.

Hair scooped into a bun, strands of curly hair escaping in every direction, she stood wide-eyed on the threshold for about two seconds, her gaze jumping from Willow's face to Brenna's and back again.

Then she was moving, shutting the door, turning the lock, crossing the room, putting one arm around Willow's shoulders, one around Brenna's.

"Who do we need to kill?" she whispered, and Brenna's sobs turned to laughter.

"Oh. My. Gosh. Addie!" she choked out before she started crying again.

They stood there for several minutes, arms wrapped around one another, a combined front against whatever foe Brenna was facing.

River?

It didn't seem possible.

Willow had seen them together at church, holding hands during the sermon, looking into each other's eyes during the hymns. They hadn't looked like a couple who was struggling. They'd looked like two people who were deeply in love.

But looks could be deceiving.

Look at her.

People thought she was confident, accomplished, brave. She'd spent her career facing down bad guys—drug dealers, murderers, rapists, child molesters. She put on a good front, portrayed herself exactly as she wanted to be seen.

But inside?

Inside, she was scared spitless.

"Okay," she said, grabbing a clean dishcloth from the drawer and wiping Brenna's damp cheeks with it. "Spill. What did the idiot do?"

"Idiot?" Addie asked, inhaling deeply, her nose crinkling. "Female or male? And . . . what the heck is burning?"

"Nothing," Willow answered, but suddenly she could smell it too. Scalded cream. Burnt chocolate. "Damn! The fudge!" She turned off the burner, grabbed the pot and tossed the entire mess into the trash can.

"That's Granddad's favorite fudge pot," Brenna pointed out, her tears nearly gone now, her cheeks and nose red from them.

"Really?"

"Yeah. I know, because I threw it away a couple of dozen times when I was helping in the shop. It always reappeared. Didn't matter how much crap it was coated with. It didn't matter how burnt the bottom was. Granddad still took it out of the trash, cleaned it, and put it back in the cupboard."

"That explains it," Addie said, grabbing oven mitts and retrieving the pot. Blobs of grainy chocolate coated the sides, and lumpy streams of it dripped off the bottom.

"Explains what?" Willow asked.

"Why it never stayed in the Dumpster."

"You threw it in the Dumpster?"

"You would have, too, if your fudge had stuck to the bottom like cement."

"You make great fudge!" Willow protested, hoping with everything she was that it was the truth. One of them needed to make the days' quota of fudge. Brenna looked worn out and fragile. Willow was an abysmal failure at fudge making.

That left Addie.

Sweet, uncomplicated, wonderful Addie who'd already set the pot in the sink and was running hot water into it.

"Now I do, but a couple of years ago"—she shook her head—"I broke knives in the cement that was my fudge. I could have crushed skulls with it. I probably could have attached it to the end of a stick, called it a mace, and conquered the world with it."

Brenna laughed again, dropping into one of the rickety chairs. "God! It's so good to be with you two. I've missed this so much."

"Are you lonely out there on Freedom Ranch?" Willow asked, filling the old tea kettle and setting it to boil. Grandma Alice had once told her that tea could fix any ill.

It hadn't fixed their father's cancer, but maybe it could fix Brenna's wounded heart.

"With all those people? Not at all."

"Then why the tears?" Adeline had scrubbed out the pot and set it back on the stove. She'd already started the heat under the double boiler and was pouring chocolate pieces into it. No measuring cup. Just eyeing it the way Granddad did.

"I found something out last night, and it's going to ruin everything." Brenna didn't break down again, but she looked like she wanted to, eyes red-rimmed, her cheeks pale.

"Is he cheating on you?" Willow guessed, hoping that she was wrong.

"River would never cheat. He doesn't lie. He doesn't

play around or say stupid things or make me feel like I don't measure up. He's as close to perfect as anyone can get. The problem isn't him. It's me."

"You," Addie huffed, pouring cream into the fudge pot and motioning for Willow to grab the sugar, "are not the problem."

"Of course I am. River and I had one deal going into the marriage. One thing we were both very clear on. We both agreed that we weren't ready for kids. Not yet. Maybe in the future. After we got things sorted out at the ranch, and Belinda was better, and . . ."

She said more.

Willow knew she did. She could hear the words, but her mind was connecting dots, putting things together, coming to a very obvious conclusion.

"My God!" she said, cutting in before Brenna finished. "You're pregnant."

And, of course, that just made Brenna cry again.

"I am!" she said through fresh sobs. "And I don't know how I'm going to tell River."

"You're going to just come out and say it," Addie responded.

"We're not ready for kids!" she insisted, but her hand was on her lower abdomen, and there was something in her face Willow had never seen before. Something soft and quiet and enthralled.

It took her breath away to see her youngest sister like that.

"No one is ever ready for kids until they have them," she said, touching Brenna's shoulder and feeling that *thing* well up inside—the warmth of family and connection and love.

How had she not realized how much she'd missed that, how much she'd needed it?

"Willow is right," Addie said, pouring melted chocolate into the bubbling cream and sugar. "I was terrified when I found out I was pregnant."

"But you'd planned the pregnancy."

"Like heck we did." Addie laughed. "We didn't even talk about it, and then I was pregnant, and we had two teens living with us and my giant dog and no room for a crib or even one of those tiny bassinets." She shrugged. "It worked out just fine. Just like things are working out for Willow. She wasn't expecting to be a mother."

"I'm not—"

"But here she is with a crib up in the apartment and plans to stay here until Miracle has a permanent home. And she's happy about that, aren't you, Willow?" Addie speared her with a look that told her she'd better darn well be.

"Of course I am."

"See?" Addie poured the fudge into a buttered pan, the beautiful chocolate streaming out in smooth ribbons. "It's going to be fine, Brenna. You're going to be a great mother. River is going to be a great father. Belinda is going to be over the moon, and Mom—"

"Don't mention this to her," Brenna cut in. "Not one word from either of you, okay? She'll be announcing it to the world and planning a baby shower before I get through my first trimester."

"You don't have to worry about me," Willow assured her, pouring hot water over a tea bag and handing Brenna the mug. "My schedule is packed. I'm not going to have much time to talk to anyone these next few days."

"When's Miracle being released from the hospital?" Adeline asked. She'd already begun a second batch of fudge. Thank God!

"Friday. Alison and I are going to pick her up around midnight. Hopefully, that will keep the reporters away."

"Are they still trying to get interviews with you?" Brenna took a sip of tea and stood, pulling ingredients out of the pantry and starting what looked like a caramel.

"Not in the past couple of days." Except for the calls she kept getting in the middle of the night. Always from the same number. Always voice mail with nothing but the sound of empty air.

"Mom said she saw a news story just yesterday morning. The reporter interviewed Wilma Strafford. Remember her?" Addie poured chopped nuts into the newest fudge mixture, poured it into another pan.

"Our seventh-grade English teacher?"

"Yes. She lives a few blocks down on the corner of Main and Windsor. She swears she saw a car drive by her place the night Miracle was born. Hand me another pan, will you? Alice is going to want to eat soon, and I'd like to be home before then."

Willow grabbed a pan, handed it to Addie, and then started chopping apricots for the fruit-studded chocolate bark Granddad sold every Monday. Six pounds of it. That's what the inventory list demanded.

She glanced at the clock.

Time was ticking away, but with her sisters there to help, things were getting done quickly. She'd be ready to open on time, and with enough stock to serve whatever customers braved the weather.

"I saw that." Brenna had finished the caramel and was layering it over dark chocolate wafers. "She said she recognized the car. She'd seen it out at the Bradshaws' farm a couple of months ago."

"Really?" Jax had mentioned something about the Bradshaws' place and a couple of young adults who were renting a house on the property, but she hadn't asked him for a follow-up.

"Yes. She swore that the car belonged to one of the hippies who have taken over the farm. Her words. Not mine. I think the reporter tried to go out and interview the people renting Sunday and Matt's house, but no one answered the door."

"I wonder if Jax knows about that?" Willow poured warm chocolate on a marble slab, smoothing it out with a spatula before sprinkling apricot bits and almonds on top of it.

"Jax . . ." Brenna murmured. "Yeah. I wonder. Maybe you should call and ask?"

"Don't tease," Addie chided as she finished another batch of fudge. It looked luscious—smooth and silky and creamy. "Willow is sensitive about her love life."

"I have no love life, and therefore," Willow argued, "I have nothing to be sensitive about."

"That's not what Mom says."

"What does she say?" Willow asked, curious and a little appalled that there'd been a conversation about her relationship with Jax.

Relationship?

Not quite.

They'd kissed.

It had been good.

Who the heck was she kidding?

It had been earth-shattering, toe-curling, soul-searing.

Addie pressed her lips together, stepped away from the stove, and wiped her hands on a dishcloth. "I think Alice is about to wake up. I'd better go."

"What you'd better do is tell us what Mom said," Brenna responded, a gleam in her eyes, a little color in her cheeks. She looked better. Happier. More confident.

"I really shouldn't," Addie hedged, opening the door and letting cold air blow in.

"You really should," Willow insisted. "Remember the pact we made after May's wedding? Remember how we swore to always have each other's backs?"

"Okay. Fine. You twisted my arm. Horribly, if Mom should happen to ask. She said that you two stopped by Granddad's house the other night. According to him, you looked really chummy. *Really* chummy."

"So he didn't mention—" *the kiss* almost popped out.

"What?" Addie let the door close, and it was just the three of them again. That silly vow between them. The one they'd sworn by candlelight after Brenna had found out her then-fiancé was cheating on her. The bond between them was still there, the threads of love woven so tightly they hadn't been broken. Not by the sorrows each of them had suffered. Not by distance or time or years when they'd barely talked.

"Willow!" Addie squealed, her eyes wide again, her beautiful curls nearly vibrating with excitement.

"Is there something else? Something scandalous. Or titillating? Or . . ."

"If it happened where Granddad could see it, how scandalous could it . . ." Brenna began, and then her eyes widened too. "Oh. My. Gosh. He kissed you. He did, didn't he?"

She didn't answer quickly enough, and Addie grabbed her arm. "He did! Was it everything you dreamed it would be?"

"I never dreamed—"

"Of course it was," Brenna interrupted. "Look at her. She's blushing."

"I'm not—"

"Jax Gordon, the town's most eligible bachelor, and you managed to snag him."

"Addie . . . it was one kiss. That does not constitute a lifetime commitment."

"That's what I told myself the first time Sinclair kissed me. But I knew I was lying. Sometimes, something is just so right there's no denying it. Now I really do have to run. Alice is like me. She loves her food!" She ran outside, snow swirling in the early-morning darkness and swallowing her up as she crossed the parking lot.

Willow stood in the doorway, watching as she climbed into her car and drove away.

She was wrong.

Of course she was.

A kiss was just a kiss. No need to overthink it. No need to analyze it. No need to remember the way it had made her feel.

"Are you trying to freeze us out of here, Will?"

Brenna asked. "Or just trying to avoid answering questions you think I might ask."

"Neither."

"Then close the door, and let's get to work. Hopefully, at some point during the prepping process, you can help me come up with a way to break my pregnancy news to River."

She was giving Willow an easy out, and there was no way she wasn't going to take it.

"It's good news, Brenna. And he's going to think so too."

"I hope you're right." She frowned, sprinkling chocolate shavings on top of white chocolate bonbons. "Speaking of good news. Granddad has a bunch of mail piled up on his desk."

"What's good about that?"

"Nothing. Just a segue into something I wanted to talk to you about. When I was in the other day, I knocked the stack of mail over. I noticed one of the envelopes had your name on it."

"Okay." She'd been too busy to pay attention to the mail situation, but she made a mental note to go through the pile.

"I recognized the return address. It was from the guy who came into the shop looking for you. He gave me that check, remember? The one you told me to burn?"

Willow had been trying really hard *not* to remember that. She'd known what the money was before she'd looked the guy up and found out he was an attorney who represented high-powered clients in the D.C. and Northern Virginia area.

Eric's family lived there.

His younger brother Josh was a senator, and people

were whispering presidential candidate along with his name. That meant his opponents would be busy digging up dirt. As far as Willow knew, Josh had kept his nose clean, but he *had* seen her the night she was raped. He'd been waiting outside the shop, ready to give Eric a ride home. Eric who'd lost his car keys when his father caught him driving drunk.

Yeah. Josh had seen her running out of the shop, her dress torn and her stockings ripped and her body shaking.

He'd called her name, but she'd just kept running.

Months later, when his brother had been accused of raping a cheerleader, he'd been the only one in the family—probably the only one in the town besides Willow—who hadn't defended the star quarterback and track champion.

"Willow?" Brenna said quietly.

"I remember."

"You never told me what that was about."

"Because, it wasn't important."

"Twenty thousand dollars is important. Twenty thousand dollars that someone burns to ashes is really important." She washed her hands, leaned against the counter, long-legged and beautiful. Married. Pregnant. She didn't need more complications in her life.

"Maybe, but it's not important anymore."

"Right." Brenna tucked a stray strand of hair under the net and sighed. "Well, the guy sent you something. Probably another check for twenty thousand."

She'd just burn it again, but she couldn't say that without opening the door to questions she didn't want to answer.

"I'll look at it later." She walked to the whiteboard that contained a list of the candy they needed for the day. She crossed off the fudge, the chocolate bark, the caramel crunch squares, the bonbons.

Her hand was shaking, but she didn't think Brenna noticed.

If she did, she didn't mention it.

Jax needed chocolate like he needed Aunt Vera to knit him another Christmas sweater. In other words, not at all. That was as good a reason as any to take his early-morning run in the opposite direction of Chocolate Haven.

Of course, he didn't.

He also didn't turn around when snow started falling and the sidewalk got slippery. He'd worked most of yesterday, graveyard shift and then extra time in the office, finding out everything he could about Eric Williams.

The most important thing he'd found out was that the guy was dead, killed in a single-car accident a few years back. Blood alcohol level three times the legal limit. The last piece of information had been a little more difficult to get his hands on, but he'd managed it. A few phone calls, a few people who were more than willing to talk about a guy who'd been dead for years.

Yeah. He'd gotten what he'd wanted. He'd found Eric Williams. There wouldn't be any confrontation or any closure, though.

Not that it should matter to Jax.

This was Willow's deal. Her past. Her story.

And, unless he missed his guess, she already knew the guy was dead. She seemed like that kind of person—one who kept her secrets, built her walls, and secured her fortress. He couldn't imagine her going through life without knowing exactly where Eric was.

He'd wanted to talk to her about it yesterday, but he'd been running late for church, and she'd slipped out as soon as it ended. Then he'd had to drive out to the Bradshaws' place again. Still no sign of renter number four. Phoebe. According to the guy who'd called himself her husband, she was eighteen.

Jax had done a little checking.

He'd asked around town and then in the next town over. He'd finally found someone who knew a girl named Phoebe. She'd worked at the feed store until a few months ago. She was one of several girls who lived off the grid with their parents.

Or, she had lived with her family.

She'd stopped coming to work and hadn't been seen since.

Jax had spent the rest of the day hunting down her family. Not easy, because they lived on fifty acres in the middle of the woods. Three teenage girls who'd been hidden away in a back room. Father named Josiah who'd had cropped hair and an attitude. Mother named Mary who looked about twenty years younger than he was, her hair pulled back from a tired face, her smile a lot kinder than the guy's scowl.

She'd invited Jax into a cabin that had probably been hand-built by the family, offered him coffee, told him all about their oldest daughter. Phoebe had been gone for six months. She'd run off with a twenty-year-old whom she'd met at a church revival.

Jax couldn't say he blamed her. The place was rustic, and that was putting it kindly. No electricity. No running water. She'd probably gotten sick of living in antiquity and even sicker of living under her father's thumb.

Or maybe she'd gotten pregnant and had been terrified of his reaction. Jax planned to ask. Once he finally met her.

He was off the clock until Wednesday, but he wasn't going to let the case go. He planned to make a few more trips out to the Bradshaws' farm.

For now, a quick jog to clear his head and get his blood pumping. Then, work on the house. He had floor tiles to put in and a bedroom to paint. The place was coming together. Which should have made him happy, but the more he worked on it, the more he realized how big it was and how empty. Bedroom furniture in his room, an old couch and a rocking chair in the living room. A card table and a couple of chairs in the kitchen.

Plenty for a guy like him.

Lately, though, it hadn't seemed like enough, all the emptiness reminding him that houses should be filled with people and noise and laughter.

He frowned, jogging along Main, the streetlights illuminating the sidewalk and road, everything coated with a dusting of powdery snow. He could see the lights from Chocolate Haven, and he knew Willow was working.

He'd be smart to jog past.

But, of course, he didn't do that, either.

Two cars were parked in the back lot. Willow's and an old Chrysler that he knew belonged to Brenna. He'd heard that Byron was out of town. The sisters must be working together to open the shop.

He didn't even bother telling himself he should leave them to it. He wasn't going to.

He knocked on the back door.

When it opened, he found himself looking into Brenna's face. She grinned.

"Speak of the devil," she said, stepping back so he could enter.

"Is that what they're calling me now?" he asked, his gaze drifting from Brenna to Willow. She stood near the sink, a dishrag in one hand and a chocolate-coated spoon in the other.

"No one was calling you anything. We hadn't even mentioned your name," she responded.

"In at least ten minutes," Brenna intoned, and Willow swatted her with the dishcloth.

"Bren! Enough."

"I'm just telling the truth. We *were* talking about Jax."

"We were talking about Miracle and her mother, and you asked if I'd heard anything from the sheriff's department. That's all it was," she added, looking Jax square in the eyes.

No tears this morning. Just smooth, pale skin and kissable lips, and the kind of beauty that could take any man's breath away.

It sure as hell had stolen Jax's.

"I've told you everything we know. I've been following up on a few leads. So far, we're coming up empty."

"You heard that news report, right?" Brenna dropped a chocolate-coated pretzel on waxed paper.

"There have been a lot of reports. Which one are you referring to?"

"The one where they interviewed Wilma Strafford."

He'd heard it, but none of the information she'd provided had been new to the sheriff's department. "I heard it."

"Well, maybe you should follow up on it. See if she

knows more than what she told the reporter," Brenna suggested.

"Bren, he and Kane know what they're doing. I'm sure they've already followed up." Willow grabbed a cookie sheet filled with chocolate hearts and carried it from the room.

If he hadn't been watching, he wouldn't have seen her hesitate at the entrance to the hall. If he hadn't known her story, he wouldn't have thought anything about the split-second pause, the deep breath, the hurried footsteps as she nearly ran into the service area.

But, of course, he *had* been watching and he *did* know.

"You could go help her put those in the display cases," Brenna said. "Or, if you were feeling really industrious, you could grab the bonbons from the walk-in and bring them out to her."

"You're putting me to work on my day off?" he asked, but he walked into the fridge and grabbed what looked like a tray of bonbons.

"You have days off?" Brenna grabbed a tray filled with white chocolate bark and stood right in front of the doorway, blocking him from exiting.

She had an agenda.

He could see it in her eyes, in the slight tilt to her head, in the way she was studying him like he was a problem she needed to solve.

"Doesn't everyone?"

"Yeah, but it seems every time I see you, you're in uniform."

"Probably because most of the time you see me, I'm pulling you over for speeding."

She laughed. "You're right about that! So . . . big plans for the day?"

"Just working on the house."

"Yeah. That's a big project," she said, still blocking the door, her blue eyes a shade darker than Willow's, her hair a shade lighter. She was the tallest of the three sisters, the sharpest edged, too, but Jax had always liked her, so he'd play her game for a few more minutes.

"It'll be worth it when it's done."

"Just like Freedom Ranch. River and I are up to our eyebrows in renovations. He's torn apart the entire kitchen, and now we're piecing it back together."

"Need some help?" Maybe that was the purpose of the blocked door and the twenty questions.

"Now that you mention it." She glanced over her shoulder. "I do. See, I can't be here and there at the same time, but Willow is in over her head."

"I can head out to the ranch. What time—"

"Oh. No. I don't need you to do that."

"Then what do you need?"

"I need you to hang around here until Chase is finished at school. He'll be in at one."

"I know squat about chocolate making." It was as good an excuse as any to avoid what would be a colossal mistake. Spending a few hours in the shop with Willow?

Yeah. *No.*

He was already having trouble staying away.

Look at him now—standing in the walk-in with a tray of bonbons in his hands.

"Willow knows plenty. She'll teach you."

"Brenna—"

"Come on, Jax. It's just for a few hours, and I could really use the help. Plus, you owe me."

"How do you figure that?"

"My tickets probably pay half your salary."

"That's—" *Not how it works,* he started to say, but she'd already walked out.

He followed, telling himself he wasn't going to agree to help and knowing he was lying.

He'd come to the shop because he wanted to.

He'd stay because he wanted to.

Whatever else happened?

It would because he wanted it too.

And what he wanted? It was a hell of a lot more than he should, because he didn't want to see Willow hurt, and he didn't want to be hurt, but he couldn't make himself stay away from her.

No matter how hard he tried.

"Well?" Brenna demanded as he closed the walk-in door. "Would you be willing to help out? I can pay you, if that's the issue."

"I never need payment to lend a hand," he replied, and she smiled, the kind of sly smile that said she had more on her agenda than getting his help in the shop.

"You're a good guy, Jax. A really good one, but if you hurt my sister, I will, for sure, hurt you. That's just a little free advice," she added, and then she set her tray on the counter, took off her apron, and left the shop.

Chapter Ten

It should have been awkward, irritating, difficult, but working with Jax? It was like walking through a forest at dawn—easy and calm and natural.

Willow tried not to think about that.

She tried not to think about anything as she set the last Chocolate S'more Delight in the case and slid the glass closed.

Done. Finally.

Every piece of chocolate in place. Internet orders boxed. Deliveries ready to go.

All with six minutes to spare.

"We win!" she said, turning to high-five the one person she should *not* be high-fiving. Because he shouldn't have been there. In the shop. Helping her fill penny candy jars and display cases. Carrying trays of chocolate. Counting change for the register. Standing beside her while she cut fudge and piped dark chocolate over milk chocolate–covered strawberries.

"*You* win," he said. "All I did was follow instructions."

"You made brittle without any help from me, and it tastes great."

"Thank you for not mentioning how many tries it took for me to get an edible batch."

"Only two. Not that I was counting."

"Were you counting how many chocolate drops I ate? Because I think I owe the shop a few hundred bucks," he said, and she smiled, moving out from behind the counter and opening the blinds in the front windows.

"If you'll take your day's wage in chocolates, we'll call it even."

"I'd rather take my wage in something else," he murmured, suddenly right there beside her, his hand on her back, his fingers trailing up her spine.

"What did you have in mind?" she asked.

"Fudge," he murmured in her ear, his lips brushing her hair, his breath a warm whisper against her skin.

She could have turned right then and kissed his lips, let her fingers trace the line of his scar. Just like she had the other night. She could have done a half-dozen things that would have sealed the bond between them.

The bond she shouldn't want.

The one he *didn't* want.

Hadn't he said that he couldn't risk it? That love was too dangerous? She stepped away, because their closeness was tempting, and she wasn't sure what either of them really wanted.

Or maybe she was, and maybe she was just afraid of it.

Just like she was afraid of so many other things.

Like coming home.

Working in the shop.

Facing that hallway again and again, walking through it and remembering. Only today . . .

Today, the memory had been a kernel of a thought

in the back of her mind, a grainy image of what had been, a backdrop to what was.

"What kind fudge do you want? Addie made milk chocolate, peanut butter, rocky road," she asked.

"I want," he responded, stepping toward her again, closing the distance that she'd put between them, "whatever fudge you made."

"Me?" She laughed, and she could hear the nervous edge to it, feel her heart thumping frantically. "My fudge is trash. Literally. I've tossed every batch."

"Why?"

"Because it tastes . . . normal."

"There's nothing wrong with normal."

"No, but Lamont fudge is special. It's creamier and richer and more decadent than any other fudge on the market. It tastes like . . ." She hesitated, because she'd sound like a fool saying it.

"Like what?"

"Love," she admitted. "Family. Home. That's why people come year after year on their anniversaries or birthdays or special occasions, because they can taste all that in their fudge, and it reminds them of all the best things in life. At least, that's what my father always told me. Once I got older, it seemed silly."

"Maybe that's why you're having trouble making it, because the idea seems silly to you. Because you don't believe in the magic of it now."

"It's just a recipe, Jax. A simple one. There's nothing magic or mystical about it. Even someone who hates it should be able to make it."

"Do you?" he asked.

"What?"

"Hate it?"

"It's the cornerstone of the family business. My great-great-grandfather—"

"That wasn't the question, Willow, and I'm not in the mood to play the game," Jax said, flipping the sign on the front door from CLOSED to OPEN.

She glanced at the clock.

Sure enough, it was time.

"What game?"

"The one where I ask and you avoid, so I ask again." He turned, and grayish daylight streamed across his face, turning his scar dark purple.

"Is that what we've been doing? Playing a game?" she asked, knowing she was staring at the scar and telling herself to stop.

She'd seen it hundreds of times before.

Like everyone else in school, she'd been fascinated by the stories she'd heard whispered by adults. She'd wondered about Jax's family. She'd wondered about the scar. But she'd been caught up in her own drama, and she'd never really considered what the experience had done to him.

Now . . .

Now she was an adult, and he was a man with a past that was way more violent and traumatic than hers.

Somehow, he'd managed to make a good life for himself, and that scar? It seemed like a badge of honor, a symbol of strength.

"I never play games," he said.

"I'll make a note of that." She looked away from the scar, told herself that she had to keep things light, because Jax wasn't the kind of guy who wanted forever, and she wasn't the kind of woman who could settle for anything less. That's why she'd left Ken, because she couldn't see him ever wanting more than what they had—the easy, simple friendship that would only have lasted until he'd gotten up the energy to find someone more exciting.

"Make a note of this, too: I don't wait around for answers. I go out and find them. Eric is dead. You know that, right?"

The words were so unexpected, it took a minute for them to register.

When they did, she stiffened, every muscle in her body going tight and tense. "Who told you it was Eric?"

"It was easy enough to figure out."

"So what'd you do? Try to look him up?"

"You're damn right I did."

"Why?"

"Why do you think? He was a grown man. You were a little girl—"

"It wasn't your business."

"Wrong," he retorted, his tone cold, his eyes colder. "Guys like that don't change. They don't stop victimizing kids. Not unless they're caught. It was every bit of my business to make sure he wasn't out there hurting someone else."

"And you didn't think I'd have already made sure that he wasn't?" She wasn't angry. Not really. She'd have done the same thing if she'd been in his shoes, but . . .

She wasn't used to having it out there—all the ugliness of it, all the horror.

"What you'd done or hadn't done wasn't part of the equation," he responded, his jaw tight. He *was* angry. Either with Eric, or with his helplessness to change what had happened.

"You could have asked me about it. That would have saved you some effort and time."

"How about a little honesty?" He stepped close, and she could see the flecks of silver in his eyes. She could smell the chocolate on his skin, mixed with soap and fresh winter air.

"I *am* being honest," she lied.

"No." He shook his head, his hands sliding up her arms. "You aren't. We both know you wouldn't have told me anything, and I would have spent time beating my head against the brick wall of your silence. Then I just would have gone and done exactly what I did."

"I might have told you," she muttered.

"You said silence was its own kind of monster, Willow. I haven't forgotten that." His hands settled on her shoulders, his fingers warm through her shirt, and she wanted to lean into him, rest her head against his chest, listen to his heartbeat and let it drown out the voice that always seemed to whisper from the past—*Scream and you die.*

She swallowed bile, the hallway behind them suddenly darker and longer and more horrible.

"It is, but I still might have told you what you wanted to know," she finally managed to say.

"Because, you've done it every other time you've been asked?" he said, his thumbs brushing her collarbone, gently, tenderly, as if he was afraid of scaring her.

God!

She wanted to cry again.

She wanted to let every tear she'd never shed over what she'd lost slide down her cheeks, puddle on the floor, flood the chocolate shop, and wash all the ugliness away.

"I've never been asked," she said, her throat tight, her heart thudding against the wall of her chest. *"Never."*

That *was* the truth. All those years ago, no one had questioned the changes in her. Her parents hadn't asked why she suddenly slept with the lights on, or how she'd gotten the cut under her chin. Her grand-parents hadn't asked why she had a million excuses for not working in the shop. Her friends hadn't asked why she spent recess in the library and her free time locked away in her house. Her grades had slipped, and the teachers had patted her on the head and told her that it was tough having a father who was sick.

No one had asked, and she hadn't told, because she'd been terrified Eric would follow through on his threats and hurt her younger sisters.

"Hey," Jax said quietly, leaning down and looking into her eyes. "Breathe."

And she realized she was holding her breath, seeing stars, feeling light-headed and nauseated.

"I'm okay," she murmured, because what else was she going to say? That she was falling apart. Again. Spinning into the vile memory and the vicious night-mare.

"You will be." He kissed her then—her temple and her cheek, and, finally, her lips.

She levered up, her hands clutching his sides, her heart still thumping painfully. If she could have lost herself in him, she would have. If she could have climbed into the comfort of his arms and never left, she might have, but the bell above the door rang, and cold air swept in.

"Excuse me!" a woman said loudly, and Willow jumped back, nearly stumbling over one of the tables.

Jax grabbed her arm, steadying her as she turned to face the customer.

Millicent Montgomery. Tan skin. Blond hair. Forehead so tight from Botox, she couldn't manage a scowl.

She was completely capable of shooting daggers out of her eyes, though. If looks could kill, Willow would be dead and buried.

"Millicent," she said, offering a smile that was almost as fake as Millicent's double-D breasts. "How are you today?"

"I'd be better if I hadn't had to witness your PDA," she huffed, her gaze sliding from Willow to Jax.

"Hello, Jax. It's been a long time."

"We spoke yesterday at church," he responded, offering a kind smile that probably made Millicent's heart sink, because there was no interest in it. Nothing but a simple, polite gesture that couldn't be construed as anything else.

Poor Millicent!

Her fourth husband had died nearly two years ago, and she was still looking for number five. At forty-two, she'd hit a wall in the romance department. A new thing for a woman who'd always had a man on the back burner. At least, that's what Addie and Brenna were saying.

"Yes. Of course. You're right." Millicent blushed, and Willow couldn't help pitying her. She'd made a laughingstock of herself—bleaching her hair, plumping her breasts, Botoxing and waxing and wearing clothes that were a few sizes too small. In a town like this one, that was noticed, and what was noticed was talked about.

"Are you here for some of our fudge, Millicent?" Willow asked, moving behind the counter and lifting one of their prettiest boxes from a shelf.

"I'll let you know what I'm here for after I decide," Millicent barked, and then sighed. "What I meant to say is, I'm not sure yet."

"Take your time."

"Thank you, dear." Millicent eyed the candies displayed in the case, her fingers tapping against the glass. "I wanted to buy something for my housekeeper. She's been feeling a little under the weather the past few days. I thought chocolate might cheer her up."

"What does she like?"

"That's the problem. I don't really know. She usually doesn't stay with me, but I've let her spend a few nights, because she looked so exhausted." Millicent speared Willow with a hard look. "Don't spread that around. I don't want people to think I'm getting soft."

"I'm sure no one would think that," she responded.

Jax coughed, and Willow met his eyes, saw amusement gleaming there.

"I should certainly hope not. I wouldn't want people trying to take advantage of me. Now, about the chocolate . . ." Millicent pointed to a tray of peanut butter fudge. "How about a quarter pound of peanut butter. A half dozen chocolate pretzels. Are those almond clusters on the bottom rack there?"

"Yes. Made fresh this morning."

"I wouldn't expect anything less. I'll take three of those. One for me. Two for Phoebe. She's such a skinny little thing. She needs the calories."

"Did you say Phoebe?" Jax asked, something in his

voice making Willow look up from the fudge she'd been weighing.

"Yes. Phoebe Tanner. She's been working for me for a couple of months. Very hard worker, that girl. My house has never been cleaner."

"Does she live around here?"

"Why do you want to know?"

"There's a woman named Phoebe who lives out on the Bradshaws' farm," he offered, and Willow's heart skipped a beat. "I've been wanting to meet her."

"If you're thinking of adding her to your list of conquests," Millicent growled, "you can forget it. She's married. Happily. And she's very young. Innocent. I simply would not approve—"

"I don't make conquests," he cut in. "I'm interested in speaking to her about a case I'm working on."

"She's not a criminal."

"I'm sure she's not."

"Then what in the world do you want with her?"

"*Is* she the woman who lives on the Bradshaws' farm?"

"As a matter of fact, she is."

"And she's currently staying with you?"

Millicent pressed her collagen-enhanced lips together and crossed her arms over her chest.

"Millicent," Jax said, his gaze hard. "I know you don't want to stand in the way of an investigation. I also know that you don't want to be charged as an accessory to a crime."

"What crime? You said you didn't think she was a criminal!"

"Is she at your place?"

"Yes." Millicent's face was red, and Willow thought she might be about to cry. "But I just can't stand the thought of you dragging her off to jail. She's such a sweet girl. Like the daughter I always wanted and never had."

"I just want to speak with her." He untied his apron, handed it across the counter. "Sorry to do this to you, Willow, but I really do need to talk to her. I'll pick you up at seven. We'll head to the hospital together."

"Okay," she said, before she realized what she was agreeing to.

She thought about calling him back, telling him to forget it, that she was afraid her heart was getting too involved and that her head was taking a lunch break. That she didn't want to fall for someone who would never let himself fall for her, but he was already heading into the back for his coat, and Millicent was actually crying, tears sliding down her face and leaving tracks in her foundation.

"It's okay," she said, setting the box and the fudge aside, and pulling Millicent into her arms.

"No. It isn't. He's going to take her to jail, and then I'm going to be in that big old house, all alone again," she sobbed.

"He's not going to take her to jail."

Hopefully.

But if she was Miracle's mother?

All bets were off, because if there was one thing she was learning about Jax, he was as keen for justice as she was, as driven to make things right. He might feel sorry for Miracle's mother. He might sympathize with her, but he wasn't going to ignore the fact that she'd left her baby out in a storm that could have taken her life.

Willow didn't say that to Millicent. She just patted her back and told her everything would be okay.

She was a kid.

That's what got to Jax most.

A scrawny kid who looked like she hadn't eaten a good meal in months, her floor-length dress sagging to the floor, covering her from neck to toe. Not a hint of skin showing anywhere except on her hands, her neck, and her face.

Her very pale face.

"Can I help you?" she asked, peering out at them from behind Millicent's storm door.

He met Kane's eyes, glad that he'd asked his boss to come along. He'd didn't want to be too hard on the young girl, but he didn't want to be too soft on her, either. If his suspicions were correct, she was Miracle's mother.

"We're looking for Phoebe Tanner," Jax said, and the girl flinched.

"This is Millicent Montgomery's house. She's out," she murmured. "You'll have to speak with her when she returns."

She started to shut the door.

"Phoebe," Kane said, and the girl froze, her hand on the door, her eyes wide. "We know who you are."

"And?" she said, brushing strands of long black hair over her shoulder, the nervous gesture making her look even more vulnerable.

"We'd like to speak with you." Kane opened the storm door, and now there was nothing for Phoebe to hide behind.

She looked . . . tired. Worn down. Like a person who was carrying a burden that was much too heavy. "What if I don't want to talk to you?"

"Then we'll obtain a warrant and bring you down to the station."

"On what charges?" She might be young, but she was well-spoken, and she wasn't stupid.

"Child abandonment." Kane said it before Jax could, and Phoebe blanched.

"I don't know what you're talking about."

"I think you do." Jax took a picture from his wallet, one he'd been carrying since after Miracle's surgery. The hospital had provided copies to the press, and he'd taken one. "She's doing pretty well for a little one who's just had her heart operated on."

He held out the photo and wasn't surprised when Phoebe didn't look at it.

"I'm glad she's doing well, but she's not my baby."

"You live on the Bradshaws' farm, right?" Jax changed tactics, tucking the photo away.

"Yes. With my husband and a couple of friends."

"Is there some reason why you haven't been back there in a few days?"

"I've been back. Just . . . I spent the last couple of nights here, because Millicent needed me."

"She said it was because you were sick."

"I've been . . . under the weather, but it's nothing serious. I just thought she seemed lonely lately, and I felt bad leaving her every night."

"Leaving her to go to your husband made you feel bad?" Kane asked, and Phoebe blushed.

"Elias understood."

"How long have the two of you been married?"

Kane pressed for more information, and Jax hoped to God it would lead somewhere other than another dead-end.

"Six months. We got married the day I turned eighteen."

"Was there some reason for that?" Jax asked.

Her lips tightened, and she looked like she was going to cry. "I loved him. He loved me. That was reason enough."

"I spoke to your family." He pressed his advantage while he had it.

"Elias is my family."

"Your father. Your mother."

"Family keeps loving you. No matter what. The people who raised me aren't family."

"I'm sorry you feel that way, but legally, they are your folks. They said you ran off."

"And?"

"Why?"

"To marry Elias. They weren't going to approve it. He was too modern for them. My . . . father doesn't think we need things like electricity and running water. Elias is smarter than that. He doesn't see anything wrong with a few modern conveniences. God gave us brains, and there's nothing wrong with using what we create with them. That's what he always says."

"I couldn't agree more. God expects us to use the gifts He's given us," Kane said, offering a warm smile that seemed to put Phoebe at ease.

"We still are very careful to not be worldly," she said earnestly. "We make our own clothes. We don't have TV. We believe that God heals. Not doctors. We worship in small groups rather than big, fancy churches."

"You have a small group meeting?" Jax asked, but he didn't really care. He was thinking about what she'd said about doctors. About letting God do the healing, and he was thinking about Miracle, born with a hole in her heart. About the little bow in her hair, and the way she'd been wearing clean footy pajamas. She'd been dressed and cared for before she'd been put in the fruit crate.

By a mother who'd loved her?

Who'd been afraid for her?

Who'd thought she had no choice but to leave her with someone who would seek the medical treatment that her husband would not allow?

"Well, just me and Elias. Clementine and Josiah. We have Wednesday night prayer meeting and Sunday morning worship. We never miss."

"Do you believe in infant baptism?" Kane said casually, and Phoebe frowned.

"What does that have to do with anything?"

"It seems to me," he responded, "that might be important if you had a baby who . . . say . . . had a heart defect."

"I . . . don't."

"Then I guess you won't be opposed to letting us bring a DNA kit to your place? It's just a swab of the inside of the cheek."

"Why would you want that?"

"You don't have TV, but you can't have missed the news about the baby who was found in town." Jax watched her reaction carefully, saw the slight clenching of her fists, the subtle shifting of her shoulders beneath the huge dress.

"Everyone is talking about it."

"And I'm sure you've heard them say that we're looking for the mother."

"What does that have to do with me?"

"We're just ruling people out, Phoebe. DNA testing is the easiest way to do it. So how about we come back in a half hour? We'll bring the kit and—"

"That's not legal." She didn't sound like she believed it, though. Which might work to their advantage.

"It is if you agree to it."

"I'm not going to."

"You do understand that we can get a warrant for that, too, right?"

She bit her lip, grabbed the edge of the door.

"If you want to talk to Millicent," she said, "you'll have to come back."

She closed the door with a quiet snap.

Left them standing on Millicent's wide front porch.

"She's the mother," Kane said before Jax could.

"I know."

"So let's go put our case together and present it to the judge. We should have the warrant by tomorrow."

"That'll be great. If she hasn't skipped town by then."

"Where would she go?"

"Far enough away to make things difficult."

"She's got no phone. Very little money. And she loves her daughter. She might have done something stupid because of that, but love was the motivation. I think she'll stay, because I think her heart won't let her make another choice."

"You've got more faith in humanity than I do, Kane."

"Maybe just a little more hope in it. Come on. The sooner we get everything to the judge, the sooner we can get the warrant."

Jax followed him to his cruiser and climbed into the passenger seat. They were pulling out of the driveway when a curtain in a lower window shifted, the movement catching his eye. Phoebe was there, watching them drive away.

Jax couldn't be sure, but he thought she might be crying.

Chapter Eleven

The day passed quickly.

Very quickly.

Dozens of customers. Dozens of orders. Plenty of things to distract Willow from her memories. She had moments when she almost forgot the fear, long minutes where she barely felt the shivery awareness of the hall and its dark shadows.

"Looks like that was it," Chase said, closing the register and eyeing the clock. "Last customer came in just under the wire. You want me to turn the sign?"

"Sure." She grabbed a few empty trays from the display case. "And you don't have to stay and help me shut things down. I know you have a lot of schoolwork."

"Meh," he shrugged, his shoulders scrawny beneath a white button-down shirt. Like Byron, he'd worn that and slacks to work. His were a little more wrinkled than Granddad's, but she thought that it was sweet that he tried.

"What's that mean?"

"I've just been thinking that I might need to work

a little more. Lark is growing up, and she's smart. She deserves to go to college one day."

"Your mother had life insurance, right?"

"No. We were barely making it, and she didn't have extra to spend on something like that," he said defensively.

"I'm not judging, Chase. Just asking."

"She didn't," he said in a softer tone.

"So you're paying for college with what you earn here?"

"I took out a loan for my tuition. I'm saving as much of what I earn as I can, so Lark has the opportunities she deserves."

"She doesn't expect you to do that. You know that, right?"

"I know that it's what my mother would have done. I'm not going to do any less."

"I don't think your mother would want you to curtail your own education for your sister."

He shrugged again, reaching past her to grab a few empty trays from the display case.

"Chase," she said when he started to walk away.

"What?" He didn't turn to look at her, and she knew she'd stepped on his toes, questioned the plans that he'd made, made him feel like a young, foolish kid instead of the young man he was trying to be.

"I think what you want to do for Lark is one of the nicest things I've ever heard of, but you're family. I'm going to treat you like family. So let me make this very clear. You're going to keep going to school full-time. You'll work here when your schedule permits, and you'll get paid accordingly."

"You don't have any right—"

"No. I don't. But I can tell you this—once you get

your degree, you can get a job that pays way more than what you're making here. With that, you'll really be able to help your sister."

"I hadn't thought about it that way." He finally met her eyes and offered a sheepish smile.

"Well, maybe it's time you did. If you drop out of college, you're going to limit your earning potential, and that will limit what you can do for Lark."

"You know what?" he asked.

"What?"

"I guess maybe I *should* go home and get some studying done."

"Good plan," she said, and he grinned.

"I'll be in tomorrow at one. See you then." He walked into the kitchen. She heard the trays dropping into the sink, the back door opening and then closing, and then she heard the silence. She was alone. The store closed, darkness pressing in against the windows. The nightmare just a thought away.

Eric is dead.

Jax's words, voicing a fact she'd already known.

If only knowing it could take away her knee-jerk fear of the hall, she'd be just fine.

"You *are* just fine," she reminded herself, jumping when she heard the back door open again.

Chase coming back for something he'd forgotten.

That's what she thought, and she walked through the hall she hated and into the kitchen to prove it to herself.

Only, Chase wasn't there.

The kitchen was empty.

Just Willow and a pile of dirty pans that needed to

be scrubbed, trays that needed to be washed and stacked, ingredients that needed to be put away.

"Hello?" she called, the shakiness of her voice pissing her off. There was nothing to be afraid of.

Nothing.

But fear had dug its talons in, and it wasn't going to let her go. Not until she checked every inch of the shop to make sure she really was alone.

She opened the walk-in, searched the pantry, then, when she couldn't avoid it any longer, walked back into the hall. Her skin was clammy, her heart thumping erratically. The hall was brightly lit, but it felt dark. She glanced in the tiny bathroom. Empty. Of course. Walked into the office.

It was empty, too, the stacks of mail Brenna had told her about lying on the desk, the old wall safe closed up tight, the cookbooks still on the shelves. Everything looked normal, and she thought she must have imagined the sound of the door closing, because there was absolutely no one there.

"No one," she said, the words echoing loudly in the silence.

She grabbed the mail, rifling through it until she found the envelope with her name on it. Sure enough, the return address was the office of the attorney she thought must be representing Eric's family.

As if they needed an attorney.

Maybe they thought they did. Josh had to have known what had happened. Or at least suspected it. Was this his way of buying her silence?

Or maybe his way of making amends?

With Eric dead, she had no need for revenge and no desire to bring his family down. She'd have to call the lawyer and tell him that. She should have done it before, but every time she'd picked up the phone, she'd chickened out.

She wasn't sure why.

Maybe she'd been afraid that the voice on the other end would sound like Eric's.

She frowned, carrying the envelope into the front of the house. No one was there, either. It was just as empty as it had been when she'd walked out of it.

Her imagination getting the best of her, and she'd let it, because no matter how much she tried to shake the past, it just didn't seem to want to let go of her.

She tore open the envelope, angry and irritated and tired, because she'd barely slept since she'd been back. There was a check inside. *Of course* there was.

Twenty thousand dollars. Just like before.

The note was different this time.

With warm regards.

That was it, and it pissed her off.

Warm regards? From a family whose golden child had raped her?

She strode back into the kitchen, turned on the gas stove, ready to burn the hell out of the damn thing.

But the back door opened, and a man stepped in, his face shadowed by a hood, his coat wet from winter rain.

Suddenly she was back in time, walking into the shop after delivering chocolate to Sally Jefferson's birthday party, hearing Eric call to her, seeing him standing in the hallway, blocking her path.

Feeling his hands, smelling his breath—alcohol and mints and something foul and horrible.

Scream and you die.

She was there again, only this time she *was* screaming, fighting the hands that were reaching for her,
shoving against a chest that was rock-hard and immov-
able. Screaming and screaming and screaming, like
she hadn't been able to do before.

She slammed her palm into his jaw, would have hit
him again, but he grabbed her wrist, pulled her arm
down. His grip . . .

Light?

Gentle?

"It's okay," he said, and she realized he'd been
saying that all along, that the words had been bouncing around in her brain, ricocheting off neurons alive
with panic and fear, slipping right back out of her
head again.

The last scream died in her throat, and she was
looking into blue eyes with flecks of silver in them.
Staring into a face filled with compassion and understanding and sorrow.

"Damn it," she muttered, yanking away from Jax's
hand, sinking down onto the floor, her back against
the cupboards, her head resting on her bent knees.

God! She was shaking, every muscle twitching.

Jax slid down beside her, not touching her, just . . .
there, waiting while she caught her breath, centered
herself, and remembered that she really was okay.

Then, as if he knew she'd reached that point, his
hand settled on her nape, his warm fingers kneading
muscles that ached with tension.

"It's okay," he said, the words as soothing as his
touch.

She melted against him, because she had nothing
left to hold her up. Every bit of her strength had seeped

out. She leaned into his side, let herself be wrapped in his arms. He didn't speak again, and she couldn't speak, so they just stayed where they were, the silence of the shop broken only by the soft patter of rain against the windows.

They sat for a while.

Twenty minutes. Maybe longer. Jax wasn't keeping track of the time. He was too busy calling himself every kind of idiot.

He should have knocked.

He'd been in too damn much of a hurry, his mind still on the evidence report he'd handed over to the judge. He'd been calculating how quick the turnaround time might be, how soon he could have the warrant in hand, how far Phoebe might get before then. That was his only excuse for entering the shop as if he were family and belonged there.

"I'm sorry," he murmured against Willow's hair.

"I'm the one who should apologize," she said, her voice hoarse from the screams that had seemed wrenched from the deepest part of her soul. "I'm pretty sure I was trying to break your jaw."

"You barely touched me."

"That's not the way I remember it." She lifted her head, and they were looking into each other's eyes. Hers were glassy, the pupils dilated. A few strands of hair had escaped her bun, and he brushed them from her cheek, his fingers lingering on warm, silky skin.

"How do you remember it?"

"I got in a pretty good hit." She touched the place where her palm strike had landed. "I don't see a bruise."

There wouldn't be one, because she'd landed a

glancing blow. A good hit, if he hadn't seen it coming and dodged it.

He knew she wouldn't remember that.

She'd been gone, sucked into a vortex created by her fear and his piss-poor timing. He'd had it happen to him—disparate things all coming together to form the perfect storm, the mega-trigger that sent him over the edge into full-out panic. It hadn't happened in years, but he could still remember the feeling of terror that had overwhelmed every rational thought and taken away any choice he had in how he would act.

He could also remember the humiliation that came after it.

"I don't bruise easily," he said lightly, and she offered a tentative smile.

"Good, because I wouldn't want to have to explain—"

"You're not going to have to explain anything. Because the only two people who need to know the details already do."

"I know, but—"

"Willow, I've been where you are, weak-kneed and wrung out, embarrassed because something completely innocent made me go into full-out fight mode. When you go through hell, sometimes the demons follow you out. That's just the way it is. Every survivor knows it." He stood, offering her a hand up.

"Thanks," she said, and he wasn't sure if she meant for the help or for the words.

He didn't ask.

The best thing he could do was clean up the shop and then get her out of it. A visit to the hospital, a nice meal, a few hours away. They'd do her good.

They'd do him good, too.

He needed to know that she was okay, because

watching her panic, knowing she was reliving the attack, it had shattered the hard shell he tried to keep around his heart.

He handed her a glass of water, and then turned off the gas burner. She'd had something in her hand when he'd walked in, something that he'd thought she was trying to burn.

There. Next to the stove. A piece of paper that looked like a check. He lifted it, frowning as he realized what it was. "This is a lot of money."

"Yes."

"It looked like you were getting ready to set it on fire."

"I was."

"Can I ask why?"

"You can ask anything you want."

"Are you going to answer?"

She hesitated, then shrugged. "I think it's from Eric's family."

He looked at the check again, read the name of the issuer. James Rhodes, Attorney-at-Law.

"Looks like a law firm to me."

"I did a little research. He works for some high-powered politicians in the D.C. metro area. Eric's family is—"

"Close to there."

"Right. I don't think it's a stretch to think that there's a connection." She took the check from his hand, shoved it into her purse.

"Have you called?"

"It's a lot easier to just avoid," she admitted.

"What are you afraid will happen?"

"Nothing that is realistic."

"Tell me anyway."

"I keep imagining that I'll dial that number, and someone will answer, and I'll hear Eric's voice. Every time I get up the courage to call, that thought runs through my mind, and I don't."

"Then I'll do the calling."

"Jax, it's not your problem, and you don't need to handle it."

"You've been making it a habit of being wrong about what I should and shouldn't do. First you thought I shouldn't be worried about where Eric was and what he was doing. Now you think I shouldn't help you out."

"You shouldn't."

"Says who?"

"Me. You've already said that you don't want to get involved with anyone."

"Did I?"

"You implied it, and I'm good at taking hints."

He didn't deny the truth, even though there were a lot of moments lately when he wasn't sure if it *was* the truth.

No denial. Instead, he took the coward's way out and ignored her comment, and what might have been her unspoken question.

"Helping you out isn't the same as getting involved."

"And rain isn't the same as melted snow," she replied. "Except that it is."

"Would it be so bad if I did get involved, Willow?" he asked, and she frowned, grabbing a handful of ingredients and heading for the pantry.

"I guess you're the only one who knows the answer to that."

"And I guess for right now it wouldn't be."

"You know what the problem is with that?" She turned, her freckles dark against her pale skin, her eyes spring-blue and beautiful, and he knew he wasn't just an idiot. He was a fool, because she wasn't just any woman. She was Willow, and only a fool would keep his mouth shut and let the possibilities turn into what-might-have-beens.

"I don't just want right now," she continued. "I had it for years and years, and in the end, what I got out of it was a good friend and a nice life and nothing that I couldn't walk away from."

"That says a lot about your ex," he said.

"It says a lot about me, too, but we weren't talking about that. We were talking about us."

"There will be no us, because I couldn't live with myself if something happened to you because of me," he admitted, running steaming water over chocolate-coated pots. The scent of it wafted into the air, mixing with vanilla and the tangy aroma of rum-soaked cherries. There was a jar of them beside the sink, opened and nearly empty.

"Shouldn't I be the one to decide if the risk is worth the gain? Or at least be part of the decision-making process?"

"Let's try not to be too logical. Okay, Willow? It's an unreasonable fear. There's no logic to it."

She smiled. A real smile this time. "I guess that's something we have in common. Unreasonable fears."

"And Miracle. We have her in common, too. I think I met her mother this morning." He offered the information as a distraction, and she seemed happy enough to take it.

"Millicent's housekeeper?" she guessed, taking a clean pot from his hand and drying it.

"We'll have to get a DNA test to prove it. She refused to allow it."

"You've petitioned the court?"

"I just sent the file over. We asked to have it expedited. I'm hoping we'll get the warrant by morning. Once it's in hand, we'll obtain a DNA sample. If she doesn't take off before then."

"She won't."

"That's what Kane said. I hope you're both right."

"I do too. She needs to answer for what she did, but she also needs a chance to make it better."

"She abandoned her baby in an alley. Left her behind a Dumpster when temperatures were below freezing. It would be damn hard to make that better."

"Poor choice of words. I guess I just meant she needs a chance to explain in a way that Miracle might understand one day."

"Would you understand?"

"Maybe. It would just depend on motive. Is she young?"

"Eighteen. She looks younger. Skinny as a stick and pale. She needs some good food and some rest."

"She probably needs to see a doctor. She gave birth a couple of weeks ago, and she's cleaning house for Millicent. That can't be healthy."

"We'll take her to the hospital once we get the warrant. The doctors will know if she's recently given birth. If she's got any health issues, they'll treat her."

"I'm sure she'll love having her privacy taken away from her," Willow said, her sarcasm as obvious as the freckles that dotted her cheeks.

"She gave up her rights when she broke the law.

You know that, Willow. Don't let your emotions make you forget it."

"*If* she broke the law. You're assuming Miracle is hers."

"I don't assume. I gather facts and evidence. What I've gathered points to Phoebe Tanner. If the judge agrees, we'll move forward. Do I feel sorry for her? You're damn right I do, but I'm not going to let my feelings get in the way of justice."

For a moment, she didn't respond. Just put away the last pot and wiped down the counter. Then she turned to face him, those stray pieces of hair dancing around her cheeks and her nape.

"I'm not letting my feelings get in the way, either. But . . . she's a kid. Kids do stupid things, and she's going to be scared out of her mind when you bring her to the hospital."

He hadn't thought about that. Not much anyway.

He'd compartmentalized things, broken it down into bite-size pieces of information that made sense. Phoebe had given birth to Miracle. She'd left her to freeze in an alley. She needed to be charged with child abandonment and, probably, child endangerment. She needed to be brought to justice.

And she needed compassion.

He knew that.

Just like he knew that she was young and naïve, and that she might have thought giving her daughter up was the only way to save her.

We believe God heals.

But maybe she'd also believed that God sometimes used modern medicine to do it. Maybe she'd been fighting a losing battle with Elias, begging him to let her take Miracle to the doctor. Maybe she'd been just desperate enough to try to do it herself.

And then what?

Had the clinic been closed?

Had she been too afraid to drive to Spokane by herself?

He'd seen the way she'd been raised—in a cabin in the woods, with nothing and no one around. How much did she really know about the world and how it worked?

"You're frowning," Willow pointed out. She'd untied her apron, pulled it over her head, and hung it from a hook near the door.

"Just thinking that I'd hate to go up against you in court. You'd always win. I'll make sure Susan comes to the hospital when we bring Phoebe. She can explain what's happening." The only female deputy in Benevolence, Susan was tough as steel, but she had three daughters. All of them teenagers. Jax figured she'd know how to comfort a scared young woman.

"It's the right thing to do, Jax. Which means we both win." She pulled a couple of pins from her hair and it fell around her shoulders, thick strands of deep red silk that floated and fluttered as she moved.

She'd worn a dress again. A soft blue one that matched her eyes. He'd noticed it before, but only in a perfunctory way. He'd been focused on calming her down, making sure she was okay.

Now . . .

He wanted to run his hands along her sides, let them settle at the curve in her waist, tell her how beautiful she was.

It would be dangerous as hell, but he thought he

could do it anyway. Maybe they'd both be okay with it. Maybe they would be more than okay with it.

Maybe that thing called hope—the thing that made Kane and Willow believe that Phoebe would stick around—would well up inside him one day, take hold of his heart and convince him that it was better to go after what he wanted than it was to stand around wishing that he could.

Then again, maybe he'd go to the hospital, look at Miracle, and remember his baby sister. Remember how it had felt to watch her die. Remember all the reasons why he couldn't, shouldn't, wouldn't open his life to those possibilities.

"Are you okay?" Willow asked, and he met her eyes, realized that she'd grabbed her coat and her purse and was standing at the door.

"Yeah."

"Are you sure? You look like . . ."

"What?" he asked, his voice gruff.

"Like I feel when I walk into the shop." She took his hand, tugged him to the door. "Come on. Let's get some fresh air. That always helps."

So does being with you, he almost said, but hope hadn't quite landed in *his* heart, so he just flicked off the lights and followed her out into the rain.

Chapter Twelve

Her hands were shaking. Still.

An hour after they'd arrived at the hospital, and Willow's stomach was in knots, her muscles twitching with the aftermath of sheer terror. She didn't think anyone noticed. Except, maybe, Jax. He was watching her as she fed Miracle, his expression neutral, everything about him still and quiet.

He'd been like that since they'd left the shop, and she thought it might have something to do with the look she'd seen in his eyes. She'd asked him about it on the way to the hospital.

"We both have our monsters."

That's what he'd said, and then he'd flicked on the radio and sped down the highway. Silent. Just like he was now.

Which, of course, had made her wonder about his family again. Killed because of his father. That's what Jax had seemed to be implying. It matched with stories she'd heard when she was younger, whispers that had traveled farther than adults thought they had: police work. Gangs. Drugs. A hit on an entire family.

Everyone should have died.

But Jax had survived.

She'd figured all that out, but she hadn't known enough to have her heart break over it.

Embarrassing now, but she'd been young and stupid.

Like Miracle's mother.

She studied the baby's face, her delicate earlobes and tiny nose. Her cheeks and lips were pink, her face filling out. She didn't look gaunt like she had when Jax had lifted her from the box. She was making gains, and the surgeon had said that there should be no long-term impact on her health.

She was tiny, though. Fragile.

And the world was filled with things that could hurt her.

"Knock-knock," someone called, and Alison walked into the room. She had coffee in one hand and a thick folder in the other. "The nurse told me you were here. If I'd known ahead of time, I'd have brought more coffee. Had to attend the most boring meeting in the world. An hour of information spread out over six. I am in desperate need of a little pick-me-up. I hope you two don't mind me drinking in front of you."

"Not at all," Willow said.

Jax didn't respond, just eyed the folder that she'd tossed on a table.

"Looks like you've been busy," he finally said, gesturing to the thick sheaf of paper.

"That? Didn't take me any time at all. I simply compiled the information from doctors and nurses, put together feeding charts and schedules, and included blank pages for journaling."

"Journaling what?" Miracle had finished the bottle,

and Willow patted her back, careful of the healing incision on her chest.

"Your feelings. Mothering is hard work, and you have no experience. All the classes in the world can't prepare you. So, the journal? My way of checking in on you without daily phone calls. Just jot a few notes, scan them into your computer, and send them along. If anything pressing happens between my weekly visits, we'll talk, but otherwise . . . I want to give you some space."

"With my family around, there won't be any of that happening," she said dryly, and Alison smiled.

"The more the merrier when it comes to family. All your relatives passed their background checks, and your mother has already finished her certification course for respite care."

"That was fast." Very fast. Which might explain why she'd barely heard from Janelle the last few days.

"She was motivated. A great lady, your mom. We're going out for lunch one day soon." She took a careful sip of coffee, grimacing a little. "Bitter. I should have put more cream in it. How about we run down to the cafeteria? I can get cream, and maybe . . . a salad. Or, better yet, a doughnut."

"I—" *Don't want to leave Miracle.*

"You don't mind staying with our princess, do you, Jax?" she asked, lifting the folder and heading to the door, acting like everyone was going to simply follow her instructions.

It seemed like they were, because Jax was reaching for the baby, his large hands sliding between Willow's. She made the mistake of looking into his eyes.

There was something old and tired and sad there.

"Jax—" *You don't have to do this,* she was going to say,

but he already had the baby and was settling back into his chair, holding her like she was the most precious, most breakable thing in the world.

"Don't worry," Alison said. "She won't break."

"Right," he muttered, his eyes never leaving Miracle's face.

"And we won't be long," Willow assured him.

"We might be. I'm starving." Alison walked out into the hall, and Willow should have followed. She seemed frozen there, though, her mind telling her to go, her heart telling her to stay.

"I don't have to go," she said, and his gaze shifted, his eyes settling on her.

"You don't need to stay either. I'm fine."

She didn't think he was.

She thought that there might be tears in his eyes, but she couldn't imagine a guy like him crying.

"You don't look fine."

"I had a sister. Did I ever tell you that?" he asked, his gaze dropping again, his hand shifting so that he was touching Miracle's cheek, smoothing her downy curls.

"No."

"She was six months old. Big blue eyes and chubby cheeks. Aside from our mother, I was her favorite person. She died in my arms."

"My God," she breathed.

"That's the reason I can't do the family thing. I think about how nice it might be to fill my house with people I love, and then I think about her."

"Jax—"

She didn't know what she wanted to say. She didn't know what she could say.

Except *I'm sorry* over and over again.

Meaningless words that changed nothing.

"What?" he asked, a hint of impatience in his voice. How many times had he heard the platitudes? How many times had he told the story and been given empty words in response?

"What was her name?" she asked, because it was important. Because *she* was important. That little baby who'd barely lived before she'd died.

"You're the first person to ever ask me that," he responded. He wasn't smiling, but his expression had softened. "We called her Dot. Her name was Dorothy. After my mother's favorite grandmother."

"Dot," she said, and she could picture the chubby cheeks and the blue eyes, and Jax holding her while she died.

Her chest hurt with the image. Her eyes burned. She could have cried for him and for his sister, but he was watching her, steadily, silently, and she knew he was waiting for something more.

"It's a sweet name," she finally managed to say, her voice thick with unshed tears.

"She was a sweet kid. She should have had the chance to grow up, but she didn't. When I see stuff like this . . ." He touched Miracle's cheek again. "It pisses me off. You don't throw a life away. It doesn't matter how scared you are. I understand your compassion for her mother, but I have more compassion for her. She did nothing to anyone, and she still had to suffer."

Miracle? Or Dot?

She didn't ask, because Alison peeked her head back in the room, her eyes wide, her cheeks pink. "There you are! I was halfway down the hall when I realized you weren't with me. Not a big deal, except

I was talking nonstop the whole way. No wonder the nurses were looking at me like I was crazy." She grabbed Willow's arm, nearly dragging her out of the room and closing the door.

Willow went. Mostly because she didn't think Jax wanted her to stay. He'd said his piece. He'd explained his position succinctly and without emotion. He would never be a family man, because he would never lose his family again.

Straightforward truth, and Willow couldn't argue with his logic. Flawed as it was, it made sense to him. Just like staying away from the shop had made sense to her. She'd been protecting herself. At least, that's what she'd thought.

Really, all she'd done was cut herself off from the people she cared about the most.

That wasn't a lesson you could teach. It was lesson a person had to learn on her own.

Or *his* own.

Maybe Jax would. Maybe he wouldn't. But she wasn't going to push him. She wasn't going to keep falling into his arms, leaning on his strength, silently demanding all the things he didn't feel capable of giving.

He was too good a guy, and she was too strong of a woman.

He knew her secret, but that didn't mean he had to help carry the weight of it. She'd tell him that. Once they were alone again.

Apparently, getting coffee took a hell of a lot longer than Jax had imagined. He watched the clock, listening to its quiet tick as one minute passed into another.

Fifteen minutes.

Twenty.

They hadn't returned, and he hadn't moved.

He was still sitting in the chair, Miracle's head in the crook of his elbow, her tiny body balanced on his forearm.

She didn't look anything like Dot.

At least, not the Dot he remembered most—the giggly, wiggly six-month-old who'd reached for him every time he'd walked into the room. He'd been just old enough to pretend it didn't matter to him, but being the brother she idolized, the one she wanted to giggle with, had made him feel ten feet tall.

Funny how he'd put that out of his mind, forgotten how his chest had swelled with pride when his mother had come to pick him up at school and all the kids had oohed and ahhed over his sister.

Dot had been his first experience with giving love. Real, true, unconditional love. He'd have done anything for her. He'd have given his life if it would have meant she lived. He'd failed her, because he'd been a kid, too weak to fight off the bastards who had murdered his family.

He'd made peace with that. It had taken him years, but he'd finally done it. Not through counseling or therapy or any of the other methods his aunt and uncle had encouraged him to try. No. He'd done it, because he'd seen himself in little kids he'd interviewed. Kids who'd tried to protect their mothers from abusers, their siblings from molesters, their friends from the drug dealers who hunted the streets of LA. He'd seen the helpless fury in their faces, and it had been a reflection of the kid he'd been.

He sighed, standing up and crossing the room, Miracle still in his arms. It wasn't as difficult as he'd thought it would be to hold her and not remember his sister's bloody, broken body.

Different kid.

Different place.

Different person standing in his shoes.

He was older, hopefully wiser, and more than capable of protecting Miracle if she needed it. He shifted, making sure the blanket covered her little arms and tiny toes.

She was sound asleep, content to dream whatever dreams babies had. He set her in the bassinet, pulled a little knit hat over her head.

"You're a cute little thing," he said, and he thought he heard someone sigh. Just a whisper of air in the quiet room.

Or maybe outside of the room.

He moved to the door. Silent. Slow. No hurry because there were security cameras all over the hospital, and if someone was standing outside the door, he'd know it whether he caught the person or not.

A woman.

He could hear her more clearly now, soft little breaths that were more sob than sigh. He almost didn't open the door, because he knew whom he'd see, and he didn't want to deal with tears from a person who'd left her baby in a cold alley.

Then again, he *did* want to prove that Phoebe was Miracle's mother, close the case, move on.

He opened the door, and Phoebe stumbled backward, her hair a tangled mess, her eyes red-rimmed, tears streaming down her face. She looked like death warmed over, her dress wrinkled, her knuckles raw and red. She had a splotch of something on the front of her dress. It took him a second to realize what it was. Breast milk. Had she been pumping milk? Maybe hoping to nurse her daughter again?

She crossed her arms over her chest in a protective gesture that made Jax feel like the lowest kind of scum.

He met her eyes.

She wasn't saying anything, wasn't trying to leave. Was just standing there looking like she expected to be slapped.

Damn!

He wanted to despise the kid for what she'd done, but all he could do was see her for what she was: a terrified girl who'd somehow managed to slip past nurses and make it to her baby's hospital room.

"You need to sit down," he said, because it was obvious that she did.

He couldn't let her in the room, though. Not until CPS had been notified and approved it. They probably wouldn't, but he wasn't going to tell her that.

"I just want to see her. Then I'll leave."

"You know that I can't let you do that."

"She's mine. I have every right to see her." She tried to duck past him, but he blocked her path. Not touching her. Just standing between her and the open doorway.

"You gave up your rights when you left her in the alley." It was a statement. No judgment in it, but she ducked her head, her hair falling over her face.

"I love her," she moaned. "I just wanted her to get better."

"Jax?!" Willow called. "What's going on?"

He looked up, saw her running toward him, her

red hair flying behind her, her pretty dress hiked up around her thighs. She skidded to a stop beside him, her gaze on Phoebe.

"Is everything okay?" she asked as Alison jogged up behind her.

Wheezing, gasping for breath, she still managed to cling to her coffee and whatever food she'd bought.

"Who's this? How'd she get past the nurses?" she demanded.

"This is Phoebe Tanner," he responded. "Miracle's mother."

"Are you sure?" Alison reached over, lifted the heavy fall of Phoebe's hair, looked into her face, then down at her dress and that telltale stain spreading across the gray fabric.

"Geez," she whispered. "She's not more than a baby herself. I'm getting a nurse. You keep her here."

She hurried away, and Willow took Phoebe's arm, urged her to sit on the floor, then knelt beside her.

"It's going to be okay," she said, and Phoebe shook her head.

"No. It's not. I sinned, and this is my punishment."

"You're not being punished. You made a mistake. There are consequences to that, but—"

"You don't understand. I was pregnant before I got married. That's why she was sick. God took her from me, because she should never have been mine in the first place."

"That's not the way God works," Willow said, pressing her palm against Phoebe's forehead. "She's got a fever."

"I'm fine. I just wanted to see her. Then I was going to the police station." She shot a look in Jax's direction, then lowered her eyes again. "I really was. I just . . . I knew I was going to jail, and I figured I'd never see

her again. I just wanted to hold her one more time."
She pulled her legs up to her chest, her long dress
billowing around her feet as she sobbed.

Homespun fabric?

Handmade dress. That was for sure. Jax could see
the tiny white stitches against the gray. Neat, but not
perfect.

For some reason, that made him feel worse.

He crouched beside Willow, waited until Phoebe
met his eyes. "You're not going to jail. Not tonight. I
can't promise you anything else, but I can promise
you that."

"Can I see her?"

"I'm afraid not." He took out his cell phone and
texted Kane. They needed to get a uniformed officer
here, because they were going to have to make an
arrest. It sucked, but the wheels of justice had already
been turning before Phoebe showed up at the hospital. There was no way to stop them now.

"That's all I wanted, was to see her," she sobbed. "I
hitchhiked all the way here, so I could look at her face
one more time."

"You hitchhiked?" *In the state known for its serial
killers?* He didn't add the last part. She'd made it.
Hopefully, she'd never repeat the mistake.

"Elias is at work. He has the car."

"You could have waited for him," Willow said gently,
smoothing hair away from Phoebe's face.

"He wouldn't have brought me. He said it was
God's will. We sinned. God was taking our baby from
us. We'll have other babies," she spat the words out.
"I'm so sick of hearing that. I don't want other babies.
I want Eden. She was my new beginning. I was going
to be the mom my mother never was. And then she
was born, and she was so tiny and perfect, and I was

sure . . . but, she wouldn't eat, and her lips were blue. I wanted to take her to the doctor, but Elias said—"

"Let me guess," Willow said, "It was God's will."

"Yes, but I didn't believe that. I didn't believe God would want my beautiful baby to die. So, I—"

"Tell you what," Jax cut in. "How about you think about how much you really want to tell us? Because what you did was a criminal offense, and anything you say can be used against you." He needed to read the kid her Miranda rights. He knew it. Willow knew it. It seemed like the wrong time, though. Kane would be there soon enough. He'd be in uniform and on the clock. He could read her rights and make the arrest. For now, it was enough to have her there and to know she'd confessed.

Willow got to her feet. "Did you contact Kane?" she asked quietly.

"Yes. He'll be here soon."

"She needs a doctor before you book her."

"She'll get one."

"I know you see a criminal," she continued, her gaze on Phoebe. The girl had dropped her head to her knees, her long hair puddling on the floor around her hips. "I see a tragedy."

"I see both. It's a shame, Willow, but I can't change what she did. I can't reverse time and counsel her into a different decision."

"I know." She frowned. "I just wish . . ."

"What?"

"That you could?" She smiled, but he could see the sadness in her eyes.

"Me too." He tugged her closer, let his arm wrap around her waist. She leaned into him. Just for a second. Just long enough for both of them to feel how perfectly they fit.

There was a commotion at the end of the hall, a woman yelling. Feet pounding, and Willow jumped back, turning toward the sound. He turned, too, saw a small woman with blond hair and a long black skirt ducking past a nurse who was trying to block her way.

He knew her, had met her at the Bradshaws' place. Clementine Warren.

And she was hopping mad, her face red, her eyes flashing.

"What the hell is going on here?" she demanded, ducking past Willow and crouching next to Phoebe.

"Language," Phoebe said, but she didn't lift her head, and the word sounded listless, her voice hollow.

"Right. Sorry, kid. I'm a little upset. Jeb Winthrop called and told me that he'd given you a ride here. He said you looked sick as a dog." She glared at Jax as she said it. "Well? Are you going to answer the question? What's going on?"

"I think you probably know."

"What's that supposed to mean?" She shrugged out of a multicolored wool coat and tucked it around Phoebe's shoulders.

"Just that I find it hard to believe you had a pregnant teenager in the house and didn't know it."

"And?"

"I asked if you knew anyone who'd given birth recently. You said no."

"Of course I did. I don't squeal on family."

"Even when they've broken the law?"

"What law? She was trying to get Eden help. She made a mistake in judgment. If she'd told me what she was going to do . . ." She shook her head, dark green eyes flashing with irritation and anger. "It doesn't matter. She didn't tell me, and that bonehead husband of hers—"

"Clementine! Please!" Phoebe got to her feet, her movements slow, her face pale.

"He's an idiot," Clementine said, and then her expression softened, some of the fire leaving her eyes. "He means well, but he is."

"So all of you knew about the baby." It wasn't really a question. He already knew the answer.

"Sim and I delivered her." She flipped one of her long blond braids over her shoulder, the gesture somehow defiant. "And we offered to take her to the doctor as soon as we realized there was a heart problem. Elias insisted that God was going to heal that kid. I insisted that Elias had his head up his—"

"Stop." Phoebe swayed, and Clementine wrapped an arm around her.

"Okay. Fine. I'll stop. But this is a mess. A big one, and your husband is responsible."

"Where is her husband?" Jax asked.

"Supposedly at work, but when I went to find him, he'd left for the day."

"He's probably at home," Phoebe said, her voice faint.

She looked like hell.

Worse, she looked like she was about to fall over.

"We need that nurse," he said, and Willow nodded.

"I'll go find one," she said, but Alison was hurrying toward them, a tall blond woman pushing a wheelchair beside her.

"Sorry that took so long," she called, her gaze cutting to Clementine and then to Phoebe. "This is Dr. Whitney. She's going to make sure you're okay, Phoebe."

"I'm fine."

"You don't look fine." Dr. Whitney lifted her wrist and checked her pulse. "Fast. And you feel warm. Have you been running a fever?"

"I don't know."

"How about we find out?"

"I really just want to go home."

"Honey," the doctor said gently, "going home isn't going to solve your problems. Let's see what's going on with you, okay? And then we'll work everything else out." She helped Phoebe into the wheelchair and rolled her through the hall.

Jax followed, Willow and Clementine beside him.

They didn't speak. There wasn't a whole lot to say. Miracle's mother had been found, and she was a sick young girl who needed a mother almost as much as her baby did.

Chapter Thirteen

Friday morning dawned just like every other morning since she'd been back—a little gray, a little dreary, cold rain drizzling from the sky. Willow didn't mind. She could smell spring in the air—a mixture of grass and sunshine and better things to come.

She hoped.

The week had been difficult. Lots of drama. Lots of people with lots of opinions about what should happen to Phoebe and Miracle.

Of course, the only opinion that mattered when it came to the baby was Alison's. She and her team had met. They'd discussed options, and they decided to proceed with the original plan. Willow would bring Miracle home tonight. She'd be keeping her until the family court date. A month from now.

Which was fine.

She was prepared. She had the nursery set up, the drawers stocked with baby supplies. She had cases of the formula the hospital had recommended. She didn't have the breast milk that Phoebe had pumped and stored in the freezer at her house.

Poor kid.

She'd been released from the hospital and allowed to return home. She hadn't been allowed to see the baby. As far as Willow had been told, she wouldn't be allowed. Not until the criminal case against her was closed. The fact that her husband had run off and left her to deal with things on her own . . . It sucked, but there wasn't anything Willow could do about it. She'd been asked to keep her distance. Alison didn't want sympathy for the young woman to cloud Willow's judgment and make her do something stupid.

"You get too close to her, and you'll start feeling sorry for her, and then you might end up doing something stupid." Those had been her exact words.

Obviously, she didn't know Willow very well. She *never* let her emotions rule her decisions, and she didn't do stupid things because of them.

"Except for this," she muttered, tossing her latest batch of fudge in the Dumpster—disposable pan and all.

At least she'd been smart about *that.*

No more chopping cement-like fudge from Grand-dad's good pans. She was using tinfoil ones. Byron had noticed, of course, but he hadn't said a word. He'd probably also noticed the disappearance and reappearance of hundreds of dollars' worth of ingredients.

Thank goodness she hadn't been in a financial hole when she'd arrived. Her fudge-making failures would have put her in the poor house. As it was, she'd reordered from suppliers twice in the past week.

She sighed, rubbing the back of her neck.

At least everything else was going well. She'd perfected old-fashioned marshmallows, mint chocolate bars, and about three dozen other recipes that she'd known how to make once upon a time, and now knew how to make again.

It was the just the fudge she was struggling with.

Her archnemesis.

"Because you don't believe in the magic of it now."

That's what Jax had said.

Jax.

She hadn't seen him since their trip to the hospital. He'd driven her back to the shop, walked her to the door, said good night, and walked away.

She'd known that she probably wasn't going to see him again. Not in the shop, anyway. Not in her apartment or his car or the hospital. Not any place that they might be alone together. They'd shared too much, and that wasn't comfortable for either of them. So, staying away from each other? It was for the best. They both had their demons, and they'd been fighting them alone for a long time. It didn't seem natural to share the burden.

She thought she might want to, though. She thought she just might be willing to take a chance on what she'd seen in Jax's eyes, what she'd felt in his tender kisses.

The problem was, he didn't seem willing to take a chance on her.

She walked back into the shop, grabbed fresh ingredients, and started the fudge all over again. Everything else was ready for the day. Byron would be in at seven. He'd open the doors at nine. They'd follow the same routine he'd been following for decades—serving customers, making chocolate, serving more customers. Always with a smile. That's what customers expected. Great chocolate. Great service. Willow had been doing everything she could to follow her grandfather's example. She might not be able to make the fudge, but she sure as heck could smile.

Even on the bad days.

Even when the fiftieth batch of fudge hadn't worked out, and she'd woken up screaming from the nightmare. Even when the hall seemed just as dark as ever and the shadowy corners seemed filled with danger. Even then, she smiled.

A key scraped in the lock and she pasted the damn smile on her face, sure that her grandfather was on his way in. To her surprise, Janelle was there. Hair damp, face makeup free. No mascara. No lipstick. No dress or heels or skirt and jacket.

She wore yoga pants, a fitted T-shirt, a down vest and . . .

Running shoes?

It couldn't be, but it was. They were right there on her feet—black and teal sneakers that matched her vest.

"Mom?" she asked, and then felt like an idiot.

Of course it was her mother.

Just not the mother she was used to seeing.

"Who else would have a key to the door and walk in at this time of the morning?"

"Byron?"

"He's never in until seven. It's only six thirty."

True, but still . . .

Janelle in Chocolate Haven? Wearing running gear?

"What are you doing out so early?"

"I finished my run and was heading back to the

house when I saw the lights. I thought I'd pop in and see if you needed a hand."

"An extra hand is always good. I'm just starting a batch of peanut butter fudge." *And I'm hoping to heaven you know how to make it, because I sure as heck don't.*

"Peanut butter? That was your father's favorite."

"I remember."

"He loved to add marshmallow to it. Just a little. Do you make it that way?"

"I haven't yet."

"Well, let me just wash up, and then I'll show you how he did it. If my muscles don't cramp up on me first. Running isn't as easy as it used to be."

"I didn't realize you were ever a runner."

"Oh. I was. When I was younger. I gave it up when I met your father. We were so busy making a life together, I didn't have time for it. Of course, back then, I didn't have so many worries. Now . . ."

"You worry about everything?"

"Of course. I've got three beautiful daughters, and I want their lives to be perfect."

"You know that's not going to happen, right?"

"Hope springs eternal, honey." She sighed, measuring out chocolate and peanut butter and a scoop of marshmallow fluff. "Noah says . . ." Her voice trailed off and she blushed.

Blushed.

Janelle Lamont—the Realtor voted most likely to make a deal, the widow who'd never shown any interest in dating after her husband's death, the mother who'd walked into PTA meetings like she owned the school—was blushing.

"Noah Story?" Willow guessed. He'd taught high

school years ago, moved away, and had just recently returned.

"That's right." She'd turned on the burner and was stirring the ingredients as if her life depended on it.

"You two hang out a lot?"

"Actually, he's my running partner."

"Could you have been any more nonchalant about the fact that you go running with a very nice-looking man?"

"It's not a big deal. We were having dinner together one night—"

"You had dinner together?"

"I do have a social life, Willow."

"I know. I just didn't think you socialized with men." That sounded just about stupid, so she pressed her lips together and handed Janelle the vanilla.

"Noah and I go way back. We were friends in high school. Anyway, we were having dinner together, and he told me that I'm too tense. He said I worry too much, and it was going to take a toll on my health if I didn't start burning off some of my anxiety. He's coaching football at the high school now, and he runs every morning to stay in shape for it."

"So . . . you decided to go running with him?"

"It took me a while to get on board with the idea, but eventually he wore me down. Now we run three mornings a week."

"Do Adeline and Brenna know this?"

"Why would they?"

"Because you're their mother, and you're going out with an old high school flame."

"I didn't say he was an old flame. I said we were friends." But her blush had deepened. "I also didn't say we were going out."

"You went to dinner, and you run together three times a week," she pointed out, surprised and a little . . .

What?

Not upset.

Unsettled?

"That doesn't mean we're going out. It just means we enjoy each other's company. Besides . . ." She poured the fudge into a pan. "We're both too busy for relationships."

For people who were too busy, they sure did seem to be spending a lot of time together.

Willow decided not to point that out. She didn't want to embarrass Janelle, and she didn't want to make her feel defensive. "You still might want to mention it to the girls, Mom. People talk and—"

"I know." That was it. Two words. But there was something in them that made Willow take a closer look at her mother's face.

She looked younger without makeup. Softer. She also looked upset, the commas that bracketed her mouth a little deeper, her eyes shadowed.

"What's wrong, Mom?"

"I need to ask you something, Willow, and I want you to be completely honest with me." She'd started another batch of fudge, was working through the recipe with ease.

Apparently, Willow really *was* the only Lamont without the magic touch.

"I'll try." Because if her mother had seen the twenty-thousand-dollar check, if she'd heard about it from Brenna or from Jax, if she asked questions about *that*, honesty might not be part of the discussion.

"No. Really. I need you to tell me the truth. Am I . . . difficult to talk to? Hard to confide in? Am I someone who people just don't . . . open up to?"

Those were questions she *wasn't* expecting. "What do you mean?"

"I'll take it from your lack of response that I am," Janelle said, pouring dark chocolate morsels into the fudge base with grim determination.

"I didn't say that. I'm just wondering why you're asking."

"I ran into Millicent yesterday."

"If she told you you're difficult to talk to, I think it's safe to say you can ignore her."

"I don't care what she thinks, and that's not what she said. She said . . ." She glanced at the door, then into the hallway, lowering her voice as she continued. "Did you know that Miracle's mother was cleaning Millicent's house? I guess she'd been hired as the housekeeper and was nearly a live-in."

"I'd heard that."

"And you also know she's sick and can't work."

Not a question, but Willow nodded. "Yes."

"That wasn't working for Millicent. You know how she is—everything beautiful and over-the-top. She likes her house to shine every minute of every day. So, of course, she hired someone else to come in until her regular housekeeper recovered."

"I'm not sure what this has to do with your question, Mom."

"She hired Angel."

Angel? Brenna and River's loudest, brashest guest?

"But . . . she's already working at the diner."

"She wanted a second income. She does have the

baby to support. And since she's young and seems to have an unlimited amount of energy, I don't think having two jobs will do her any harm."

"Maybe not." The fact was, Angel *was* young. She was also a hard worker. She was a good mother. If she had one major fault, it was that she liked to talk. About things. About people. About private matters that were better left unspoken. If she'd overheard Brenna telling River about the baby . . .

God! Had she told Millicent?

If she had, the entire town had probably heard the news by now.

"I'm sure you're right. She'll be just fine," she said, trying desperately to reroute the conversation to something that wasn't going to leave Janelle with hurt feelings and ruffled feathers.

"We'll help her out if she isn't. That's how our town is, but that's not what this conversation is about."

"No?" Willow grabbed butter from the walk-in and got busy cutting it into tablespoon-sized pieces. She wasn't sure if they needed it, but she absolutely knew she didn't want to look her mother in the eyes when she asked about the pregnancy.

And that was coming. She could feel it like a gale-force wind. So, yeah . . . butter cut into chunks, big bars of chocolate broken into smaller ones. Anything to keep her head down.

"Angel told Millicent something, and she told me."

"Sounds like gossip."

"It is."

"Then maybe you shouldn't repeat it."

"It was about River and Brenna."

"Mom—"

"Brenna's pregnant. Don't tell me you didn't know, because I'm sure she told you."

"There were extenuating circumstances."

"So she did. And I'm sure Adeline knows. Angel knew, so Millicent found out. It seems to me, the entire town knew about Brenna's pregnancy before I did."

"Angel must have overheard, Mom. I know Brenna was planning to tell you after she told River."

"She told you girls first? Before she told her husband? Now I feel even more left out."

"You weren't left out."

"I was just not told? Same thing, Willow. Obviously, I *am* difficult to talk to. My own daughter doesn't dare confide in me," she murmured.

"That's not true."

"It is. You know it. How much have you told me about what happened with Ken? How much did Brenna say about what Dan had done? Cheating on her, stealing from her?"

"We just don't want you to worry."

"Well, that just makes me worry more." She poured more fudge and turned to face Willow. "I love you girls, but Noah is right."

Noah.

Again.

Interesting.

"I need to have my own life. One that isn't tied so closely to you girls' accomplishments."

"Mom—"

"It's true, Willow. I've spent the past few decades trying to make sure you girls had happy, successful lives. But really, all I did was put a wedge between us. You were all fine without my input. You'll continue to be fine, because you're wonderful, hardworking people. Just like your father."

"And you."

She smiled. "I do work hard, and Noah says I should play hard too. He says that I should let down my hair sometimes, have some fun, enjoy these years when my girls are grown and doing great and I'm still young enough to hike and explore and visit exotic places."

That was three times now that she'd mentioned Noah, and Willow wasn't naïve enough to think it didn't matter.

"He's right. You've worked hard. You've sacrificed a lot to make sure we had good lives. There's nothing wrong with having a little fun now."

"Yes. Well, he's been saying that for months. Just like running, though, it took me a while to agree. But yesterday? After I heard my own daughter didn't want to tell me she was pregnant? I called Deanna Witt. She's a travel agent, you know."

"I didn't."

"She is, and she's been begging me to go on a cruise with her for five years."

"You're going on a cruise?!"

"An Alaskan cruise at the end of May. She's already booked it."

"Mom! That's wonderful!"

"It will be. Noah was right about me needing to take some time for myself. Maybe while I'm on the cruise, I can figure out what I've done wrong that Brenna . . ." She shrugged, pouring pecan-studded fudge into a pan.

"She didn't mean to hurt you." That, Willow knew, was the truth. Brenna and Janelle butted heads a lot, but neither would ever do something to knowingly hurt the other.

"You know that saying, 'Hurt people hurt people'?

I spent a lot of time thinking about that last night and wondering what I'd done to hurt Brenna. Because that's the only explanation I can think of for being kept in the dark. I hurt her, and she feels like she can't trust me."

"Mom—"

"It's okay, Willow. Really. It was a catalyst for a good change, right? Me on a cruise? Can you imagine?"

"You're going to have the time of your life." She dropped the butter into a bowl, told herself not to ask the question that was on the tip of her tongue.

She asked anyway, because she really wanted to know. "Will Noah be there?"

"Where?"

"On the cruise?"

"Of course not. I'm way too old for that sort of thing."

"You're not even close to old, Mom." She kissed Janelle's cheek and was rewarded with a smile.

"Honey, I'm fifty-six, and I'm feeling every bit of that, but thanks." She glanced at her watch and frowned. "I've got to go. I'm showing a property in an hour, and I can't show up dressed like this."

"You could."

"Not if I want to impress the client. He's looking at some retail space, and he has plenty of money to make it into the pub he's thinking of opening."

"In town?"

"Where else?"

"I didn't realize there was retail space available."

"There is. Right on the corner of Main and Wesley. That brick building that used to be a bead shop."

"It closed?"

"Not enough people in town are interested in

crafts. There will be a lot more interested in good pub food. Now, I really do have to leave. I've got a full schedule today, but tomorrow my day is wide open. I'll stop by in the morning to see how you and Miracle are getting along. Unless . . . you've got someone else coming to help out?"

"Just the nurse, but I'd be happy to have an experienced mother there."

"An experienced mother whose daughters don't tell her anything."

"We do, Mom. The thing is—"

"She can explain. Or not. When she's ready. Do me a favor. Don't tell her I know. I don't want her to think that I'm upset."

"You are upset."

"I don't want her to think it. She's pregnant. The last thing she needs to worry about are my feelings."

"I won't tell her."

"Promise?"

"Of course."

"Thanks, sweetie." She walked outside and closed the door, and Willow was alone in the kitchen, three pans of beautiful fudge sitting on the counter, her mother's words still ringing in her ears.

"I'm too old for that sort of thing."

But of course she wasn't. Willow could see it in her face and in her eyes.

Byron wasn't, either.

Willow's siblings weren't.

Willow seemed like the lone holdout, the one Lamont destined to always be too old for *that sort of thing.* She'd sure as heck felt like it when she and Ken were together—already settled in like a couple who'd been married for sixty years. That wouldn't have been so bad if there'd still been fun times doing interesting things together. All there had been were long nights watching ball games or talking sports or rehashing their busy days and crazy schedules. They'd made dinners for each other and talked politics or weather or work while they ate. It had all been so . . . nice. No arguments. No disagreements. Plenty of compromise. But she hadn't needed Ken, and he hadn't needed her.

Which was fine.

It was easy.

It might be what some people wanted.

But Willow? When she'd listened to her mother talk about the way Noah challenged her to be her best self and dared her to try new things, she knew exactly why it had been so easy to walk away from the only long-term relationship she'd ever been in.

"Enough," she grumbled, grabbing a cutter and pressing it into the peanut butter fudge. The cuts were clean, the fudge beautiful. Janelle had managed what Willow could not.

And not just with the fudge.

She frowned, cutting the second and the third batch.

She was happy for her mother. She was happy for her siblings, for her grandfather, for every love-besotted person in town. She was happy for herself, too, because she could have stayed with Ken. She could have accepted the mediocre relationship and called it good. She could have continued pretending that what they had was enough. She could have spent the next fifty years returning to a silent house, a silent partner, a guy who was more interested in the television than he was in her.

She could have.

She hadn't.

And she was ecstatic to be free, to have no obligations, to go home to the silence and not have to struggle to fill it.

She dropped the dirty pot into the sink and filled it with water, knowing damn well she was lying.

Truth? She'd gotten a glimpse of what *that sort of thing* really was. She'd felt it in the gentleness of Jax's hands, the heat of his lips, the warmth of his breath against her cheek. She'd heard it in every word he'd said to her, all the little secrets they'd shared, all the big ones.

Dot.

His sister's name.

She'd been thinking about that a lot these past few days. Every time she went to the hospital, every time she held Miracle, she thought about Jax holding his baby sister while she died. That was the kind of thing a person never got over. She understood that. Just like she understood why he'd stayed away.

Yeah.

She understood, but she'd still thought about calling him a dozen times. She'd talked herself out of it, because she didn't want to start something that would only break both of their hearts.

It would. How could it not? They were both a little broken.

But sometimes broken things were the most beautiful.

And he was.

She glanced at the phone, tempted again. By him, and by the thought of what they might have together.

That's all it was, though—a pretty little daydream that wasn't doing a darn thing for either of them.

She scowled, dragging more ingredients from the pantry and starting the fudge all over again.

Aunt Vera had a hankering for fudge.

At least that's what she'd been saying every other minute of every other day since Sunday. Jax had ignored her. He knew matchmaking when he saw it, and he'd seen it plenty when it came to his aunt. She'd been trying to set him up with daughters of friends, granddaughters of friends, cousins of friends, and acquaintances of friends since he'd moved back.

Now she wanted to set him up with Willow.

Usually, her efforts amused him.

Not today.

Today, he was tired. He'd worked graveyard and then attended a preliminary hearing for Phoebe Tanner. She'd had a court-appointed attorney with her and had sat silently through the proceedings. She'd been wearing another homemade dress, her hair pulled back in a long braid that made her look like a middle-school kid. He wanted to see her as the villain in the story, but she'd looked more like a victim. By the time he'd left the courthouse and made the hour-long drive to town, he'd been ready to call it quits for the day, but Aunt Vera had begged him to stop for dinner, so there he was, sitting at the dining room table, shoving meat loaf in his mouth and hoping to God he didn't fall asleep in his mashed potatoes.

"If I just had a *small* piece of fudge," his aunt was

saying, her eyes big behind thick-lensed glasses, her short hair fluffing around her head. "Just a *little* one, mind you, I'd feel like the meal was complete."

"It's seven. The shop closed an hour ago," he pointed out.

"Oh, I know that. I placed my order a couple of hours ago. Just one little piece of fudge and then a pound of brittle for you and Jim." She stood, bustling to the stove and scooping more potatoes onto her plate. She was a tiny thing. Barely five feet and just under a hundred pounds. She ate like a linebacker, though. As a matter of fact, the only time Jax had ever seen his aunt skip a meal was when Uncle Jim had been in the hospital.

"I may have to skip that for tonight. I have a lot of work to do on the house, and I'm planning to go straight there. No stops after this." Jax loved his aunt, but he wasn't going to Chocolate Haven to pick up chocolates. Not anytime, but especially not when the place was closed.

He'd already gotten too close to Willow.

He'd already let his thoughts go in directions they shouldn't. The last thing he needed, the last thing he should want was to be alone with her.

"No worries. Byron said he'd have the order delivered."

"He's stopping by?" Jim looked up from the plate of food he'd been picking at. He'd once been a big guy. Huge muscles and broad shoulders. Now he was a shell of himself—thin and weak, but still madly in love with his wife and completely determined to do everything he'd once been able to.

"Not tonight. Someone else is bringing the order."

"Should I ask who?" Jax asked, carrying his plate to the sink.

"Oh . . . probably one of the girls."

"One that you specifically requested?"

"Why would I do something like that?" she hedged, her cheeks red.

"Because you've got a desperate need to see me married off, and there's only one Lamont sister who is still available?"

"I'll have you know that Byron suggested Willow bring the candy. Who was I to argue with the shop owner?"

"Aunt Vera, I love you to pieces, but your match-making efforts are never going to work."

"I'm not matchmaking, and even if I were, what would be wrong with that? You're thirty-one. A wonderful, handsome, successful young man, and you deserve to have a woman in your life who appreciates that."

"I do have one in my life." He finished washing his plate and set it in the drying rack.

"Really? Why didn't you tell us before?" She grabbed Jim's hand, her eyes wide with happiness. "Did you hear that, Jim? He's finally found someone! Who is she, Jax? Anyone we know?"

"That's a pretty good possibility. Since she's you."

Jim laughed. "Good one, kid!"

"Good one? It was horrible. Getting my hopes up like that, only to dash them!" Vera said, but she was smiling, and Jax knew he'd amused and pleased her.

Good. Because he was about to *dis*please her.

He was leaving.

Before Willow arrived.

If that made him a coward, so be it. He knew his strengths, and he knew his limitations. He also knew

damn well that he couldn't keep spending time with
Willow and not fall for her.

Hell! He'd probably already fallen.

He grabbed his coat from the back of his chair,
kissed Vera's cheek. "I need to get home. Thanks for
a fantastic dinner."

"But . . . you haven't had dessert!"

"You can have my share."

"But Jax, really! You and Willow would be perfect
together."

"I know you mean well, but I'm not looking for
anyone to be perfect with," he said gently, because she
did mean well.

She just didn't understand.

Honestly, there'd been a few nights this week when
he hadn't understood either. Intellectually, he knew
that there was a greater chance of Willow's getting
struck by lightning than there was of her being tar-
geted and killed because of Jax's job.

In his heart, though, deep down in that pain-filled
empty spot that had once held his parents and his
siblings, he was still afraid to risk it.

He opened the door, ready to inhale cold fresh air
and let it wipe away the scent of blood and death and
fear. He smelled . . . chocolate. Rum-soaked cherries.

Willow.

She'd just reached the top of the porch stairs, and
she stopped there, her eyes wide with surprise and
pleasure.

She didn't say anything, just smiled, holding up a
cream-colored box.

"Fudge," she said. "Peanut brittle. And six Bitter
Cherry Bonbons."

She handed him the box, her fingers brushing his. And just that touch was enough to drive every thought out of his head, every worry from his heart.

He should have told her that. Right then. While they were standing on the porch, the quiet sounds of small-town life drifting around them. While he was looking into her eyes and into her face, and thinking that he could have studied both forever and still not learned enough.

"The bonbons?" She spoke into the silence. "I made them just for you. Tell your uncle and aunt I said hello, okay? See you around."

Then she turned and headed back down the stairs, her wool coat billowing out, her oversize purse slapping against her side, her hair bouncing against her collar. All of her focused on walking away.

And all of Jax was focused on not going after her.

Chapter Fourteen

She'd left because she'd had to.

Not because she had to get to the hospital. Which she did. Not because Granddad was waiting for her to return to the shop. He wasn't.

No. She'd left because if she'd stood on Vera's porch for one more second, she'd have done something stupid.

Like . . .

Smooth the frown line from between Jax's brows.

Knead the tension from his shoulders.

Run her hand over his thick blond hair.

Press her lips to his. Not just because she wanted to kiss him, but because she wanted to see if what she'd felt before was as earth-shattering as it had seemed.

"That," she muttered, "would have been really stupid."

"What?"

She whirled around, realized that Jax was right behind her.

"God! You scared me!"

"Sorry." He still had the chocolates in his hand, and he was still frowning. "I wasn't being all that quiet."

"My thoughts were pretty loud. They probably masked the sound of your footsteps."

He smiled at that. "What were you thinking about?"

"You." She answered honestly, because she didn't see any reason to deny it.

"Were they good thoughts?"

"Do you care?"

"Of course I care, Willow. That's the whole damn problem," he muttered, taking her arm and leading her toward Main Street.

"In that case, they were good thoughts."

"Want to share one of them? I need a distraction."

"From what?"

"You," he said simply, and she laughed, because she thought it was a joke.

Only Jax wasn't laughing. He wasn't even smiling. He was watching her, his gaze skimming the navy dress she'd worn to work, the cute little boots she'd shoved her feet into before she'd walked to Vera's place, the scarf she'd tossed around her neck. That all would have been just fine, except his gaze shifted to her face, settled on her lips. Just for a moment. Just long enough for Willow to remember the way it had felt to be in his arms.

"Maybe you should bring those chocolates to Vera," she suggested, her pulse racing with a longing she had no business feeling. Not for a guy who'd made it very clear there'd never be more than right now.

"I would, but you said the bonbons were for me."

"They are."

"Then how about we share?" He veered to the right, cutting across Williamsburg Lane and out onto

School Run. The elementary school was at the corner of the street. Empty now, the windows dark.

They bypassed the building, walking across the blacktop and then into grass still wet from the day's rain. She didn't ask where they were going. She almost didn't need to know. She was with Jax, and as dangerous as the darkness seemed, as alarming as the shadowy alcoves of the doors and windows, she felt . . .

Safe?

That surprised her, and she would have rolled it around in her head for a while, tried to decide what it meant, but the schoolyard was straight ahead, the old swing set still exactly the same as it had been when she attended school there.

"Remember playing here when you were a kid?" Jax asked as he pulled her down onto a bench that faced the playground.

"How could I not? We all lived for recess. It was the one time we got to run around and act like lunatics." She eyed the old swing set, the metal slide, the old-fashioned monkey bars. "I bet this thing was put in in the fifties. There's probably some code the school is violating by keeping it up."

"Probably."

"I didn't notice how old it was when I was a kid. I didn't notice how small it was, either."

"I'm pretty sure the slide was at least fifteen feet tall the year I got here. Now it looks more like four." He opened the box, handed her one of the bonbons, and then popped one in his mouth.

"What are we doing, Jax?" she asked, putting hers back in the box. She wasn't hungry. Not for chocolates. She'd taste-tested about sixteen pounds of fudge

in the last few days, and she'd had about all she could
take of candy.

"Sitting on a bench. Sharing a treat."

"You know that's not what I mean."

"Maybe," he admitted, lifting another chocolate and
eating it.

That was it.

Just maybe.

"I missed seeing you this week," she said quietly,
telling another truth. One she didn't think he wanted
to hear.

He didn't respond, just set the box on the bench
and stood.

When he held out his hand, she took it, and when
he pulled her into his arms, she went willingly.

There was no kiss.

No warm caress.

Just Jax, swaying to a rhythm that only he could
hear.

She didn't question it, just let herself move with
him, her head pressed to his chest, his heart beating
steadily beneath her ear.

They were dancing in the moonlight without
music, and she didn't think there'd ever been a
moment so beautiful. If it could have lasted forever,
she would have let it, but life was waiting beyond the
moonlight and the wet grass and the old-fashioned
swing set.

"Jax," she said, and the moment was broken, the
dance finished.

He stilled, and she thought he'd step away, but his
hands moved from her back to her shoulder and then
to her face. Warm palms to her cool cheeks, and his
lips pressed to hers in a tender, soul-searing kiss.

She wanted to cry from the beauty of it.

She wanted to cry because she thought that was all there would ever be. Just that one silent dance and that last beautiful kiss.

She wanted to cry, but she wouldn't, because this wasn't a tragedy. It was a bump in the road, a little dip in the smooth path she'd thought she'd be on after she'd left Ken.

"I need to get to the hospital," she said, her voice husky with longing and with tears.

She'd spent years searching for peace. She'd spent a lifetime searching for solace. She'd found it in Jax's arms, but she wasn't going to beg him to give her more than he could.

"I'll take you."

"You don't have to do that."

"I know."

"I don't want you to do it," she said, and he raised a brow.

"No?"

Yes!

That's what she wanted to say. Of course she wanted him to come with her. Of course she wanted to spend more time with him. She wanted more dances and more kisses and more of everything she thought they could be together.

"I've got the infant car seat installed in my car. It's a pain in the butt to get in properly, so it's better if I just drive myself."

"You're upset," he said, pulling the edges of her coat together, his fingers sliding along her nape as he tugged her hair from the back of it.

"I'm practical."

"Meaning?"

"I want more than this, Jax. I'm not going to pretend I don't."

"That's good, because I'm not into women who pretend."

"And I'm not into relationships that aren't going to be more than a few stolen kisses and a couple of dances in the moonlight." She grabbed the chocolate, handed it to him. "I like you. A lot. If you want more than this, I'm all for it. Otherwise, let's just call it a lifetime and say good-bye."

He didn't say a word.

She hadn't expected him to.

But she'd hoped.

God! Had she ever hoped!

She walked back the way they'd come, knowing he was following her. She made it all the way to Main Street before he moved into step beside her, took her arm again, his fingers cupped lightly around her bicep.

"I keep telling myself to stay away from you, Willow. I keep listing all of the reasons why we're not a good idea."

"I figured that was the case." She didn't look at him. She couldn't. She didn't want to see the darkness in his eyes, the sadness of all his losses. She didn't want to be pulled any deeper into his heart, because she knew she wasn't going to be allowed to stay there.

"Did you also figure that I wouldn't be able to stay away? That I wouldn't be able to come up with one idea that wasn't based on what-ifs and speculation?"

"Jax—"

"Look." He turned to face her, holding her still when she would have walked away. "I know what you want. Promises that I'm willing to keep going with this, assurance that we're not just going to have today or tomorrow. That there's some bright and wonderful future out there for us."

"I didn't ask you for that."

"But it *is* what you want."

She wasn't going to deny it, so she kept silent, waiting while he studied her face, touched her cheek, his fingers trailing down the column of her neck and resting near the hollow of her throat.

"See?" he said gently. "It is what you want, but every time I think about the future, I see the past. That's my issue. Not yours. I'm working on it, but I can't promise I'm going to be done anytime soon."

"At least you're honest," she said, and he sighed.

"I didn't follow you so that I could piss you off again."

"I'm not pissed off."

"Then what are you?"

"Hungry for something that doesn't taste like chocolate, smell like chocolate, look like chocolate." It was a cop-out, because she didn't want to tell him that she was hurt. That she'd wanted to be enough to wipe out all the bad memories.

"We can stop somewhere on the way to the hospital," he said as if they'd already agreed that he would go with her.

They hadn't.

And he shouldn't, but being with him was so much nicer than being alone.

"Don't you need to bring the chocolates to Vera?"

"She'll understand if they arrive a little late."

"My grandfather won't. He told me to bring them there stat."

"He'll understand too."

They'd reached the shop.

Byron had already closed up for the night, and a lone light glowed above the door. Everything else was dark as pitch, the blackness behind the windows filled with monsters and memories.

Those were the things that kept her from walking away from Jax. Those were the things that allowed her to understand his reservations and his fear.

They were also the things she hated most.

She hurried past, knowing she was running and not caring. She wanted to get to her car, climb in, go find some real food. Eat enough to fill the emptiness.

Only she wasn't sure it was her stomach that was empty.

The hollow ache seemed to be coming from somewhere in the region of her heart.

Jax jogged behind Willow as she sprinted through the alley, ran into the back lot, and jumped into her car. He figured the demons were chasing her, and he wanted to pull her to a stop, tell her to take a deep breath, and let them catch her.

Sometimes you had to face them down to be rid of them.

He knew that for a fact.

He also knew that saying anything would be about as hypocritical as claiming to be a teetotaler while guzzling one-hundred-proof vodka behind closed doors.

He had no right to talk.

Not when he'd just refused to tell her what she wanted to hear because of *his* demons. He was running

from them still. Even after all these years. He wasn't
proud of that, but he'd been as honest as he could.
He'd given what he could.

He'd wanted to give more.

He'd held her in the moonlight, felt her melting
into him, and he'd known that if he'd allowed it, they
could become something more than two people living
separate lives. They could become *us, we, them.* Two
people who were so connected, they finished each
other's sentences, felt each other's joy and sorrow
and pain. Needed each other as much as they'd ever
needed anything or anyone.

Hell! That was already happening, and they weren't
even trying. Look at them now, getting in her car,
heading off to get some food and then to pick up a
baby who didn't belong to either of them. They were
drawn to each other despite their demons.

Or maybe because of them.

"What do you feel like eating?" Willow asked. She
was trying to act like she hadn't just run the hundred-
meter dash, but her voice was shaking, her hand trembling as she shoved the key into the ignition.

He should have ignored both those things.

He should have just told her that he'd already
eaten, and he wasn't hungry, and that she could go
wherever she wanted.

He touched her leg instead, that bit of thigh right
above her knee, and his hand just . . . settled there, his
palm resting against warm, silky fabric and firm,
sinewy muscle.

"It's okay," he said, his thumb caressing the side of
her knee.

She stilled, and he could feel the tension seeping
out of her, the fear flying away.

"God!" she whispered. "How do you do that?"

"What?" He let his hand fall away, because if he didn't, he'd do more than touch her thigh and caress her knee. If he didn't, he'd be pulling her closer, and taking way more than one kiss.

"Make me forget all the things I'm afraid of." She turned on the engine, pulled out of the parking lot, sighed. "Well? Where's it going to be? Are you in the mood for burgers? Salad? Chicken?"

Her voice had gone from fearful to chipper, from sincere to fake. He knew the difference. Just like he knew when someone was feigning emotion she didn't feel.

He wasn't going to point it out.

They could play this game for a while. The one where they were just friends going out to dinner together.

"I already had meat loaf."

"Did Vera cook?"

"If she hadn't, it would have been canned soup."

"What'd she make with it? Potatoes?"

"And string beans. Homemade rolls."

"Tell me more," she moaned as she pulled into the drive-thru at the Daily Grind. "Because I don't have the energy to stop in the diner and get a real meal. I'm going to settle for coffee and a muffin."

"I could run in the diner for you, or we could stop somewhere in Spokane. A fast-food place maybe. That way you wouldn't have to get out of the car."

"Bite your tongue, Jax."

"You don't eat fast food?"

"I did. Until River entered my sister's life. Now I have been schooled on the value of a good meal, and convinced that fast food isn't really food."

"And coffee and muffins are?"

"Probably not, but they're quick, and I need a pick-me-up that doesn't include chocolate." She placed her order. Two coffees. Two muffins. Blueberry. One shortbread cookie. No chocolate in any of it, but there sure as heck was plenty of caffeine and sugar.

"Planning to energy-up before bringing Miracle home?" he asked as she dug in her purse and pulled out the money to pay.

"You bet your life I am. But one cup of coffee should be enough. I don't drink it that often." She grabbed the cup carrier and a white bag from the barista. "One is for you. You're looking a little tired."

"Thanks?" he said.

"I didn't say you didn't also look good. Did you work graveyard again?"

"Yes. Did the dark circles give it away?"

"No. Alison did. She said court had been scheduled for the afternoon to accommodate your schedule. How did it go?"

"Court? About like I expected."

"I don't have any idea what to expect. I'm scheduled to give testimony next week. I hate to do it. Every time I think about the way Phoebe looked, sitting on the floor of the hospital . . ." She shook her head, handed him one of the muffins. "I keep telling myself she did something wrong, and she has to pay for it, but she looked like a little girl, and all I wanted to do was mother her."

"She didn't look any more mature at the court-house today."

"Were her parents there?"

"Were they supposed to be?"

"I was hoping they would be. Alison said she spent

a half a day tracking them down. She thought Phoebe could use their support. The mother seemed like she might be willing to be there."

"And I'm sure the father put an end to that idea. He didn't seem like the kind of guy who'd stand by his kids once they broke free of his control."

"You met him?"

"Briefly. She's better off with Clementine."

"Was she in court too?"

"Different court date. I'm hoping the judge is lenient. She didn't know Phoebe was going to abandon her baby, and she didn't skip town when she found out that Phoebe was turning herself in. That's what the two guys they were living with did."

"Their husbands?"

"Elias and Phoebe were married. Supposedly."

"They weren't?"

"There's no record of it. No marriage license. Nothing to prove it. I'm thinking Elias had his pastor perform the ceremony, but they didn't get the state involved. Not that it matters. In Phoebe's mind they're married, and she can't understand why Elias ran off."

"I could answer that question for her," she muttered, taking a sip of coffee. "He's a coward."

"Not in her eyes, Willow. In her eyes, he's a hero. He helped her escape the fanatical control of her family. Now she's expecting him to help her escape this." He'd interviewed her. He'd heard all the childish assumptions and naïve beliefs. Elias had built himself up in her mind. Either that, or she'd done all the building up. Either way, she was going to be disappointed.

If Elias had been around, Jax would have been

tempted to shake some sense into him. A young
woman like Phoebe needed someone in her life who
could help her understand how the world worked.
Faith was great. Belief was wonderful. Having a relationship with God? That was the thing that had gotten
Jax through some of his toughest times.

But . . .

A person shouldn't be walking through life with
blinders on. It was a really good way to get sideswiped.

"That's sad," Willow said.

"The whole thing is sad." He sipped the coffee and
held the muffin. He wasn't in the mood for sweets. He
was in the mood for Willow. Her soft skin and velvety
lips, they were an addiction he needed to break.

So far, he hadn't been successful.

"At least Miracle should be okay," she said. "Unless
I somehow screw up her care, and she isn't."

She hadn't touched her coffee or the food, and he
wondered if she was really as hungry as she'd said or
if nerves had stolen her appetite.

"Are you nervous?"

"About bringing her home? Absolutely. I think
anyone would be. That's why I want to get to the hospital early. The nurse is going over a lot of the discharge
instructions with Alison. Alison is planning to go over
them with me."

"But, you want to hear them firsthand?"

"It makes sense, right?"

He didn't think she was actually looking for reas-
surance, but he gave it anyway. "Yes."

"That's what I thought. Of course, it's not like I
haven't already had a ton of training. I know how to
feed her. How to change her. How to change her
bandages and make sure nothing is getting infected.

I was given a packet yesterday. Pages of information about Miracle's heart defect and the surgery and what to expect during the next stage of recovery."

"You have help lined up, right?"

"Alison has everything on a spreadsheet. Nurse visits. Therapist visits."

"For you or Miracle?"

"Probably me," she said with a quiet laugh. "She's worried that I'll be overwhelmed taking care of a post-surgical infant."

"Will you be?"

"I won't know until I try." She merged onto the highway, her face pale in the light from passing cars. She had high cheekbones like her sister Brenna, a sharp chin like her mother, and eyes that were as soft as her sister Adeline's. The family resemblance was pretty incredible, and he tried to remember her father. Tried to see the resemblance to him in her face. Brent Lamont had had red hair. That's about all he could remember. That and his kind smile.

"You're staring," she said quietly.

"Just thinking you look like your family."

"Is that a compliment or a criticism?"

"Why does it have to be either?" He lifted the second coffee cup and handed it to her. "Drink your coffee, Willow. You're looking tired."

"Thanks," she muttered, taking a quick sip and then returning it to the carrier.

"I didn't say you didn't also look good."

She smiled, but her eyes were shadowed, her hands tight on the steering wheel.

"You're still upset."

"I'm just wondering what we're doing, sitting in this

car together, going to the hospital, pretending we're friends."

"Are we pretending?"

"Are we friends?"

"Why wouldn't we be?"

"Jax, we can't be alone together for two seconds without ending up in each other's arms."

"We could try harder."

"Why would we want to?"

"You ask difficult questions."

"I'm an attorney. It's what I'm trained to do." She was trying to keep it light, and he needed to let her, because that was what he wanted.

Or what he should want.

"How about we just take one day at a time, okay?"

"How about you hand me the shortbread cookie?" she countered. "And grab me a napkin, too. I don't want to get crumbs all over my dress."

"Who's going to notice if you do?"

"Whatever press happens to be hanging around the hospital hoping for a picture."

"They're being kept outside. I talked to the Spokane County Sheriff's Department, and they've got deputies at the hospital, making sure there aren't any problems." He gave her the cookie, looked in the bag for napkins. "Sorry. No napkins."

"Check my purse. Front pocket. I usually have a package of tissue. That'll work."

"Most women don't like other people digging through their purses," he commented as he did what she asked.

"I'm not most women. Plus, there's nothing in my purse but a wallet, tissue, emergency lipstick—"

"And a check for twenty thousand dollars," he cut

in, because he'd pulled out the package of tissue and the damn check was static clinging to its face. Folded, but he recognized the color and the size.

"I forgot I put that there."

"Were you trying to forget it altogether?" He handed her a handful of tissue, and he tucked the check in his pocket.

"What are you doing?"

"What you can't. I'm going to call the guy who issued the check, and I'm going to find out what he wants."

"Jax, I don't need you to—"

"Right. You don't. If we were friends, I'd take that into consideration. If we were lovers, I'd probably have already called. We're not either, and I'm an officer of the law. This reeks of a payoff, and if it is, someone in Eric's family knows what he did. I'm obligated to find out who."

"Bull crap," she spat. "The statute of limitations ran out years ago. Even if you could find evidence to prove they were accessories after the crime, there wouldn't be a thing that could be done about it."

"Then call it a moral obligation. Maybe bad blood runs in the family. If it does, better to know now before anyone else is hurt."

"Eric's brother knew," she said, all the irritation gone from her voice. She just sounded . . . defeated.

"Are you sure?".

"If he didn't know, he suspected. Eric lost his license the year he worked for Granddad. Since his family lived outside of town, Josh used to pick him up after work. He was there that night. I know he saw me come out of the shop, and I know he noticed my torn dress and my ripped tights. He called my name and asked if I was okay, but I just kept walking, and he just let me go."

"That bastard."

"His brother's crime wasn't his fault."

"His hiding it was."

"You know how their father was. He wanted everything perfect."

"Are you making excuses for them, Willow? Because if you are, I sure as hell don't want to hear it."

"What are you so angry about? It happened almost twenty years ago, and it happened to me. Not you." She tossed the cookie back in the bag, her hand shaking with anger or fear or some combination of them both.

"You're not going to tell me that it doesn't matter anymore, are you?" he asked, forcing the anger out of his voice, because it wasn't directed at her, and she didn't deserve it. "Because I was the one sitting beside you on the floor in Chocolate Haven, remember? I was the one in the car when you woke up screaming from a nightmare. I held your shoulders while you puked, remember? Maybe no one else knows the truth. Maybe there's not another person in this world who understands, but I sure as hell do, and I'm not going to forget it. I'm not going to sweep it under the rug. I'm not going to pretend that it didn't happen."

She didn't say a word.

Didn't make a sound.

Didn't tell him to give her back the check or to mind his own business or to get lost.

He thought they were done. That he'd pissed her off to the point that their dance in the moonlight wouldn't matter, their kiss under the stars would mean nothing.

Maybe he was glad.

Maybe it was for the best.

He was trying to convince himself of that when she reached for his hand, her fingers twining with his. Her skin was cool and clammy, and she was trembling, and he wanted to take back every word he'd said, shove the check back in her purse, forget what he knew and what he felt obligated to do.

"You okay?" he asked, and she nodded, but she didn't release his hand. Not as they reached the Spokane city limits, not as they drove into the hospital parking lot. Not until she parked the car and opened the door, and even then, he felt like she would rather have stayed in the car, holding his hand.

Chapter Fifteen

Mothering was hard work.

Willow had always known that.

Now she was living it.

Endless bottles. Endless diaper changes. Endless nights when she and Miracle barely slept. Six days into mothering, and Willow wasn't sure how any parent survived.

She sure as heck didn't think she was going to.

Three a.m. and Miracle was up again, crying in the little bassinet that Willow had moved into her bedroom. Sure, the nursery was nice, but getting up and leaving the room sixteen million times every night was not conducive to good rest.

Okay.

That was a slight exaggeration. Miracle didn't get up sixteen million times. It was more like three. It just felt like more.

She rolled out of bed, shoved her feet into slippers, and shuffled to the bassinet, not bothering with the light.

She'd fed the baby an hour ago, so she knew she wasn't hungry.

"Hey, sweet pea," she said, lifting Miracle to her shoulder. The stitches had been removed a couple of days ago. There were no more bandages. No more monitors. No more twice-weekly visits from the nurse, either.

Thanks to Miracle's stellar appetite, she was gaining weight like a champ, her little fingers and toes dimpled. Her thighs and arms filling out. The nurse would be coming out once a week for the next month, and then every other week after that.

Miracle might still be with Willow then.

Or she might not.

Things were still up in the air. One thing was for sure: She wasn't going back to Phoebe. The judge had revoked her parental rights and granted custody to the state.

It wasn't unexpected, but from what Willow had seen in news reports, Phoebe was devastated. The only good news was that the judge seemed to be sympathetic, and it didn't look like the young mother would have to serve time behind bars. Currently she was living with Clementine, working for Millicent, and trying to get her life back on track.

At least that's what Janelle had said.

She'd been out to see Phoebe. She'd also bought so many little girl outfits for Miracle that there wasn't room in the apartment for them.

She was getting too attached.

Willow had tried to warn her.

Of course, that had been like the pot calling the kettle black since she was getting too attached too.

"It's because you're so sweet," she whispered, kissing Miracle's forehead and laying her back in the bassinet.

She *was* a sweet baby.

Despite the late night and early morning feedings
and the million daily diaper changes, she was mostly
content, mostly happy, mostly easy.

And Willow was falling in love with her.

Just like she was supposed to.

Mothering her.

Just like she was supposed to.

Thinking about a month or two or five or a year
down the road . . .

Which she really wasn't supposed to do.

This was a short-term placement.

Alison had made that clear. Now that the judge had
made Miracle a ward of the state, it was just a matter
of time before an adoptive family was found and she
was placed in a new home.

That was a good thing, something to be celebrated.
The sooner she was in her permanent home, the
better. Willow should be jumping for joy and cheering
the loudest.

She was doing both those things.

Really.

She was.

But . . .

She'd miss Miracle when she was gone.

The baby filled a hole in her life that she hadn't realized was there. She'd never thought of herself as
overly maternal. When she'd decided to foster kids,
she'd been picturing tweens and teens, not infants. So
the feelings she had for Miracle had taken her by surprise. She'd expected to love her. She'd expected to
feel protective and maternal toward her, but she
hadn't expected to feel like her mom.

She frowned, all of her sleepiness suddenly gone.

She was wide awake, and anxious with nothing to think about except the day that she'd have to say good-bye.

Maybe Jax had been right when he'd warned her not to fall for the baby. At this point, he'd probably tell her he'd been wrong, that she should love Miracle and treat her like her own. He'd probably also say that she shouldn't worry about the future. That she should just enjoy the days she had.

Maybe she'd ask him the next time she saw him.

She wasn't sure when that would be. They didn't make plans together. They didn't go on walks or sit on benches or dance silently in the moonlight. He'd been around the past few days, stopping in for visits, walking into the chocolate shop to buy fudge or brittle or bonbons. He'd come to the apartment twice. Once to bring a baby blanket that Vera had made. Once to bring meat loaf and mashed potatoes. Because he knew she was sick of chocolate.

That's what he'd said, and she'd smiled, because it was what she knew he expected.

She guessed they were trying the friend thing, seeing each other casually, asking about each other's days, not intruding into private matters.

Like the check and the guy who'd sent it.

Jax hadn't returned it to her.

She hadn't asked.

So that was always between them. Even though she didn't want it to be. She wanted to forget it, and she wanted to forget the way he'd looked and the way he'd sounded when he'd told her he was going to find out why it had been sent. She wanted to forget how much she'd needed to hold on to him, to ground herself with his strength and his compassion.

She hadn't wanted to need him, but she did.

And she missed him.

Even though he was coming for visits. Even though he was smiling and being friendly and treating her like they were buddies.

"And that's okay, because he doesn't want to be anything more than that, and you don't want to be clingy and needy and immature. So go ahead and miss him. Just don't let him know it, because you'll just end up looking like a fool, and he'll just end up feeling guilty," she said out loud, because she needed to hear the words, and she needed to believe them.

She covered Miracle with a light blanket and walked out of the room. Tea would be good, and she started the pot, the light in the kitchen making her feel marginally better. It would be dawn soon, and her mother would be arriving at six. Willow had to be in the shop early. Because of Byron.

He'd left town again.

This time for the weekend. He and a few of his buddies were going on a road trip.

Friday and Saturday and part of Sunday. She could expect him back on Monday. He'd said it like it didn't matter, acted like she had everything under control. When she'd protested, he'd reminded her that Lamont fudge ran through her veins.

Maybe, but having it running through her veins wasn't going to help her make fifty pounds of fudge for Jenny Bates's bridal shower. A half pound for each of her guests. And she wanted three hundred chocolate-dipped pretzels served in pretty silver boxes that she'd provided herself. All by this Sunday. Which meant extra time in the kitchen, and more wasted ingredients, because Willow still hadn't perfected the fudge. Fortunately, she had perfected the pretzels. They were done, wrapped up in boxes and ready to go.

But the fudge?

Yeah. *No.*

It wasn't happening.

She'd tried.

God knew she had, but no matter how carefully she measured, no matter how carefully she watched the temperature, no matter what she did, the fudge would not turn out.

So she was going in at six, and she was working on the fudge, because Brenna and Adeline both had plans for the weekend. Chase hadn't been given access to the fudge recipe, and Janelle was more interested in cooing at the baby than stirring up batches of chocolate. That left her, and she wasn't going to fail. Not this time, because there was too much riding on it. One hundred people who may or may not have ever had the family fudge before. She had to make a good impression, because good impressions led to more customers.

And bad impressions?

They could drive away old customers and new ones.

"What a mess," she muttered, pouring hot water over a tea bag and tensing when Miracle started to cry again.

It was going to be one of those nights.

Barely any sleep for either of them.

She waited a minute, listening to see if the crying

geared up or calmed down. When it continued, she grabbed the baby carrier from the nursery and strapped it on.

If she was going to be awake, she might as well make herself useful. No way was she going to make the fudge while she was carrying Miracle around, but she could read the recipe again, see if she could figure out exactly what she was doing wrong.

Nothing. You just don't have the magic touch.

The thought whispered through her mind as she wrapped Miracle in a blanket and settled her in the carrier. She ignored it. There was nothing magic about the fudge. She was making a mistake somewhere. She just needed to set her mind to the task of figuring out what the mistake was.

Not the temperature. She was certain of that.

Not the ingredients. She measured them to the quarter ounce.

Not the—

Someone knocked on the door, the light rap making her heart trip and race.

No one visited at this time of morning.

Ever.

The knock reminded her of the one she'd heard the night she and Jax had found Miracle. This time, though, she didn't think there was a young girl waiting on the stoop, a sick infant in a box in her arms.

Willow flipped off the light, moving out of the living room and into the hall, the nightmare clawing at her mind, daring her to let go of control, run screaming into her room, call the police.

Call Jax.

That was what she really wanted to do.

And she didn't see why she shouldn't. He was close. Just a few blocks away. He could be there quickly.

More important, he *would* be there quickly.

If she needed him.

And maybe she wouldn't. Maybe whoever had knocked would go away.

Another soft rap, and she grabbed her cell phone, dialed Jax's number as quickly as her fear-numb fingers would allow.

He answered on the first ring, his voice groggy with sleep. "Hello?"

"It's me."

"Willow?"

"Yes."

"What's wrong?"

"There's someone at my door."

"Doing what?" He sounded more awake now, and she could picture him getting up, pulling on jeans and a T-shirt, shoving his feet into shoes.

"Knocking."

"Don't answer it."

"I wasn't planning to."

"I'm on my way. Stay on the phone, okay?"

"Yes."

Whoever it was knocked again.

This time more loudly.

The baby startled and started crying, and Jax said something Willow couldn't hear. Her heart was beating too loudly, the hollow pounding in her ears mixing with the sound of Miracle's cries and drowning out everything else.

"Shhhh," she soothed, her focus on the door, on the handle that seemed to be turning.

Was it turning?

Oh God! Was it going to open? Was—

"Ms. Lamont?" a woman called, and the doorknob rattled as if whoever was out there was trying to get in. "Willow?"

"I've called the police," she responded.

"Oh. No. There's no need for that. I just . . . I wanted to see my grandbaby, and it took me a while to find my way here."

Grandbaby?

Was she Phoebe's mother?

"I'm sorry. I can't—"

"Open the door!" a man shouted, and she screamed, jumping backward, nearly stumbling in her haste to get away.

"I said open it!" he yelled again, pounding on the door with so much force she thought it might break.

The phone dropped from her hand and she wrapped both arms around the carrier and the baby, running into her room, slamming the door, the nightmare that had been chasing her for years finally catching up to her.

Jax sped into Chocolate Haven's parking lot, squealing to a stop a few inches from an old VW van. He could still hear the echo of Willow's scream. It pounded through his skull, zipped through his blood, filled him with adrenaline.

He'd heard screams like that before.

He'd heard the silence, too. The one that came after the scream. The one that, all those years ago, had signaled the end of everything Jax had loved.

He gritted his teeth, jumping from the truck and

racing into the alley. He could hear sirens, and he knew Kane and Susan were on the way. He'd called for backup while he was sprinting to the truck, because Willow's scream hadn't been one of surprise. It had been filled with stark terror.

God! Please let her be okay.

If he was too late, if she died because he hadn't gotten there in time, he wouldn't be able to forgive himself. He wouldn't be able to look in the mirror every day and face the man he saw there. He wouldn't be able to forget that he'd denied them everything they could have been together and that it still hadn't been enough to save her.

He was halfway up the staircase when he noticed them.

Two black shadows beside the Dumpster, still as stone and completely out of place. At first, he thought they were trash bags, leaning against the metal container.

He almost ignored them, almost continued up the stairs and to the apartment, but something stopped him. Maybe one of the shadows shifted. Maybe he saw a glimmer of pale skin.

Whatever the case, his hair stood on end, and he froze, watching, waiting.

The night had gone still, the sirens background noise to the silence that filled the alley. Nothing moved. Not a breath of wind or the scurry of an animal. No papers fluttering in the breeze. Just Jax standing there, looking at two shadows that shouldn't have been there.

"Come on out of there," he said, and one of the shadows jerked, then went still again.

"You heard me," he said. "Come out, and keep your hands where I can see them."

Still nothing.

"You've already got one night of jail to look forward to. Keep making my job harder, and it may end up being more. You want resisting arrest added to trespassing?"

"Josiah," a woman whispered. "We can't go to jail. What about the girls?"

"Hush, woman," a man barked.

Too late. Jax already knew what he was dealing with. Not a murderer bent on destruction. Grandparents who wanted . . .

What?

To see their granddaughter?

To take her?

The second seemed more likely than the first. Why else would they have arrived at this time of the morning?

He walked back down the stairs, waited at the bottom, figuring it was just a matter of time until one or the other of them made a break for it.

Lights flashed at the end of the alley, illuminating the brick building, the green Dumpster, the man and woman who were crouching there.

"Josiah. Mary. You need to come on over here and explain yourselves," he said, but what he really wanted to do was run up to the apartment, knock on the door, and make sure Willow was okay.

Mary moved first, straightening to her full height and looking straight at him. "We didn't mean any harm. We just wanted to see the baby."

"How did you hear about her?" Not from any televised news report. That was for sure.

"Josiah was in town getting supplies—"

"Hush," Josiah said again, finally getting to his feet. "He doesn't need to know our business."

"I do if you're going to keep from going to jail tonight," Jax responded.

"Everything okay in here?" Kane called, walking into the alley, Susan beside him. They were both in uniform, both with their hands on their guns. Prepared but relaxed. That was the impression Jax got. It was the impression he always got from them. They were as good at their jobs as any other cops he'd worked with, and he'd worked with plenty of them.

"I think so," Jax responded, glancing at the apartment door. It was intact and closed. No way had Willow opened it. There hadn't been enough time between the scream and his arrival for Josiah and his wife to break into the apartment and get out of it again. "From the look of things, they didn't make it into the apartment."

Josiah frowned, stepping between his wife and Jax.

"Now, you hold on a minute," he said, raising his hand as if he could stop any of them from approaching with the sheer power of his will. "We weren't trying to get in the apartment. Not without permission. We knocked on the door, and we were waiting for someone to answer. I don't know why you were called out here, but we've done nothing wrong, and you can go on back to wherever you came from."

"Sorry. We got a call about trouble, sir, and we can't leave until we check things out," Susan responded. "Since it looks like you two are part of whatever happened here, we're going to have to have a discussion."

"All we wanted to do was see the baby," Mary said, peering out from behind her husband. She looked like she was in her mid-thirties, her skin unlined, her shoulders straight.

She must have been a baby when she'd had Phoebe. That shouldn't have made Jax feel sorry for her, but it did.

"I understand how you feel, but you have to petition the court for permission to see her," he said, and Josiah frowned.

"Now, why would we have to do that? She's kin." Josiah straightened to his full height and puffed out his chest like an overconfident rooster. Maybe that worked with his family, but it didn't work with Jax. It didn't work with anyone from the Benevolence Sheriff's Department.

"She's a ward of the state. The court decides who gets to see her and who doesn't." Kane had moved closer and was standing just a few feet away from the couple. "I take it you're her grandparents?"

"That's right." Mary smoothed a hand down her long skirt, brushed dirt off her long-sleeved shirt. "We thought that maybe . . ."

"What?" Jax asked, his gaze on the apartment and the door that was still closed.

Willow had to have heard the sirens.

Was she terrified?

Frozen in place?

Caught in her nightmares and her memories?

"Well, Josiah and I, we thought that maybe we could raise the baby. She's our blood, after all, and that seems like it should count for something."

"Blood counts for squat, ma'am, when it comes to these kinds of things," Susan said bluntly. "You want to adopt the baby, you're going to have to fill out the paperwork and wait in line with every other Tom, Dick, and Harry who wants her."

"But she's ours," Josiah said. "It's as simple as that."

"It's not simple at all," Kane corrected. "Especially now that you've come for an unapproved visit at three in the morning. That's not what most people do, Mr. . . . ?"

"Sanders. Josiah. This is my wife, Mary. Phoebe is our daughter. She's always been rebellious, always skirted the rules." He shook his head, ran a hand over his cropped hair. "I tried to keep them away from worldly things. I tried to give them a good life free of the kinds of temptations that could get a person in trouble. She had her own mind, though, and she did what she wanted."

"We all have to make our own choices, Josiah," Kane said. "How about we go to my office and talk things out? I can put you in touch with a lawyer who can help you learn about custody laws."

"You're arresting us?" Mary said. "We have daughters, and they're expecting us home by dawn. They'll be worried sick, if we don't return."

"You're not being arrested. Yet," Susan said. "We just want to ask a few questions. If it takes too long, and you think you're going to be late getting back, you can call them and let them know what's going on." She took Mary's arm and started leading her to the patrol car.

"We don't have a phone!" Mary said. "And our youngest is only twelve. She gets scared. She's going to—"

"Calm down, ma'am," Susan said. "I'm a mother too, and I know how it feels to not be able to get in touch with your kids. I'm off-duty in an hour. If you're not done by then, I'll go over to your place and let the kids know what's going on."

"We don't need strangers on our property," Josiah growled.

"If you tell her not to go out there," Mary said quietly, "it's over. I mean that, Josiah. I've given up everything so you could have the kind of life you wanted, but I'm not going to scare my girls for the sake of your paranoia."

"I'm not paranoid," Josiah said. "I'm realistic. The world is filled with evil. It's—"

"How about we work it out at the station?" Kane opened the back door of the cruiser, and the couple climbed in. Not another protest out of either of them.

"That was easy," Susan said, taking off her uniform hat and smoothing her hair. "Reminded me of dealing with my kids. Lots of loud noise but not a whole lot of backbone. Have you checked on Willow and the baby yet?"

"I'm going up there now."

"You want us to stick around?" Kane asked, glancing up at the apartment door. "I doubt we're going to need to take her statement. This looks pretty cut-and-dried, and unless Willow wants to press charges, I don't see any reason to make an arrest."

"You're bringing them down to the station," Jax pointed out.

"Just instilling a little fear of the law in them. No one gets to come into our town and bother our people. That's just the way it is. I'll bring them back for the van later. As long as they agree to leave without getting anywhere near Willow and the baby, they should be home before dawn."

"I'll let Willow know."

"Thanks. I'll see you tomorrow. Graveyard again," Kane reminded him, and climbed into the cruiser.

Seconds later, he was pulling out of the parking lot, lights flashing, sirens off. He'd do the right thing by the Sanderses. He'd ask his question and let them tell their story, and then he'd probably buy them coffee and send them home.

Jax had no worries that the couple would return and bother Willow again. They'd both seemed pretty innocuous. Like Susan had said. Lots of noise. Not a whole lot of action.

He jogged up the apartment stairs, the metal clanging against brick as he moved. When he reached the door, he knocked. Waited a heartbeat and knocked again.

"Willow?!" he called. "It's Jax. You two okay in there?"

She didn't answer, and for a moment, memories flooded his head and he was swallowed up by them. He imagined she was lying on the other side of the door, bleeding. Imagined Miracle in her crib, blood pouring from her head and chest, her mouth open as she gasped for air. Imagined he could smell death and dying and fear.

He knocked a third time, reaching for his cell phone, ready to call and try to get Willow to the door that way.

The door flew open, and she was there. Pale. Shaking. Alive. Miracle was cocooned in a bright-colored carrier, nothing but the top of her head visible. No blood. No gasping breaths. No smell of anything but chocolate and cherries and baby powder.

"Thank God," he said, pulling Willow into his arms. Gently, because the baby was between them. "I was scared out of my mind."

"So was I," she murmured, her voice filled with relief mixed with the remnant of her fear. "There was a man out there, Jax. Banging on the door, and I kept thinking that it was Eric. That somehow he wasn't really dead, and that he'd found me again."

She shuddered, and he tilted her chin, forced her to look into his eyes. She was pale, her freckles dark, her eyes that sweet spring blue that he loved so much.

"He *is* dead," he said. "You don't ever have to worry about him finding you. If he weren't, I'd kill him, and you still wouldn't have to worry."

"You're too good of a guy to kill someone out of revenge."

"I'm not that good." But she was right. He hadn't shot the man who'd put the hit on his family. He'd had the opportunity. He'd had the guy in his sights. He may have even been able to convince a jury that it was an act of self-defense. The problem was, he'd have known the truth, and he was the one who'd have to look at himself in the mirror every day.

"Liar," she murmured. "We both know that you really *are* that good."

"What gave it away?"

"Everything you've ever done for me. Thank you, Jax." She levered up on her toes, kissed his lips, and if the baby hadn't been between them, he would have pulled her in for more. He would have deepened the kiss. He would have let himself forget all the rules he'd made for himself, all the limits he'd set to keep from having to lose someone again.

"What was that for?" he asked.

"For being a good friend. One who comes at three in the morning to rescue me."

"You didn't need rescuing. The guy on your stoop was Phoebe's father. His wife was with him. They just wanted to see Miracle."

"You still rescued me, because I had no idea I wasn't in danger. Neither did you when you came running to help."

"Don't make me your hero, Willow."

"Because you don't want to be one?" She stepped back, brushed a strand of hair from her face. "I understand."

"No. You don't." He touched her cheek, let his palm rest against her cool, silky skin.

God! She was beautiful!

Everything about her. Not just her hair, her skin, her eyes.

Her smile.

Her laughter.

The way she looked when she was singing Miracle a lullaby.

The way she'd felt in his arms when they'd danced in the moonlight.

He'd spent six days keeping his distance, playing the friendship game, because he'd wanted to keep her safe.

And then he'd heard her scream, and he'd known the truth. Life was what it was. All the twists and turns, heartbreaks and sorrows, they happened no matter how much a person tried to stop them.

So maybe the point wasn't to avoid the hurt. Maybe the point was to grab as much joy as possible, to love as deeply as possible, to be as much as possible to the one person who wanted to be as much as possible to him.

"If you don't think I understand, Jax," Willow said quietly, "maybe you should explain it to me."

"I don't want to be your hero, Willow, because heroes? They're there for the big things. They come running when dragons need to be slain and monsters need to be killed. They're there for the glory and the fame and the worship. Me? I just want to be there for you."

She blinked, opened her mouth. Closed it again.

"Unless," he said gently, kissing her the way she'd kissed him—lightly and sweetly. No expectations. No demands. "You don't want me to be."

"I don't think there's anything I want more," she responded, her hands sliding into his hair, her eyes staring straight into his. "Unless, of course, it's you helping me make fifty pounds of fudge."

He laughed, because she meant him to, and because *she* was laughing, her eyes sparkling with amusement, her cheeks pink with it.

The baby whimpered, and Willow looked down at her, a smile still hovering on her lips. "Much as I'm enjoying this enlightening conversation, Miracle is going to want to be fed in a couple of hours, and I have to study the fudge recipe while she's sleeping. Otherwise, I'm never going to figure out where I'm going wrong and fix it before Sunday."

"Sunday?"

"A wedding shower. We've got an order for—"

"Fifty pounds of fudge?" he said, and she met his eyes, her face still soft with amusement.

"Right. Only, one of the Lamonts can't make fudge, and she's the only one available this weekend."

"I take it that Lamont is you?"

"You're batting a thousand, Jax." She patted his cheek, and he caught her hand, pressed a kiss to her palm.

She froze, all the amusement disappearing from her face.

"I hope you meant it."

"What?"

"What you said about not being my hero, because I guess I don't need a hero, Jax. I guess I just need you."

"You've got me," he said, and then he took her hand and walked her out into the still-dark morning.

Chapter Sixteen

Batch number sixty-five of Lamont Family Fudge? A bust.

Just like batch number sixty-four, sixty-three, sixty-two . . .

"How's it going?" Jax asked, and she met his eyes, tried not to let him see how frustrated she was. He'd said all those pretty words to her, and then he'd walked her to the shop and into it. He'd been there for an hour and a half, holding Miracle, handing Willow ingredients, and doing everything she'd expect a good friend to do.

Except she didn't want a good friend.

Or a hero.

She wanted Jax to step into her life and become something she couldn't even put a name to. Not a boyfriend or a lover or her other half. Not something so big it took over everything. Or something so small that it didn't matter.

She wanted what he'd said—the guy who ran to her because she was and he was and they were meant to be together. Not just for big dramatic moments but for all the moments in between.

"It's going about how it looks like it's going," she responded, glancing down at the mess she'd created.

"It looks like . . ." He leaned over her shoulder, peering into Granddad's favorite fudge pot.

It wouldn't be his favorite if he could see it now. Coated with chocolate and cream, bits of nuts and sugar and caramel seared to its sides.

"The portal to fudge hell?" she asked. "Because I'm beginning to think that's what it is."

She stabbed at the hardened goo in the bottom of the pot. "I followed that recipe exactly, and this still looks like a big pile of dog—"

He pressed his finger to her lips, stopping the words.

"Little ears," he said, gesturing to Miracle.

She lay against his shoulder like she belonged there, her blond hair and dark lashes so similar to his, they looked like a matching set. Father and daughter spending time together while the mother . . .

Nope.

Not going there.

Sure, Jax had said a lot of really great things, and she wanted to believe them. God knew she did! But they'd both been riding an adrenaline high, and they'd both probably said things they didn't mean. Well . . . *she* hadn't, but that didn't mean the same was true of Jax.

She stabbed at the chocolate goo again. "I was going to say *crap*."

"You think that's appropriate for a kid to hear?"

"My grandfather said it the whole time I was growing up, so . . . yeah?"

"So Byron has become the standard by which you judge appropriateness? You must be really frustrated." He lifted the pot and set it in the sink, then ran hot water into it.

She'd done the same three times already.

Every time she'd started over, she'd tried to instill a little more gusto into the fudge-making process. She'd hummed while she'd added the ingredients. She'd thought good thoughts about things like butterflies and flowers and spring. She'd envisioned beautiful, glossy streams of fudge pouring from the pan.

She'd even tried to think of magic and happiness and family, hoping that it would help her capture the essence of what the fudge tasted like.

The stuff still tasted like a pile of dog vomit.

Maybe not quite that bad, but it sure wasn't good enough for a bridal shower. It wasn't good enough to sell as yesterday's fudge or last week's. It wasn't good enough for anything but the trash can.

So . . .

Yeah. She was frustrated, but she didn't want Jax to know it, because they were friends, buddies, two people who'd shared a beautiful kiss after a really scary moment.

No pressure.

He could be what he wanted to her, and she'd be okay with it, because in a few weeks, Miracle would be with her family and she'd be back in Seattle, living in her cute little rental and throwing herself into the cases she had on the docket for the spring.

"What's wrong?" Jax asked as he scrubbed the pot one-handed. She should have nudged him out of the way and taken over, but she'd scrubbed so much fudge out of so many pots, that her hands were raw and her wrists were tired.

She took Miracle instead, smiling as the baby sighed with contentment. "Nothing."

"I'm surprised."

"About?"

"You not being honest. Usually, when you're not sidestepping or avoiding my questions, I can count on you for that." He didn't look up from the pot, and she was glad. She didn't want him to see the sadness in her eyes.

She'd thought she'd hate her time in Benevolence.

It had been a means to an end, a way of trying to shake off the talons of the past. She hadn't expected to enjoy it, but she had. It was everything she remembered, but without the thread of terror running through it. Sure, she still got spooked. Sure, the hallway was still the place she hated most.

Slowly, though, slowly she was learning to be okay.

And while she was learning that, she was relearning what it meant to be home.

"I am being honest. There's nothing wrong. Except the fudge."

"Willow?" He stopped scrubbing and met her eyes. "I'm a lot of things, but stupid isn't one of them. You've been on a mission since we walked into the shop, and I don't think it's got anything to do with the fudge."

"It has everything to do with the fudge. That shower—"

"Is Sunday. You need fifty pounds of fudge. We've already established that. Now, how about we move on to something more interesting?"

"Like?"

"Like why you're tiptoeing around me like I'm a giant pile of *crap* that you're trying not to step in."

"Do you think that's appropriate language to use in front of the baby?" she joked, because it was easier than answering the question or avoiding it.

Jax didn't crack a smile. "I'm not in the mood for jokes."

"I'm not in the mood for games, but we were playing one all week. You coming over for quick visits, acting like we were buddies and then leaving. If that's what you want, I'm cool with it. I just don't want to get my hopes up that there's going to be more. I don't want to start pinning dreams on all those things you said upstairs, because I don't think you want what I do, and I don't want to have both of us be disappointed in what we get."

There. How was that for honesty?

Jax eyed her for a moment, then grabbed another pound of chocolate bits from the pantry, a half gallon of heavy cream from the walk-in. Butter. Sugar. Vanilla. Salt. Evaporated milk.

"What are you doing?" she asked, irritated by his silence as much as she was by her tripping heart and churning stomach.

He hadn't denied the friendship thing.

He hadn't said he wanted more.

He was leaving her to come to her own conclusions, and none of them were as pretty as his words had been.

"You're holding the baby. I'm making the fudge."

"You can't. The recipe is top secret."

"I watched you make it four times, Willow. It's not a secret anymore."

"Fantastic. Not only can I not make the darn stuff, I've leaked the recipe. Granddad is going to kill me."

"Only if he finds out."

"Am I going to have to pay a price for your silence?" she asked, the words grumpier than she'd intended.

She'd wanted them to be a joke, but she guessed she was all joked out, too frustrated and tired to do anything but stand there holding Miracle.

"If I made you pay me to keep your secret, that would be extortion. I'm an officer of the law, so that's out of the question. I only need one thing, and it's not money."

"Okay. I'll bite. What do you need?"

"You." He grabbed her hand, pulling her close to the stove. "I know the ingredients, but I don't know the method. You'll have to coach me."

"Uhm, Jax?" she said as he scooped sugar and cream into the double boiler, then added evaporated milk to it.

"Yes?"

"You did see my last four tries at this, right?"

"I did."

"And you still think it's wise to ask me to coach you?"

"Here's what I think, Willow," he responded, grabbing a wooden spoon and stirring the mixture gently. "You've got fifty pounds of fudge to make. There are three people in the shop. One of them only knows how to eat and sleep."

"And poop," she muttered, and he finally smiled.

"That, too, but I don't think it'll help with our mission."

"Which is?"

"Fifty pounds of fudge? You seem to be losing track of the conversation."

"I'm not losing track. I'm protesting. You're not supposed to be helping me, because this is a family recipe and—"

"Byron is going to kill you if he finds out I know it?"

"Yes. Exactly."

"First, Byron wouldn't hurt a fly. Second, this is a family recipe, and maybe we're not family, but you need the help. I'm here. It seems to me, you may as well let me lend a hand." He was still stirring the fudge base, his movements slow and smooth. Just like . . .

Byron's?

"Did my grandfather show you how to do this?"

"He showed me how to melt chocolate. Is that the same thing?"

"About as close as the rain forest is to a desert climate," she responded, grabbing the salt and adding a pinch of it. "But whatever he taught you, it's paying off. The base is looking good."

"Is it?" He sounded pleased, and that pleased her.

She didn't know why.

Or maybe she did.

"You know it is. It looks about sixty times better than anything I've made."

"Can you grab the evaporated milk? I think it's time to add it."

"Not yet," she said, moving closer, Miracle snuggled in her arms, the scent of sugar and cream drifting in the air.

It reminded her of her childhood. Of all those early mornings standing on a footstool, helping her father or grandmother or grandfather, stirring the

base with the same slow, deliberate movements Jax
was using.

"Smells good," he murmured, his free hand sliding
around her waist, and then she was right up against
his side, watching the base start to bubble, reaching
for the milk, pouring just the right amount in.

She didn't measure it.

She knew exactly how long it took for the right
amount to pour. How long the mixture had to bubble,
and how it looked when it was time to add the vanilla.

She inhaled deeply, letting the sweet, rich smell fill
her nose and replace the scent of sweat and alcohol,
mint and tears that seemed to be there every time she
worked in the shop.

"It really does," she responded, her body shaking
just a little, those memories never more than just a
thought away.

"You okay?" he asked, dropping a kiss to her temple,
his lips lingering just long enough for her to feel their
warmth.

"I will be."

He didn't question that, just continued to stir, and
she finally reached for the spoon, planning to take it
from his hand, stir it a little herself so she could feel
the thickness of the base.

Only, he didn't move his hand, and hers just en-
veloped it. Her fingers curved around his, and they
were stirring together. She could feel his pulse thrumming beneath his skin. She could feel her own heartbeat jump in response.

She could feel the hallway behind her, and all the
old memories that lingered there. She could feel the
weight of Miracle in her arms, and the weight of
the past trying to pull her down.

But she was here. In the moment, stirring silky cream and sugar in her grandfather's favorite pot, and she thought that maybe it was time to let it go, to release the sadness that had been inside her for so long, she'd almost stopped remembering it was there.

"Don't cry," Jax whispered, his free arm tightening around her waist.

"I'm not." Only she was, a few tears slipping down her cheeks as the cream and sugar bubbled and thickened.

"It's done," she said, and she didn't know how she knew. She just did, the memory of the way it was supposed to look and feel and smell filling her heart, chasing away everything else. And she thought that maybe it wasn't just the fudge base that was done. Maybe her old life was done too. The one where she stayed in Seattle and avoided Benevolence, and tried to pretend that there wasn't still a scared little girl living inside the trappings of a confident adult.

"You're sure?" he asked, but he was already removing the pot from the stove, reaching for the chocolate bits.

They added them together, and he stirred them in, the scent rich and heavenly and just exactly right.

"Good?" Jax asked, and she nodded, watching as he poured the silky mixture into a prepared pan.

"Perfect," she said, and she almost couldn't believe it, because it *was* perfect.

She didn't have to taste it to know.

She could see it and smell it and feel it, all the contentment of a perfect batch of fudge sitting on the counter.

* * *

The fudge?

It looked about as perfect as any fudge could be.

Willow? She looked perfect too.

She stood a few feet away, the baby in her arms, her cheeks still damp from tears she'd said she hadn't been crying. Of course, she had been, and he knew why.

They were in the shop, and he didn't think she could be there without remembering.

He frowned, cleaning the pot and starting a second batch of fudge.

After watching Willow struggle with the first four pans, he'd thought it would be impossible to get it right. It probably would have been impossible on his own, but with Willow there, it had been a breeze, the ingredients coming together into something she seemed pleased with.

She wasn't going to be pleased when she heard what he'd done.

He knew that, and he'd been trying to think of just the right way to tell her. It had been easy enough to avoid the subject when he was trying to keep his distance.

He could still avoid the subject.

She'd find out eventually, though.

The lawyer Jax had contacted was going to send a copy of Eric Williams's will and a copy of his father's. There was a confession somewhere in there, scribbled on a piece of paper that Eric had stapled to the document. Willow's name was mentioned. It was mentioned again in Derrick Williams's will. He'd left twenty thousand dollars to three women who'd grown up in Benevolence. That was about all James Rhodes had said. That and that Derrick Williams had died a year ago. Liver cancer.

An old friend of the family and the executor of the will, James had been charged with the task of tracking all three women down and giving them what Derrick had set aside for them. Including notes that he'd handwritten before his death.

The messages Willow had gotten? They'd been from Derrick.

The guy had had a screw loose.

That was Jax's opinion, and if he could have his way, he'd have kept the Williams family from ever touching Willow's life again.

"You've gone quiet," Willow said, shifting her hold on Miracle and murmuring something he couldn't hear. The baby quieted, her little fist pressed to her mouth.

"Just thinking."

"About?" She dropped butter into the pot and added a few dashes of salt. She'd been convinced she couldn't make the fudge. That had been the problem. He'd watched her and known that she knew it like she knew her own heartbeat. Every ingredient, every stir of the spoon, she'd had it in her, but she'd been too tense and too worried to let it out.

Now?

Now she scooped in sugar one-handed, poured in cream, did it all like she'd never struggled with it before.

She met his eyes and smiled. "Why don't you just tell me, Jax?"

"Because you've been hurt enough, and I don't want to hurt you more." That was the truth, and he wasn't going to sugarcoat it.

"I thought you didn't want to be my hero?"

"I don't."

"Then stop trying to protect me."

"I will always try to protect you," he responded.

"Stop trying to protect me from things I need to know. Is that a better way to say it?"

"I contacted James Rhodes."

She stilled, something dark flickering in her eyes. "I was hoping you'd forgotten about that."

"Did you really think I would?"

"I guess I didn't." She handed him the wooden spoon, and he stirred the thick mixture. "What did he say?"

"That Eric's father left you twenty thousand dollars."

"Why?"

"Eric had a will, and he left a confession. There were at least three names in it. James is going to black those out in your copy of the document."

"That's really swell of him," she said, and he could hear the bitterness in her voice.

"Willow—" he began, but she raised her hand, stopping the words.

"What else did he say?"

"Derrick died a year ago. His will stipulates that each of his son's victims receive twenty thousand dollars. It was his way of apologizing for what—"

"You know what, Jax? I actually don't want to hear this."

"Will—"

"Call Rhodes back. Tell him where he can stick that damn twenty-thousand-dollar check."

"I already told him."

"Tell him that I don't want to see the will. I don't want to see the confession. I don't want any of it."

"He has a legal obligation—"

"His client had a moral obligation. He should have contacted me as soon as he read the confession."

"I know."

"And he should damn well have known that twenty thousand dollars wasn't going to pay for what was stolen from me." She was crying again, holding Miracle close, her arms wrapped around the baby and around herself.

And, God! He wished he could take the pain from her, erase the memories, give her back the things she'd lost.

He touched her arm, and she jerked away.

"I wish you'd just listened to me, Jax. I wish you had just put that check back in my purse and let me deal with it." She swiped tears from her cheek and took a deep, shuddering breath.

"I'm sorry." It was all he could say, and it wasn't enough. Because he wasn't sorry about calling Rhodes. He wasn't sorry about getting the answer that Willow had been too afraid to seek. He was sorry for the little girl she'd been, the child who'd walked into her favorite place on Earth and had every bit of her innocence taken from her.

That's what he was sorry about.

That's what he wanted to fix.

But, of course, he couldn't.

Because he wasn't a damn hero, and he'd said he didn't want to be. Maybe, though, for Willow, he did.

She was walking to the door, her shoulders straight, her muscles taut, and if he hadn't been part of the reason why she was crying, he would have gone after her.

"You still have forty-five pounds of fudge to make," he said quietly, and she stopped her hand on the door.

"I'm . . . tired," she said, her face averted, the tears glittering on the column of her throat. "My mother will be here in ten minutes to take care of Miracle, and then I have work to do. Lots of it. I don't have time to waltz down memory lane or to try to make sense of things that will never be logical. Thanks for your help, Jax. You can go ahead and turn off the stove. I'll finish the fudge when I get back."

She stepped outside, closed the door, left him there with his unfinished pot of top-secret fudge and a baseball-sized knot in his stomach.

"Damn!" he spat, his eyes on the closed door, his hand still on the wooden spoon. He was stirring the fudge base. Just the way he'd done before, mixing the ingredients together in slow, gentle circles.

Maybe that was the way he needed to approach things with Willow.

Slowly.

Gently.

There was no need to rush.

No need to force everything into the light before she was ready to see it. No need to do anything but let their relationship grow into exactly what they both wanted.

And what he wanted?

It was more.

More than friendship. More than a few evenings spent together. It was more than one dance or one kiss or one minute of shared laughter. He'd already told her that, but maybe not in a way she could understand.

So he'd tell her again, and he'd ask if she wanted the same.

Right now, though, he was going to give her time.

He was going to make the fudge.

He was going to do what little he could to save the day.

He wasn't a hero, but he was a man who loved a woman, and he'd do just about anything for her.

Even make forty-five pounds of Lamont Family Fudge.

He heard a car pull into the parking lot, heard a door open and close. He heard footsteps on metal stairs and the soft murmur of voices above his head.

They were the sounds of normalcy, of family, of life, so he kept stirring the fudge, waiting for it to bubble and for Willow to return.

Chapter Seventeen

There were some secrets that were way past the time when it would have done any good to tell them.

Willow's rape?

It was one of those.

She'd told Jax, but she couldn't tell her mother. Not today anyway. Not when she was still so angry, still so hurt.

Twenty thousand dollars to buy her innocence?

Is that what it had been worth to Eric?

Or to his father?

She winced at the thought, the weight of her mother's gaze boring into her back.

"Are you sure you're okay, Willow?" she asked for the tenth time since she'd walked in the door.

"Positive."

"You look like you've been crying."

"Allergies," she lied, offering Janelle a watery smile. "And Miracle was up a lot last night."

"I heard there was some trouble here. Is that what kept her up?"

"Who did you hear that from?"

"Laurie Beth. I stopped at the diner to grab a breakfast sandwich, and she said she'd heard it on the police scanner. She would have called Byron, but she didn't want to give him a heart attack."

"Good thinking on her part. It really wasn't an emergency, and it was nothing to get people out of bed for." It was also a lot easier to talk about than Willow's tears.

Or her allergies.

She grimaced.

She hated lying to her mother, but she couldn't admit she'd been crying. If she did, she'd have to explain why, and she wasn't even sure she knew.

Sure, she was angry. She was disgusted. She wanted to rant and scream and throw things, but she wasn't sad.

Not really.

"If it wasn't something to get people up out of bed for, why did you call the police?"

"I called Jax. He called the police."

"I see."

"What do you see?" she asked, handing her mother the baby and a bottle.

"You and Jax have been spending time together."

It wasn't a question, so Willow didn't answer. "She should take all four ounces of the bottle, and then she'll probably nap. She's been up for a while."

"I'll give you an A for effort, Willow, but you're not going to distract me. What's going on between you and Jax?"

"Nothing." Not after she'd just had a complete breakdown in front him. Again!

God!

She just seemed to turn into a blubbering idiot

every time she was around him. And she'd left him to make the fudge. The top-secret Lamont recipe that he'd managed to make with just a little help from her.

Even he had the magic.

Willow?

She felt hollow and tired and too exhausted to return to the shop. She had to, though, so she walked into her room, hoping against hope that Janelle would settle into the recliner and feed Miracle.

Instead, she'd followed her down the hall and into the room.

"'Nothing' could mean lots of things," she said as she settled onto the bed and smiled at Miracle. "Ready to eat, my sweetie pie?"

"Sweetie pie?"

"She is." Janelle offered the bottle, and Miracle latched on, her chubby cheeks working as she drank. "So," Janelle said, because she'd never been one to let things go. "You were going to tell me about all the nothing you and Jax have been doing together."

"No. I wasn't."

She headed for the bedroom door, but she felt rude and mean and petty, so she stopped, turned to face Janelle again. "I'm sorry, Mom. I'm just . . . tired."

"You've got a lot of things you're working through, don't you, honey?" Janelle said, her gaze as soft as Willow ever remembered seeing it. Did she know? Could she?

"Why do you say that?"

"You always loved that shop, Willow. You loved it almost as much as you loved the family." She dropped her gaze to the baby, lowered her voice. "From the time you were old enough to walk, I knew you were the one."

"The one what?"

"Who was going to take over the shop. Your dad and I had three miscarriages before I got pregnant with you. Did I ever tell you that?"

"No."

"We did." She smiled sadly and touched Miracle's cheek. "So, when you were born healthy and beautiful, I was determined you were going to be my little mini-me. I planned all kinds of activities—teas and dance lessons and cheerleading. All you wanted to do was spend time at the shop."

"I'm sorry, Mom. That must have been disappointing."

"It wasn't. It made your dad happy, so it made me happy. Anyway, I'm only telling you because I didn't really notice when things changed. I think about it sometimes, and I can't remember when exactly it started."

"When what started?"

"You not wanting to be at Chocolate Haven anymore. Your dad was so sick, and I was worried about him and about paying the bills and about a million other things that you couldn't have understood then. I was distracted. That's my only excuse."

"I know, Mom. You don't have to explain."

"I feel like I do, because one day, I did notice. Your dad was already gone, and I walked into the house, and you were sitting on the sofa. I asked if you were going to help your grandfather at the shop, and you said no. You looked so lost and sad, and I didn't know how to help you, so I made you a bowl of ice cream and kissed your cheek. Do you remember that?"

"No."

"I do, because I've always regretted the fact that I didn't ask any questions. I assumed you were grieving your father, but the older you got, the more I thought it was something else."

"Like what?"

"I was too much of a coward to speculate." She bit her lip, and Willow thought she might cry. "But I never liked that boy."

"What boy?" Her blood went cold, her entire body suddenly numb.

"Eric Williams. I never liked his father, either. After a while . . ." Janelle hesitated, then took a deep breath. "I started thinking about how you'd changed after we'd hired him to work at the shop. I started thinking that maybe your silences weren't about missing your father."

She didn't ask.

Not outright.

But it was as close as she'd ever gotten, and Willow crossed the room. Touched her mother's shoulder. "It was a long time ago, Mom."

"So, I was right." Her voice sounded thick, but she didn't cry.

"Yes." There it was. The truth. And Janelle's shoulders bowed, and her head dropped.

"I don't know how to even say I'm sorry. I really don't," she whispered.

"You have nothing to feel sorry about."

"I failed you."

"No. You didn't, Mom."

"I did. I was too caught up in my own grief to see yours. And now we've spent all these years apart because of it."

"We were apart because I couldn't be here. It was too hard. But now . . ." Her voice trailed off, because she wasn't sure. Not yet, and she didn't want to say something that she couldn't follow through on.

"Now what?"

"I may stay. I probably will stay."

"Here?" Janelle looked shocked. And pleased. And still just a little heartbroken.

"Where else?"

"I guess I'm just . . . surprised. You've always said you were happy in Seattle."

"That's because I'd forgotten how happy I used to be here. Coming back reminded me of it. I had one really bad memory of this place, and it overshadowed all the really good ones. Now that I'm older, I can see the truth."

"What truth is that, honey?"

"Home is a place where all kinds of memories live. Good ones. Bad ones. Happy ones. Sad. I had them all here. I chose the wrong ones to dwell on."

"Sometimes," Janelle said, "we have to choose to make new ones. Sometimes we have to decide to let them fill the empty places."

"Are you talking about you and Noah?"

"I'm talking about you and Jax."

"Are we back to that again? You're like a dog with a bone, Mom," she teased, trying to lighten the mood, because she was already tired and worn out, and she didn't want to talk about the past anymore. Not now. Not when the future was in front of her. Little Miracle for however long she would have her. Her mother. Her sisters. Her grandfather. The shop, and day after day of finally being home.

And maybe Jax.

Maybe him.

But Janelle didn't need to know that. Not yet.

"I'm just curious, and honestly, I'd rather not be the last to know. The thing with Brenna really made me think, and what I've been thinking is that I don't pay much attention to what my daughters are doing."

"You're kidding, right?"

"Of course I'm not." She set the bottle on the bed and lifted Miracle to her shoulder, patting her back expertly. "As a matter of fact, I think I'm going to have a party next month."

"A party?"

"Is there something wrong with that?"

"No. Of course not. Unless it's a baby shower. I don't think—"

"Willow! Really, sweetie, I'm much more subtle than that. Besides, I was thinking more of a welcome home party. For you. How does that sound?"

A month ago, it would have sounded horrible.

A month ago, she would have nixed the idea, explained that home was her cute little house in Seattle.

But a lot could change in a month.

A *person* could change a lot in a month.

She sure had.

"That sounds great, Mom," she said, dropping a kiss on her mother's head.

"Really? Wonderful! Grab a notebook, and let's start planning."

"How about Sunday? I've got a boatload of fudge to make for Jenny Bates's bridal shower, and it's not making itself."

Jax was making it, and she'd left him alone in the shop to do it.

Because she'd been hurt.

But he'd been hurt too.

A person couldn't care and not have his heart broken sometimes.

"Right. I nearly forgot about the shop. Your grandfather is going to be so happy when he hears that—"

"Nothing is set in stone yet, Mom."

"Except that you're here, and you're staying." She beamed, and Willow didn't have the heart to argue, because she was right.

She was here.

She was staying.

"Just . . . don't spread the news yet, okay. I have a job. I have to make sure I can travel back and forth to Seattle to do it until my term is up."

"Right. Of course. Go on and get yourself ready. Miracle and I will keep ourselves busy while you're gone. Won't we, sweetie?" She kissed the baby's cheek, and Willow hurried into the hall. She needed to shower and change, and then she needed to go make fudge.

With Jax.

Because she didn't think she could do it any other way.

She didn't think she wanted to do it any other way.

And maybe that was the magic and the mystery of the fudge. Maybe that was the thing that made it taste like home—not some fake feeling that she could conjure by the power of her will. The deep and real and true contentment that came from finding that place called home in the arms of someone you loved.

Jax wasn't sure what the hell had happened.

He'd stirred the fudge just like he had before.

He added the ingredients. Just like before.

He'd done everything exactly the same as he had previously, but instead of a pretty pan of fudge, he had a cement block stuck in the bottom of the pan.

He'd been hacking at it for twenty minutes, and it was still stuck there.

"Shit," he growled, lifting the pan, ready to slam it on the floor to try to loosen it.

He probably would have done it if the door hadn't opened, and Willow hadn't walked in.

She'd changed into one of her pretty little dresses. No heels. Just white sneakers that she somehow made work. No coat, either, and she was shivering, her lips nearly blue.

"Were you running around outside without a coat?" he asked, setting the pan on the counter.

"I had no choice," she said, her teeth chattering.

"No?"

"My mother is making party plans." She stepped closer, and he could see the freckles on her smooth skin, the fine lines near the corners of her eyes, the burnished gold in her red hair.

"She forced you to run around without a coat because of that?"

"She asked me to get a notebook out of her car, and then she remembered that she also needed a pen. And, then—"

"Let me guess," he said, running his hands up and down her arms, trying to warm her.

She shivered. This time not from cold. He watched her eyes dilate and her breath quicken. He saw the telltale pulse in the hollow of her throat. He could have bent his head and tasted her lips and told her all the things he'd wanted to say before she'd run from the shop.

But all he really wanted to do was make her smile.

"Go ahead," she said, her hands on her slim waist, her chin jutting out in a dare he couldn't ignore. "Give it a shot."

"She wanted you to carry the car into the apartment, so she could sit in it while she was making plans."

"Close," she said with a quiet laugh. "She wanted me to get her phone. She'd left it in the glove compartment."

"You should have grabbed a coat during one of your trips."

"I was in too much of a hurry."

"Big plans?"

"Huge." She lifted the pan, stared into it, her brow furrowed.

"Care to share?"

"Well, I was planning on making fudge, but it looks like we may have to do an excavation first."

"I already tried. It's stuck like glue."

"Did you try cutting it out?"

"Yes."

"There's a small hatchet in my grandfather's office."

"Found it. Used it. Wasn't successful."

"Blow torch?"

"Almost set the whole place on fire."

Her lips quirked, and her eyes flashed with humor. "Did you try tossing it across the room? I've found that to be extremely successful."

"You've had this problem before, huh?"

"Many, many times. The only real solution is very hot water for a very long time." She set the pan in the sink and ran steaming water into it. "Or, if you're really brave, there's another option."

"What's that?"

"Making it right in the first place."

"I gave it a good effort," he said, amused by her and by their conversation. "I'm not sure what happened."

"It's simple, Jax," she said, and she touched his cheek, her fingers skimming along the scar and settling on his jaw. "You have to have the right tools."

"I'm pretty damn sure I used every tool available to me."

"Maybe." She smiled. "Let's try again. Just to be sure."

She rinsed out the double boiler, dried it with one of the dishrags, her hands trembling so hard she almost dropped it. The water was still running into the sink, and her cheeks were pink from the heat.

He took the pot and the rag, set them on the counter, pulled her in so they were just a breath apart.

"Are you scared?"

"Of the shop? Not anymore. Not much anyway, and not when you're here with me."

"Then why are you shaking?"

"Because there are plenty of other things to be scared of," she said.

"Like what?"

"Failing at the thing I want most."

"The fudge?" he asked, and she shook her head.

"No. Not the fudge." Her hands settled on his shoulders, and she was looking straight into his eyes. He could see everything there. The fear. The hope. The desire. "You're what I want most, Jax. All of this other stuff? It's just extra."

"Funny," he murmured, his lips brushing hers, his

hands sliding around her waist, pulling her so close there was no space between them. "I was thinking the same."

He kissed her then.

Like he hadn't before, and that empty place in his heart? The one reserved for the pain and the sorrow and the loss? It filled. Not with fear. Not with worry. Not with panic over what could happen if he loved too much or too deeply or too long.

Just with her.

He whispered her name, and it was a promise to her and to himself. No more holding back. No more doubts. He'd go after this with the same passion he'd gone after justice for his family, because it mattered just as much. *She* mattered just as much.

She answered, moaning softly as she pressed closer, her hands finding their way under his shirt, resting against his back. Flesh to flesh, and he wanted so much more. They were lost in that moment, and in each other, and he didn't want it to end.

Not ever.

But the water was still running into the ruined fudge, the steamy air filled with the scent of chocolate and vanilla and something he thought might be love.

"We need to turn that off," she murmured against his lips, and he nodded, his breath heaving, his heart pounding. For her and for all the things he'd thought he couldn't have.

They were there.

In her eyes. In her face.

And he had all the time in the world to find them.

Right now, he was going to help her with the fudge. He was going to let her know he was there. Always. In the little things, and in the big ones.

He turned off the water, kissed her forehead.

"Unfortunately, we also need to make the damn fudge," he said, his voice still husky with longing.

She laughed, setting the double boiler into place, pouring in the cream and the sugar and the evaporated milk, stirring it as it simmered, her movements slow and easy.

"Like our dance in the moonlight," he said, placing his hand over hers, stirring the fudge base, getting a feel for the thickness of the mixture.

"Not quite as beautiful," she responded, leaning back, resting against him. "I think that's the best thing I've ever done, Jax. Dancing with you."

"We'll do it again one night," he said, and she nodded, still stirring the fudge base.

It was bubbling now, and he could almost feel it changing from a few separate ingredients into something more. Something special.

"Is it done?" he asked, leaning over her shoulder to look, and then pressing a kiss to the tender flesh behind her ear. He could smell soap on her skin and chocolate, and just a hint of rum-soaked cherries.

"Not yet. It takes time to make it perfect."

"How much time? Because we've got about forty more pounds to make, and the shop will be open soon." *And I want to spend more time with you. Just us. No chocolate or cream or steaming water.*

He could have said that, but she knew.

And he knew that they'd have that time.

When this was done, and the shop was closed, and they were sitting in her apartment with Miracle sleeping beside them, they'd have all the time in the world to find out what it meant to be together.

"We're not making all the fudge today. This is for

our store inventory, and it's going to take just enough time to make it perfect," she responded, reaching for the chocolate bits. He helped her pour them in, helped her stir them until they melted.

He watched as just enough time passed, and all the individual ingredients became something rich and decadent and smooth.

She poured it into a pan, smiling a little as she turned to face him.

"There you have it," she said. "Perfect fudge."

"Hard to believe we managed it," he said.

"Why's that?"

"You said we needed the right tools," he reminded her.

"We did."

"Are you going to tell me what they are?" he asked. "Or is that as secret as your great-grandfather's recipe?"

"Since I've already spilled the beans on that one," she said, smiling, "I guess I can tell you the rest. The special tools? They're these."

She lifted his hands, wove their fingers together.

He should have laughed, because there was no way that the difference between his fudge and their fudge was . . .

Them?

Together?

No way, but they made another batch and another, each one better than the last, and he didn't feel like laughing anymore, because he thought that maybe she was right.

That what they'd needed was each other.

Not just for the fudge.

Forever.

When they'd finished the last batch, he helped her cut it, and he carried it into the front of the shop. She followed, walking through the hallway where her life had changed and her innocence had died. Where all her nightmares had begun.

"You okay?" he asked, and she nodded.

"The shadows aren't as dark when you're here," she said.

And he knew she meant it.

He took her hand, kissed her gently.

"Come on," he said. "It's time to turn the sign."

"It's going to be a busy day," she said.

"How do you know?"

"The weather is clearing. It's warming up. People are going to want to celebrate. There's no better way to celebrate than with Lamont fudge."

"I can think of some that might be almost as good," he said, and she smiled.

"Okay. Tell me."

"Walks in the park. Dances in the moonlight."

"Baby bottles in the early morning?"

"Only if I'm with you," he said, laughing as he kissed her again.

"Now, come on." He wrapped his arm around her waist. "Byron will blame me if we open late."

"Who's going to tell him?"

"Millicent. She's standing right outside the door."

She was. Face pressed to the glass. Glaring at them balefully.

"She's going to report on us one way or another," Willow said, stopping a few inches from the door. "So maybe we should give her something to report on."

"Do you have any good ideas?"

"Maybe a little PDA?" she said, flipping the sign to OPEN and unlocking the door. She stepped back as Millicent entered, and Jax figured she'd been joking about the public display of affection.

He wasn't.

Not when it came to her.

"You know what? A little PDA is probably a good idea," he said, and then he tugged her into his arms and kissed her.

She was laughing when she pulled away, and even Millicent was smiling.

"I'd complain," she said. "But I smell fudge, and it's making me too happy for anything to be irritating. I'll take a pound of whatever you have, Willow."

"Coming right up," Willow said, and she stepped behind the counter and started her day.

Their day.

Because Jax would always be part of this world.

Her world and theirs.

She looked up from the fudge she was measuring, and he winked.

"Keep up the good work," he said as he moved past her. "I'll go make some more cement."

She laughed at that.

He could hear it ringing through the hall as he went back to work.

Ready to take another visit to
Benevolence, Washington?
Then please turn the page for an exciting sneak peek
of the first book of a new trilogy taking place in
Benevolence and focusing on the Bradshaw brothers!

Look for Shirlee McCoy's

HOME WITH YOU,

coming soon wherever print and eBooks are sold!

Here's how it all went down:

She'd been sitting there, minding her own business, trying to eat breakfast. She'd had the newspaper in just the right position to block her view of Lu and of the little glass cup that held Lu's false teeth. Two months living back on the homestead, and she knew the routine. No internet. No TV. Five a.m. breakfast followed by mucking out the stalls and feeding all twelve of Lu's therapy horses.

So, yeah . . .

She'd been trying to eat breakfast before she mucked out the stalls. Multitasking, munching on toast and searching the help-wanted section of the paper for a job.

God knew, she had to have one of those.

Lu needed money, and Rumer was going to make sure she had it. She'd already emptied out her savings and cashed in her 401(k), but there were still medical bills to pay. She'd be able to go back to teaching in the fall, but right now things were tight.

Which made Lu worry.

That wasn't good for someone who'd had triple bypass surgery.

So Rumer was going to get a job or two and put every dime she earned into paying off the last few medical bills. When she went back to Seattle in the fall, she'd know that Lu was going to be okay. More important, Lu would know it.

And that's why she'd been sitting at the tiny kitchen table in Lu's tiny house ignoring the false teeth and looking for work. If things had played out the way they had for the past week, she'd have seen nothing in the help-wanted section, dumped her toast in the scrap bucket, and headed out to do the chores.

But in one of those cosmic twists of fate or moments of divine intervention, Lu had shoved another paper across the table.

"Rumer Truehart," she'd said. "Take a look at that."

So, of course, she had.

And of course it had been the gossipy little newspaper that was published in the next town over. The *Benevolence Times.*

"County fair is going to be there in two weeks." Lu had jabbed at the announcement. "Bet they'll have some horses."

"You already have twelve."

"There are plenty of people on the waiting list to bring their kids here. We train one more horse, I can accept three more children into the program."

"I can't stay to train horses, Lu. You know that. I have to go back to the Montessori school in the fall. Otherwise they'll give my job to someone else."

"We could still go look. I've been cooped up in this house for too long. I'm getting antsy," Lu had said.

A total lie.

Lu never got antsy. She worked hard. All day every day. Running a nonprofit center that provided therapy horses for kids with disabilities.

But Rumer had promised herself she wouldn't get in any arguments with her grandmother. So she'd nodded and skimmed the page.

Which is how she'd seen the advertisement. Right at the bottom. Boxed in with a dark line that had pulled her eyes right to it.

HELP WANTED.
PEACEFUL VALLEY ORGANIC FARM.
FULL-TIME HOUSEKEEPER/GARDENER/COOK.
EXPERIENCE WITH CHILDREN A PLUS.
LIVE IN OR LIVE OUT.
CALL SULLIVAN TO SET UP AN INTERVIEW.

It was the first help-wanted ad she'd seen in a week, and she'd jumped all over the opportunity. She'd mucked the stalls and made the call. When Sullivan hadn't answered, she'd decided to find the farm and apply in person.

And that's how she'd ended up on a dirt road just outside of Benevolence, Washington. Chugging along in Lu's old pickup, listening to the oldies station. She'd found the sign for Peaceful Valley Organic Farm and had headed up the long, windy road that seemed to lead to it. She'd been able to see the farmhouse in the distance—a two-story monstrosity that someone had painted yellow.

Yellow!

She'd taken a quick peek at the slacks she'd borrowed from Aunt Minnie. Yellow polyester. Bell-bottoms. Probably from the seventies. Minnie never got rid of anything. She had an entire lifetime of stuff shoved into the double-wide trailer that sat on the east end of the homestead.

Rumer had been thinking that maybe the yellow slacks and yellow house were a sign, a portent, a hint from God that the job was hers. That after two months of near hell, things were finally going to get better.

And then she'd looked up at the road again . . .

She'd looked up, and the girl was right there!

Wandering out from between overgrown field grass, skin glowing rich brown in the midmorning light. Pink tutu shimmering. Ivory tank top hanging loose. Boots clomping. A bouquet of early spring flowers clutched in her hand.

Rumer had had about three seconds to take it all in, and then she'd swerved, bouncing off the road and straight into a rain culvert. Nose down, steam spilling out of the hood.

She'd scrambled out of the truck, her purse hooked over her shoulder, and the girl had still been there. Standing right in the middle of the road.

And that's how she'd ended up here.

On a dirt road.

With a strange kid who was dressed in nothing but a tutu, a thin-strapped tank, a tiara, and bright green rain boots.

"Hello," she said, because what else would she do? She sure wasn't going to let the kid wander back to wherever she'd come from. Half-naked and alone. It was chilly, for God's sake. Early spring in eastern Washington, and winter still had the upper hand.

The little girl cocked her head to the side, eyeing Rumer with a look that was both suspicious and mutinous.

"Who are you?" she finally replied, every word

enunciated and precise. Surprising, because she didn't look older than three.

"Rumer Truehart. How about you? What's your name?" She crouched so that they were eye level, offering a smile.

She got a scowl in response.

"I'm not supposed to talk to strangers," the girl said, her eyes so dark Rumer could barely see the pupils. "Not even if they offer me candy. Do you have candy?"

"No, I don't. I do have a jacket, though. And it's cold. How about I let you wear it?" She shrugged out of the yellow jacket that matched the slacks. Minnie had insisted she wear both. A job interview was important, and Rumer couldn't go in the jeans and T-shirts she'd brought from home.

Rumer could have and would have.

But . . . again: She'd promised not to argue with her grandmother and that meant she also couldn't argue with Minnie in front of her. So she'd put on the pantsuit and the pretty white eyelet blouse that went with it.

She held out the jacket, and the little girl snatched it from her hand.

"I'm not cold," she declared as she struggled to get her tiny arms into the sleeves, the little bouquet still in her hand, pink and purple petals floating to the ground as she maneuvered into the jacket. "But thank you very much for this."

She had a lisp.

Which would have been totally adorable if they'd been anywhere but on that road with not another adult in sight. The kid had parents somewhere. Parents who obviously were not doing their job.

"You're very welcome. I bet your mom will be

happy that you've got a jacket," she said, hoping to break the ice and get a little more information about the girl and her family.

It was the wrong thing to say.

One minute, the girl was looking at the jacket's daisy-shaped buttons, the next she was crying. Not louds sobs. Just silent tears that were sliding down her cheeks. "Mommy is at the hothpital," the girl wailed, the lisp suddenly more pronounced.

"Are you trying to get to her?" Rumer guessed, because why else would the child be wandering around carrying a wilted bouquet of flowers?

"I'm making her medicine." She sniffed back more tears and waved the flowers in front of Rumer's face.

"Medicine?"

"Yep! Heavenly read me a book about a boy who climbed a mountain to pick a flower that would make his best friend better. One flower is good. Ten flowers is better." She waved the bouquet again.

"Who is Heavenly?" she asked.

"My sister. She's twelve. I'm six."

"You're—" Tiny was on the tip of her tongue.

She didn't say it.

Six-year-olds didn't often want to be told they were little.

"Is she taking care of you today?" she said instead.

"Nope. She's making cake for Twila. It's her birthday."

"Is Twila also your sister?"

"Yes, she is," the girl said emphatically. "And no one better say she's not! Markie Winston tried it, and I popped him right in the nose. He was bleeding and everything." She swung her free hand in a wide-arcing left hook. "Now I can't go back to school until Wednesday. The man is not happy about it."

"The man?"

"Yeah." She dropped her fist and leaned close. They were nearly nose to nose, and Rumer could see the trail of drying tears on her cheeks and a thin, pale scar near her hairline. There was another one right beside her lip.

"He's not so good at kids," the girl whispered. "Heavenly says that's what happens when you get old without ever having children."

"Who is he?" Certainly not the girls' father. Maybe a relative who'd been called in to help while their mother was in the hospital?

"My uncle. Daddy's brother. Daddy is dead, so he had to come and help out while Mommy is in the hospital." The whisper had gotten softer, and Rumer almost didn't hear the last part.

She saw the tears, though.

They were rolling down the girl's face again.

"Oh, honey," she said, giving her a gentle hug. "I'm so sorry about that."

"Me too," the girl wailed, her skinny arms wrapping around Rumer's waist, the flowers rustling as they smashed against her back.

Rumer could have cried too. That's how awful she felt.

It all just seemed so wrong and so completely horrible. The sun was warm and bright and high, the sky blue, the air crisp. The dirt road stretched toward the yellow house and the horizon, tall grass and trees dotting the landscape. All of it picturesque and perfect.

And a little girl was standing brokenhearted in the middle of all of it.

Alone except for the stranger who'd found her.

As soon as Rumer got the little girl calmed down, she was going to find the uncle and give him a piece of her mind. She didn't care if he was ancient as days. He should still have more sense than to let a six-year-old out of his sight. Sure, this area was rural. Sure, most people were pleasant, kind, and helpful, but there were predators everywhere. Not to mention the river, the woods, the roads that crisscrossed the land.

Plenty of trouble for a child to get into.

She brushed her palms down the girl's cheeks, wiping the tears away.

"How about I take you home? You can put your flowers in a vase and bring them to your mother the next time you go to the hospital," she suggested.

"I'm not bringing her flowers." The girl's chin quivered, but she'd stopped crying. "I'm making medicine. I'm going to bake it into magic cookies, and Mommy will eat them and wake up."

It would be hard for someone who was asleep to eat, but Rumer wasn't going to point out the flaw in logic.

"How about we go do that, then?" she asked. "Do you know how to get home?"

"Why wouldn't I? Mrs. Bridget says I'm just about the smartest first-grader she's ever met."

"She's your teacher?"

"Yes. She lets me read the second-grade reading books. She also sent me to the office when I punched Markie."

"Violence is never the answer."

"Maybe not, but it still felt good!" the girl responded, skipping ahead, her tiara glinting in the sun.

Rumer had to jog to keep up. Not easy to do in her borrowed shoes. Two-inch cream-colored pumps that Minnie had insisted she wear. Probably because the slacks were too long, and not one woman in the Truehart family could fix that. They could muck stalls, feed horses, teach kids. They could cook, clean, and organize. They could even run a very well-respected nonprofit, milk goats and cows, make cheese, plant and harvest a garden.

What they could not do—had never in the history of Truehart women been able to do—was find a good man or sew a straight hem.

So, yeah, she was tottering on the heels, trying to not fall face-first into the wheat grass. She didn't notice that they'd taken a sharp turn through the field until she jogged onto a gravel path that cut across a fenced cow pasture. Her foot slipped on loose pebbles, and she went down. Legs one way. Arms the other.

She landed with a solid *thump* that knocked the wind right out of her.

She must have closed her eyes on impact, because she opened them and was looking straight up at the bright blue sky.

"You okay, Rumer Truehart?" the little girl said, suddenly at her side and peering into her face.

"Fine. I'm just not used to wearing heels."

"Mommy says they take practice. Maybe you should practice more." She offered her hand, and it was as tiny as the rest of her.

"That's a good idea, poppet," Rumer said as she got to her feet and brushed dirt off her slacks.

"Poppet?" She giggled, the sound like a creek bubbling over smooth stones. "Is that the same as puppet?"

"No. It's—"

"Moise!" a man called from somewhere to their left. "Moise Bethlehem Bradshaw! You'd better get your butt moving and get back home."

The girl froze, her dark eyes widening.

"That's the man!" she said. "And he said *butt*!"

There were a lot worse things a man could say. Rumer had heard them all when she was the little girl's age.

"Moise!" someone else called. Female and young from the sound of it. "You're not even going to get one teeny tiny piece of cake if you don't hurry up home!"

"Coming!" the little girl yelled, and took off running, her scrawny legs churning beneath layers of pink tulle.

Rumer followed, abandoning her heels so she could keep up, racing across rough gravel and then onto soft grass.

The house was straight in front of her, maybe a quarter of a mile away, the clapboard siding pristine, the white-washed front porch railings sturdy and practical-looking.

Moise was beelining it across the yard. No time wasted now. She was a girl on a mission, her tutu swishing, her rain boots gleaming in the sunlight.

Must have been the threat of no cake.

"Moise?!" the man called again, and this time Rumer saw him coming around the side of the house.

She'd expected gnarled, stooped, old. She'd expected a cane or a walker, gray hair, chewing tobacco, a spittoon.

She sure as heck had not expected Mr. GQ cover model. Mr. Frilly-Pink-Aprons-Make-Me-Seem-Even-More-Masculine.

She didn't expect him to be carrying a chubby baby, but there was that, too, and the girl jogging along beside him, dark hair in cornrows, big blue eyes filled with anxiety. She was a hot mess—too-short shirt showing three inches of skin, too-tight jeans clinging to bony hips. Red lipstick smeared across her mouth.

And her eyeshadow . . .

Rumer wouldn't even go there

"Moise!" the girl cried, running over to Moise and grabbing her arm. "Where have you been! If Sunday were here she'd shi—"

"Don't," the man cut her off.

"What?" she snapped, whirling on him like they were mortal enemies about to go to war.

"Use foul language in front of your siblings. I've already been called to the school three times because your brothers are repeating you."

"Don't blame me for the tweebs' problems," the girl said. "They've been brats since the day I got here."

"They are not brats!" Moise yelled, pulling back her foot in preparation for what Rumer thought would be a well-aimed kick.

Time to put a stop to things.

She stepped forward, lifted Moise off her feet, and set her down about a yard away from her target.

"Violence," she said, looking into Moise's angry face. "Is never the answer."

"It'd sure feel good," she fumed.

"Not when I kicked you back," the girl retorted.

"Enough, Heavenly. Nobody is kicking anybody," the man said, and Rumer swung around to look at the girl.

Heavenly.

The twelve-year-old sister.

She looked sixteen, and she had trouble written all over her scrawny body and her scowling face. Rumer recognized it. She'd seen it every time she looked at her teenage self in the mirror.

"Who are you? What were you doing with my niece?" the man said, and she realized that while she'd been studying Heavenly, he'd been studying her.

"My name is Rumer Truehart. Your niece walked out onto the road in front of my truck. I almost hit her." She added the last so that he'd know just how serious the situation had been.

"Geez," he muttered, raking a hand through thick black hair. "Sorry about that. She was supposed to be napping."

"Six is a little old for a nap," she pointed out.

"It's also a little old for punching and kicking when we don't get our way. Since she still does both, I figure she still needs a nap. Are you from the county?"

"The county?"

"Social services? CPS? Whatever the heck they call it now." The baby grabbed a handful of his hair, and he winced, pulling her dimpled hand away from his head.

"I'm not from the county. I was looking for Peaceful Valley Organic Farm."

"You're from the state tax assessment board?"

"No, I—"

"Insurance adjuster?"

"I'm here—"

"Real estate agent? SPCA? School board?"

"None of the above."

"Then you must be from the church. We have enough casseroles, and I promise I'll bring the kids back to Sunday school once we get a little more settled."

"Look, Mr. . . . ?"

"Bradshaw. Sullivan."

Her heart thumped. One hard, quick jerk of acknowledgment. This was Sullivan? The guy from the help-wanted ad? The one who needed a housekeeper/gardener/cook who had experience with kids?

"Nice to meet you, Mr. Bradshaw," she said, stepping forward and offering her hand.

He took it.

He had a firm, quick handshake. The kind she'd expect from someone with confidence and very little need to prove himself.

She had a thing about handshakes. Probably because she'd met so many people when she was a kid. All the people he'd mentioned and more: CPS, social services, foster parents, caseworkers, school counselors. Police. Doctors. Clergy.

"Nice to meet you, too, but I'm right in the middle of about three dozen things. Thanks for making sure my niece got home." He was already turning away, snagging the back of Moise's tank top when she tried to dart ahead.

"I came about the ad," she called as the motley group of unhappy people moved away.

She shouldn't have said anything.

She knew it.

Heavenly wasn't the only one who had trouble written all over her.

Sullivan Bradshaw did, too.

A different kind of trouble.

The kind that could cause a woman to make mistakes, to forget her promises to herself, to lose pieces of her heart that she wouldn't ever get back. He was black-haired, green-eyed, handsome-as-the-devil trouble, but she needed the job, and his little family needed her.

They need someone.

She mentally reminded herself.

It doesn't necessarily have to be you. Turn around. Walk away. Call a tow truck to get the pickup out of the ditch. Go into Benevolence and see if the diner needs a waitress or if the church needs a janitor.

"What ad?" he asked, handing the baby to Heavenly, releasing his hold on Moise, and turning to face Rumer again.

The preteen didn't waste time. She marched up the porch steps like a martyr going to her doom, dragging poor little Moise along behind her.

"The ad?" Sullivan prodded impatiently.

"Yes. Right. You ran it in the *Benevolence Times*?" She pulled the newspaper from her oversize purse and tapped the ad. She'd circled it in blue marker.

"Housekeeper/Gardener/Cook. Experience with kids a plus." She read it out loud, and he frowned, crossing the distance between them and taking the paper from her hand.

He scanned it quickly, thrust it back. "That's my number, but I didn't pay for the ad."

Good. Great. Because he looked even better close up than he had a few feet away—long dark lashes, firm full lips, hands that were nicked and scarred and currently speckled with what looked like orange frosting. He had it on his apron, too. And in his hair.

"In that case, I'll get out of your hair," she mumbled, turning away because she definitely did not want a job working for Sullivan Bradshaw.

"Nice meeting you, Mr. Bradshaw." She called the last over her shoulder as she retreated.

Ran for her life was more like it.

As far as she was concerned, the big yellow house was filled with more trouble than any one person could handle, and Rumer? She'd already had enough trouble to last several lifetimes.

"I didn't run the ad. One of my brothers probably did. I've been a little . . . busy," he said.

She'd reached the little gravel path, and she was ready to step onto it, forget this effort in futility, this midmorning faux pas.

"But we *are* looking for help, and if you're willing to wait a few minutes while I finish up what I was doing, I can interview you and take a look at your résumé. You do have a résumé, right?"

"Of course I do. I've taught in a Montessori school for six years. I have a bachelor's in special education, and a master's in early childhood development," she huffed, sounding prissy and uptight and totally unlike herself.

But she hated when people judged the book by its cover.

Sure, she was walking around in forty-year-old bell-bottoms. Sure, she was barefooted and probably wild-haired. Maybe even grass-stained, but that didn't mean she wasn't well-educated and intelligent.

Although . . .

She *was* still standing there. Right at the edge of the gravel path. She wasn't running for her life and sanity. So, maybe the intelligence thing was in question.

"It was just a question, Ms. Truehart. Not a statement about you. No need to take offense."

"I didn't, but you're busy. I'll come back another time," she said. Meaning never.

"The position pays well," he countered.

"What is your definition of well?" She spun around, and he was right there. So close she could have reached out and brushed the orange flecks from his hair.

He named a figure that was just about half her monthly teaching salary.

"How long are we talking? Six months? A year?"

"Three months. If things stretch out longer, we'll work up a new contract."

"Things?"

"My brother and sister-in-law were in an accident a few weeks ago. He was killed. She's in a coma. We have no idea when she'll wake up. Or, even, if she will."

"I'm really sorry about that," she said, and meant it.

"Me too. My brothers and I feel that help around the house would make the transition easier for the kids. The job description is vague because we're not sure what we'll need. This is a working farm, and there are six kids living in that house." He gestured at the aging farmhouse. "If you want to interview, great. If not, thanks for stopping by."

He walked away, all smooth, graceful steps and understated masculinity.

She let him go, because, of course, she wasn't going to do the interview. The money was great, but the job sounded extensive, and she still had Lu to worry about.

She wasn't going to do it, but then she saw little Moise peeking out a window, face pressed up against the glass, a smudge of orange on her cheek.

Trouble wasn't Rumer's thing.

It *wasn't.*

But, somehow, she always found herself walking straight into it.

She hitched her purse up onto her shoulder, brushed a few pieces of grass from her slacks, and followed Sullivan across the yard.

Connect with

Us

Visit us online at
KensingtonBooks.com
to read more from your favorite authors, see books
by series, view reading group guides, and more.

Join us on social media

for sneak peeks, chances to win books and prize packs,
and to share your thoughts with other readers.

facebook.com/kensingtonpublishing
twitter.com/kensingtonbooks

Tell us what you think!

To share your thoughts, submit a review,
or sign up for our eNewsletters, please visit:
KensingtonBooks.com/TellUs.